Love Like
Hallelujah

JUL   2017

CH

Love Like Hallelujah

LUTISHIA LOVELY

KENSINGTON PUBLISHING CORP.
http://www.kensingtonbooks.com

DAFINA BOOKS are published by

Kensington Publishing Corp.
850 Third Avenue
New York, NY 10022

All Kensington titles, imprints and distributed lines are available at special quantity discounts for bulk purchases for sales promotion, premiums, fund-raising, educational or institutional use.

Special book excerpts or customized printings can also be created to fit specific needs. For details, write or phone the office of the Kensington Special Sales Manager: Kensington Publishing Corp., 850 Third Avenue, New York, NY 10022. Attn. Special Sales Department. Phone: 1-800-221-2647.

Dafina Books and the Dafina logo Reg. U.S. Pat. & TM Off.

ISBN-13: 978-0-7582-1753-0
ISBN-10: 0-7582-1753-6

First Kensington Trade Paperback Printing: January 2008
10 9 8 7 6 5 4 3 2

Printed in the United States of America

*This book is dedicated to all the readers who choose
to look at the love in their lives;
from family, friends, lovers, strangers,
Spirit . . . and rejoice!*

ACKNOWLEDGMENTS

With Gratitude . . .

The dictionary defines gratitude as being grateful, thankful, appreciative. I define gratitude as pure joy, because that's what I feel when I think of all the people who, in one way or another, helped this story get told.

Of course, a shout out to family: Mama, Daddy . . . everybody! And to friends who said, "Girl, I can't wait to read the sequel." Kai, Fadzo, Sherri, my sister Cella, and all the *Sex in the Sanctuary* readers who contacted me about this book's release. Here it is, y'all!

To my Kensington/Dafina family: Selena James, you are a writer's dream as an editor and, job aside, a wonderful person. For your spirit, positive energy, smiling personality and priceless editing . . . thanks. To everyone I met while in New York attending BEA—how great was that, huh? Hillary, Jessica, Adeola, Mercedes, Joan, everyone in sales. Wal-Mart reps, and the Zacharius family . . . you're the best! To Kristine Mills-Noble for another stunning cover design, and to Superstock for the delicious photography. Also to the people at Kensington I didn't meet, who I don't know, but who helped turn this "possible" to "actual" . . . thank you.

To the fellow Dafina writers I've met and whose works I've either already enjoyed or look forward to reading in the future: Paula Chase (I'm not getting it twisted!), Mary B. Morrison, Mary Monroe, Daaimah S. Poole, Gwynne Forster, San Culberson, Pat G'Orge-Walker, and Angie Daniels. Actually to all writers everywhere . . . it is an honor to be counted among you.

To my wonder-woman agent and friend, Natasha Kern. What a gem I found in you, Janice, and everyone at the agency. Here's to years as a successful team . . . l'chaim!

To all the fabulous readers; we writers are nothing without you. Much love to book clubs, both in-person and on-line: you guys hold it down! Clubs like CushCity (hey Gwen!), MosaicBooks, Rawsistaz (what up Tee C?!), Sistahs Sippin' Tea, APOOO, People Who Love Good Books, Baton Rouge Barnes & Noble Urban Fiction Book Club (headed by fellow writer Naiomi Pitre . . . shout out!), and every single book club on the planet. Nothin' but love for you guys! Also to libraries everywhere and the readers who use them . . . *muchas gracias!*

To friends who I presently or in the past have shared lessons in love, and/or hallelujah good times: Evan (I don't know . . . but I'm gon' sho' find out!), Holly, Charmaine, Ladymac, Carla, Ava, brothah-man, Lightfoot, and his "hallelujah," Debbie.

To Nabil Issa, a brilliant contributor to the earth's positive vibration. Much success with your book, *Untapped*. It's time for the world to "get tapped," baby!

As always, to Spirit, with whom I have the continuous, illustrious pleasure to co-create; with every fiber of my being . . . *merci beaucoup.*

Love Like
Hallelujah

1

Remember to Forget

Cy moved with calm precision, feeling perfectly at home among Victoria's Secret's wispy feminine apparel. Not the most traditional gift to give his soon-to-be wife, but Cy couldn't think of anything he'd rather see her in than a silky negligee, except her bare skin. He knew her body would show off to perfection the diamond necklace he'd just purchased at Tiffany's, and he wanted a delicious piece of lingerie to complement the eight-carat teardrop. He couldn't help but smile as he fingered the delicate fabrics of silk, satin, and lace, unmindful of the not-so-covert glances female shoppers slid his way. It hardly mattered. His fiancée, Hope Serenity Jones, had captured Cy's attention from the moment she'd appeared at the back entrance of Mount Zion Progressive Baptist Church, a piece of sanctified eye candy wrapped in a shimmering gold designer suit.

Female admirers ogled Cy as he continued his deliberate perusal. He stopped at a hanging negligee, red and pink flowers against a satiny white background. The top had thin spaghetti straps that held up a transparent gown hitting midthigh. The thong had an intricately designed rose vine for the string, a trail he would happily follow once it was on Hope, first with his fingers, then with his tongue. . . .

A perky, twenty-something salesclerk came over with a knowing smile. "Are roses your favorite flower?" she asked, flirting.

"They could become my favorite," Cy countered easily, "if worn on the right person."

"That's a very popular design," the salesperson offered, encouraging the purchase.

"I'll take it," Cy said, as he casually handed the lingerie to her.

"Will this be all?" she asked, unconsciously moving closer to the live Adonis who had walked into the store and (blessings abound!) into her area.

"No, but I'll keep shopping on my own," Cy murmured as he eyed something on the other side of the store. The salesperson followed without thought. "I'll let you know if I need any help," he said with emphasis.

"No problem, I'm here if you need me." The salesclerk turned around, a look of regret barely concealed behind her cheery smile. Cy was oblivious to the wistful stares his six-foot-two frame elicited from the saleswoman and other shoppers. His naturally curly jet black hair may have been hidden under a Lakers cap, but his raw sexuality was in plain sight. He had no idea that his sparkling white smile lit up the room like the noonday sun or that the dimple that flashed at the side of his grin was like a finger beckoning women closer.

Cy picked up a bra and panty set that had Hope's name written all over it. It was a soft, lacy, yellow number. The panty was designed like a pair of shorts—very short shorts—and Cy reacted physically as he thought of Hope's bubble booty filling them out. He quickly added this set to the black and beige more traditional sets he'd selected earlier.

While making his way to the perfume counter, another outfit caught his eye—the perfect backdrop for the diamond pendant. It was a lavender-colored sheer nightgown with matching floor-length jacket. The beauty was in its simplicity, and he smiled again as he thought of how Hope would look wearing this purple paradise. He held it up and closed his eyes, mentally picturing her ebony splendor wrapped luxuriously inside the soft material rubbing against her silken skin as he kissed her sweet lips.

Cy felt the presence of someone behind him. Figuring it was the attentive saleswoman, he turned to apologize for taking so long to make his decisions, and for the growing pile of lingerie she'd collected on his behalf. The smile died on his lips, however, as did the clever banter he'd thought to deliver as he completed the turn and stared into the eyes of the person he'd most like to remember to forget . . . Millicent Sims.

Or so he thought, initially. The woman could have been Millicent's twin sister; that's how much alike they looked. But after the initial shock subsided, Cy realized it wasn't her. The eyes were similar, but this woman's nose and lips were larger. Her face was a bit fuller, the cheekbones less prominent. One thing was definitely the same though; the woman looked at him as if he were a chicken nugget and she the dipping sauce. He quickly excused himself and went around her, making a beeline for the cash register. A close encounter of the Millicent kind had cooled his shopping frenzy.

Moments later, he closed the rear door of his newly purchased BMW SUV. It had been hard to get him out of his Azure, but looking back it hadn't made sense for a Bentley to be his main driving vehicle. As the salesman had promised, Cy found the BMW to be a perfect ride for jetting around the city. He fired up the engine, hit the CD button, and zoomed out of the parking lot. The sounds of Luther Vandross's greatest hits, redone to perfection in snazzy jazz styles as a tribute to his memory, oozed out of the stereo. Cy bobbed his head as Mindi Abair got ridiculous with her alto sax version of "Stop to Love." As he crossed lanes and merged onto the 405 Interstate, his thoughts drifted back to Millicent. His heart had nearly stopped when he thought he saw her; it had been a while since she'd crossed his mind. He wondered how she was doing, where she was. Even after "the incident," he wished her well.

The incident. It had been a while since he'd thought about that, too. But seeing Millicent's near twin in Victoria's Secret had brought the memories back with a vengeance. That crazy Sunday when out of the blue, and in the middle of a regular church service, Millicent had wafted down the aisle in full wedding regalia. It had shocked everyone in the sanctuary, him most of all.

Cy had had months to replay those events in his mind, and they'd mellowed with time. Now, he thought about the Millicent Sims he knew before she'd lost her mind that Sunday morning. He remembered the way he felt when he first saw her, tall and regal with beautiful hair, flawless skin, legs forever, and a smile that made his heart skip a beat. He'd quickly asked her out, knowing those fine looks would test the limits of his celibacy vow. But it hadn't taken him long to realize that aside from good looks and Kingdom Citizens' Christian Center, they had little in common. He also quickly felt Millicent's desire to take their relationship to another level, one of the physical kind. Though sorely tempted, he did the right thing and broke it off with her after a couple months. Now, however, he wondered what it would have been like to have those long legs wrapped around him, his dick tapping that flawless skin. His manhood jumped in response to these thoughts, the smaller head seconding the bigger head's thoughts.

As Cy exited the 90 Freeway into Marina Del Rey, Millicent's words from that fateful day of their last encounter drifted through the melodies of Rick Braun's rendition of "Dance With My Father." He could hear them as loudly as if they were actually being spoken: *Come! It is our time. . . .* Cy's dick went limp.

A horn honked. The red light he'd reached had turned green. Cy floored the gas pedal as if trying to outrun the memories of Millicent from that Sunday and his wandering sexual thoughts just now. He thought of Hope, physically different from Millicent yet beautiful both inside and out. His dick jumped again. He massaged it mindlessly, even as he once again tried to divert his thoughts and calm "Mr. Man" down. *Man, sleeping next to my baby is gonna be hard tonight!*

As Cy turned into his garage, he smiled. A yellow MG sat parked in the stall next to his. Hope. What an appropriate name she'd been given, because hope was exactly what she'd given him. Hope that he could have the love he'd always envisioned, that he'd seen his parents experience. Hope that he could find someone both spiritual and sexy, who could love God like an angel and love him like a courtesan. He now had no doubt that that was exactly what he had in the chocolate pudding waiting upstairs for him. They'd agreed to remain celibate until their wedding took place, but that hadn't prevented them from getting to know each other. He hadn't played the piano, but he'd definitely stroked the keys.

Cy turned the key and activated the elevator to the penthouse floor. Humming to himself, he looked at the lingerie packet and Tiffany box he'd concealed in a plain brown bag. He wanted to see her in something different every night of their honeymoon, before he saw her in nothing but his arms.

The house was quiet as he went inside. "Hey, baby," he called out, noting the silence of the almost always playing stereo. He entered the large open space that was the living, dining, and den area. No Hope. He continued to the kitchen, where he saw the note as soon as he turned the corner:

Hey, Baby, tried to reach you on your cell. I'm with Frieda. Hollah.
Love you, Hope.

He set down the packages, pulled the cell phone from his briefcase, and noted a couple missed calls. Belatedly, he remembered how poor the cell phone reception was in some of the mall stores. Smiling, he hid Hope's honeymoon package in the closet and decided to fix a protein drink before calling his baby. Yes, Hope was the woman he wanted to be thinking about, the one he wanted on his mind. He hoped Millicent was happy, but she was his past. The woman occupying number one on his speed dial was his future.

2

God, Always with You . . .

"Look, you know yo ass can't wait to get some dickage. God created the bone, ain't nothin' wrong with saying you want to handle the meat for a minute, damn!"

"Frieda, you have no sense." Hope laughed as she entered her cousin's newly decorated apartment near Baldwin Hills, an area of Los Angeles that at one time boasted the city's most affluent Black residents. A month after Hope had relocated from Kansas City, she'd suggested to Frieda that she do the same. One visit was all it had taken. One trip to Magic Johnson's theater followed by a stroll through the mall next door and Frieda had agreed that LA was her kind of place. "Umm . . . thirty-two flavors, just like Baskin-Robbins," she had commented after seeing the plentiful, multicultural, multiethnic mix of testosterone who shopped there.

Hope couldn't have been happier. There had not been a moment's hesitation when Cy had asked her to move in with him shortly after he proposed, but after a couple weeks she realized that a big city with millions of people could get lonely, especially with Cy's business and church commitments. When Frieda had called from Kansas City and told her she'd given notice at her job, and to the latest nucka she was seeing, Hope had started things rolling on her end. She'd liquidated one of her "rainy day" CDs so that Frieda could get a place and have rent for a couple months until she got situated. She'd helped Frieda pay for the U-Haul to move her furniture from Kansas City, and they'd had a ball going around to estate sales and swap meets to replace the things Frieda left behind.

It had been a great move for both of them. Frieda had quickly landed a secretarial job and within a month knew her way around LA enough to outrun the fool she'd turned on and then tuned out at a club three weeks after she'd arrived. It was no surprise to Hope that Frieda brought the drama with her. It was her middle name and, Hope guessed, just the way she liked it.

"So, is it good, girl? Fine as his ass is, he better be able to f—"

"We didn't do it yet," Hope interrupted. "How many times do I have to tell you that we're waiting until the wedding night?"

"Girl . . . tell that lie to somebody who'll believe you. Ain't no way you got *that* lying in bed with you at night and you ain't hittin' it. Ain't . . . no . . . way."

"Whatever, Frieda. Where do you want me to put these?" Hope had never seen any of Frieda's places look this good and didn't want to junk it up with their latest purchases.

"Put 'em anywhere, and stop trying to change the subject. You think I tell you all my business and ain't gonna get into yours? Think again, sistah!"

Hope sighed and shook her head as she placed the bags on Frieda's bar counter. Was last night's good time written all over her face? "Okay, we have fooled around, a little bit."

"That's what I'm talkin' 'bout, baby. Be real with a sistah. I know'd yo ass wasn't gonna be able to leave *that* alone." Frieda whooped as she plopped down on the couch. "C'mon in here, girl, and spill it . . . spill it!"

Knowing her cousin wouldn't let the subject rest, Hope

plopped down beside her. "Well, we haven't had actual inter-course but we've, you know, checked each other out."

"Is he big, girl? You know sometimes those pretty boys carry pistols instead of shotguns." Frieda was all ears.

Hope paused. "He's perfect. Not too big, not too little. He's just right." She hid a smile, embarrassed yet happy to be shar-ing her joy with someone else. "And it feels good, nice and thick. It's been so long since I'd seen one, that at first I didn't know whether to touch it, suck it, or frame it!"

"Don't make me hollah!" Frieda said, delighted. "So, did you take care of boyfriend? I know he tasted good, huh?"

"Frieda!"

"Girl, please!"

"I don't know how he tastes, and I'll thank you not to be wondering either!"

Frieda rolled her eyes. "Girl, I've got enough dick to suck, fuck, and fill a semitruck. I don't need yo' shit."

It was Hope's turn to laugh. "I'll be honest, I didn't want to wait. I figured that since we're engaged—and speaking for me, even married already in my heart—I was ready to do it. But Cy said we'd waited this long, a couple more months wasn't going to kill us."

"And you said speak for yourself, right?"

"I'm glad he said it actually, because he's right. It will make our wedding night extra special. I know it's going to be so good. Just from the way he kisses me and holds me; he knows all the right spots to touch. He drives me crazy!"

"Well, all I can say is you're a better woman than I am. I would have licked that piece of caramel on the first night, within the first couple hours, feel me?"

Hope's phone rang. She eyed the ID and opened her cell. "Hey, baby, we were just talking about you."

"Were you saying how much you love me, and how you can't wait to become my wife?"

"That's *exactly* what I was saying, babe, that I can't wait." Hope winked at Frieda. "What's up?"

"Not much. Just got home and got your note. I was at the mall when you called."

"Out shopping, huh? Anything for me?"

"Not today, baby. I'm sorry, should have thought about you."

Hope feigned disappointment. "Cy Taylor, nothing called out my name? Nothing had Hope Jones Taylor written all over it?"

You have no idea, he mused. "Next time, okay?"

"Okay. Any plans for dinner?"

"Just you."

"Good, I'll stop and get some salmon steaks when Frieda brings me home."

"What do we need the steaks for? I said 'just you.' "

"Ooh . . . you're such a bad boy. That's why I love you. I'll see you soon." Hope's pussy tingled as she closed the phone and leaned back on the couch.

"Can you believe it?" she said to Frieda. "Can you believe I'm actually marrying that man? It still feels like a dream. All the years I prayed and believed that my prince would come, and all the nights I cried and argued with God because he didn't. Then it was like, snap, and just like that, my life changed. I can't even begin to describe how this feels. It's more than amazing, really. It's beyond words."

Frieda got up and walked into the kitchen. "You want a wine cooler?" Hope declined but said yes to a cola. "And I've got some chips and dip. You hungry?"

"Yeah, bring it all in. I want to go over the wedding, get your final opinions. And don't try to get all crazy on me. I've decided to keep it simple. Oh, and I've finally settled on the colors—different shades of blue. What do you think? Frieda!"

Frieda came around the corner loaded down with chips, dip, leftover chicken wings, cookies, soda, and a wine cooler.

Hope jumped up. "Dang, you took me literally, huh? What's all this?"

They placed the food on the coffee table and loaded up plates. "Anytime we talk about men and matrimony," Frieda answered around a mouthful of chips, "it's a party."

They spent the afternoon fine-tuning Hope's plans for the ceremony. She'd dreamed of this for so many years one would think the details would have been easy. Now that the time was actually here though, she'd changed her mind more than once, wanting everything to be perfect. She had switched color schemes three times, but felt her idea of using various shades of blue was going to look beautiful against the scenic ocean backdrop. Cy's custom Carlo Scotti tux was a deep navy made from extrafine merino faille wool. Hope's dress was a white halter-necked, dropped waist satin wonder accented with light blue Swarovski crystals to match Cy's light blue silk shirt. Frieda was the maid of honor, her dress a mix of turquoise, aqua, and light blue. The best man, Simeon, Cy's equally fine cousin, would wear a light blue suit. Hope had snagged the Musical Messengers to provide the music, a blend of jazz, R & B classics, and contemporary gospel for both the ceremony and sit-down dinner afterward, as the boat cruised around the marina. She and Cy had decided to recite traditional vows and keep the ceremony simple: a duet of "their song," Eric Benet's "Spend My Life With You," a recitation of The Lord's Prayer, and a poem Hope wrote, titled simply, "The One." Knowing how close their pastors were and how much church meant to them, it was easy to decide that both pastors, Derrick Montgomery and King Brook, would officiate.

"Do you think his wife will come?" Frieda asked.

"I don't know," Hope answered. Frieda was talking about Tai Brook, first lady of Mount Zion Progressive Baptist Church, Hope's former church in Kansas City. Hope had told Frieda about how Tai once suspected Hope of wanting her husband,

King. Being a single female in a church with a fine pastor wasn't always easy. Some had thought Hope's exuberant praise was for the King of Mount Zion instead of the King of Kings. King was very attractive, but Hope could never have imagined stepping out with Queen Bee's man. And then go to church and dance with the ministry's dance troupe, the Angels of Hope? Twirl around to the melody of "My God Is an Awesome God?"

"It is your wedding, after all," Frieda continued, sipping on her cooler. "You'd think she'd come just to make sure the deed got done."

"I like Queen Bee and I know she and Sistah Vivian are best friends. I included a personal note with the invitation, saying how much I wanted her there. She seemed to warm up to me toward the end, so I hope she'll come."

"Vivian's your new pastor's wife, right?"

"Uh-huh, the one you met on your one and only visit."

"Now, don't give up on me, cousin. There's some fine brothahs in that building; I'll be back."

"And you didn't even see Darius. He was out of town the Sunday you visited."

"Darius . . . who's that?"

"Kingdom's newest most eligible bachelor since Cy got engaged. He's our minister of music. He's got a new CD coming out and it's supposed to be fire. Cy says some major record labels are trying to sign him."

"Oh, he ain't signed yet? Tell a brothah to hollah when he gets that advance check!"

"Frieda, you should marry for love, not money."

"Don't worry. If he's got money, I'll love him."

Hope just shook her head. "Maybe God has other plans for you. There are some fine associate ministers at Kingdom. You might end up a pastor's wife."

"Ah, hell no. Ain't that much holy water in the world!"

Hope laughed. "Remember, they're men first and foremost. Look at Cy; he's a minister."

"Yeah, and he's marrying yo ass. I can't be hooking up with somebody who wants me in church every Sunday. Give me a hit every now and then, maybe a song at Christmas and an Easter egg, and I'm good to go. Feel me?"

"No, I don't feel you, but it's all to the good. God is with you no matter where you are."

"Ooh, don't tell me that. 'Cause there's some places I'd rather He not tag along. Let a sistah roll solo, okay?"

Hope looked at Frieda, her countenance serious. "No, Frieda. God is with you *all* the time."

"Shut up, girl. Next time I'm fuckin' I'll be lookin' up at the ceiling expecting to see a big ass pair of eyes staring down at me." Frieda drained her wine cooler bottle and jumped up to get another.

Hope almost spit out the soda she was swallowing. "You are a bona fide fool," she said, laughing so hard her sides hurt.

Frieda returned from the kitchen. "No, I'm a bonin' fool," she said. "There's a difference." She sat on the couch, leafing through pictures of the yacht Cy was leasing for the wedding. "And speaking of fools, I wonder what happened to that girl who went gangsta on your boy, showing up at the church with demands and what not."

Hope's humor dimmed. "Millicent?"

"Yeah, her. I know what she did was whack, but that was some bold shit."

"I don't know where she is, nor do I care," Hope said with finality. She didn't want to discuss Millicent. Hope didn't want that woman, or even her name, anywhere near her wedding plans.

3

From Dreams to Reality

The hustle and bustle of LAX, Los Angeles's busiest airport, greeted Millicent as she stepped through the Jetway. Hard to believe she was back in Los Angeles. When she left four months ago, whether she'd return at all was anyone's guess. Even now, she felt vulnerable, not sure if she was ready to step back into the real world. But she couldn't hide out at her mother's forever. Her therapist had encouraged her to accept the marketing contract she'd been offered, felt that working would help her life return to normal. Problem was, Millicent wasn't sure she'd recognize normal when it arrived.

Millicent made her way to baggage claim, keeping her hat pulled low and sunglasses firmly in place. The last thing she wanted was to be recognized. That was the main reason she'd decided to return to California but not live in Los Angeles— she did not want to see or be seen by anyone she knew. Before coming back from her mother's home in Portland, Oregon, Millicent decided to sell her condo and had enlisted her real estate agent to find another one in La Jolla, about a hundred miles from the City of Angels, near San Diego. Based on her therapist's diagnosis, she'd gotten disability through her insurance company and was thankful she'd played it safe with her investments. The time off from work hadn't hit her too hard financially. Plus, at her therapist's suggestion, to occupy her mind productively, she'd freelanced for a couple clients in Portland.

Her contract with Innovative Designs, a computer technology firm, began at the end of January, two weeks away. For now, Millicent was anxious to get her luggage and go to the condo that she no longer called home. That would be where the test of her healing really started, when she walked into the place that held so many memories, so many dreams, the dreams that had led to . . . *No. Not those thoughts, not right now.* She dealt with thoughts of Cy every day, had even dreamed of him. But she didn't want to think about him right now.

Standing near the carousel, Millicent looked around and saw a man holding a sign that read "Sims." It was the town car she'd hired. She waved him over, just as the first of her many suitcases came into view. It wasn't long before the driver saw what he was dealing with and went to find a porter. Fifteen minutes and several suitcases later, they headed out of the airport and into the LA night.

Millicent smiled slightly as familiar sights and streets passed by. It hadn't been that long, but things looked different somehow, a stark contrast to the clean, calm city of Portland, that's for sure. One thing hadn't changed—traffic. Settling back for a long ride, she pulled out her Blackberry and checked e-mails. There weren't many new ones, as she'd expected. One from Jenny, her real estate agent, confirming their noon appointment the next day; one from Alison, her good friend and one of the few who knew about "the incident" with whom she'd remained in contact; a couple from inspirational sites; and her monthly music selection from BMG. She replied to both Jenny and Alison, read the inspirational messages, and declined the BMG selection before pushing delete.

When she looked up, the car was crossing Wilshire, a main boulevard through the heart of Los Angeles. Her heart tightened a bit. This was the street she regularly took to her old church, Kingdom Citizens' Christian Center, or KCCC, as it was sometimes referred. Thinking of the church made her think of Cy. Tall, handsome, Cy Taylor, the man she'd believed with all her heart was her husband. *Husband! No, stop it. Don't play the tape again.*

Millicent used the techniques her therapist had taught her and switched her thoughts to something different, positive. *That's it, refocus.* She thought about the glowing recommendation she'd received from the company in Portland, the one that helped seal the deal at Innovative Designs: "Ms. Sims's talents and skills are superb; your gain will be our loss." She remembered the feel of her mother's arms around her, the unending encouragement that life would get better: "No matter how long the road, dear, eventually there is a turn in it." She thought about the profit she'd made from the sale of her condo. *Six figures in my savings! Maybe Cy will—No, Cy won't.* There were plenty investors in San Diego County. She took a deep breath, counted to three, let it out. *Yes, breathe, focus on the breath, positive thoughts.* She thought about her mom, the one person on earth who could make her feel better, no matter what. Just then, her phone rang.

"Mom! I was just going to call you!"

"Millie, dear, you all right?"

"Yes, I'm fine. I was just thinking of you, that's all, and wanted you to know that I made it back." Millicent paused. "I'm on my way to the condo."

"How are you feeling about that?"

"A little nervous, but I'll be okay."

"Oh, Millie dear, I wish you'd let me come with you. I don't know that going there is something you should be doing all by yourself."

"Mom, I'm a big girl."

"I know, but with all the upsets you've been through lately . . ." Mrs. Sims didn't finish. They both knew all too well what Millicent had been through.

"I love you for caring about me. But I feel like I need to do this alone. Take back control of my life, you know?" Again they were silent, thinking of how Millicent's life had temporarily spun out of control. "But I will never be able to thank you enough, Mom. You were my rock when I stood on very shaky ground."

Mrs. Sims laughed. "That's what mothers are sometimes. You'll see, when it comes to your children, you'll do anything."

Millicent changed the subject. To think about children, she'd have to think about a husband, and that was the last thing she wanted on her mind. "My agent left a message; she has a couple condos in La Jolla for me to check out."

"Oh, that's great, Millie. I think your moving out of LA was the best idea."

"I do, too. La Jolla is a beautiful area, and the people at the computer company seem really nice. Lots of work coming up in these next few weeks and that's just what I need, to stay busy."

"That's right. And you need God, too, dear. Don't forget to start looking for a church home."

Millicent wasn't going down that road either. She was sure she'd find one eventually, but she was not in any big hurry to join another church. "We're almost at the condo, Mom. I'll call you later. I love you."

"Love you, too, dear."

The driver turned the corner and there it was—the condo Millicent had proudly called home for almost five years. She'd leased it out on a month-to-month basis during her time in Portland, but now with it sold, she needed to move what furniture remained to storage and say good-bye to a chapter of her life that was forever closed. The driver was already out, placing her suitcases on the sidewalk. With a sigh of resignation mixed with determination, Millicent got out of the car and walked into the lobby.

"Nice place," the driver commented cheerfully, putting suitcases near the elevator.

"Yes," Millicent responded simply.

"Wish I could afford to live in a neighborhood like this. I can't imagine coming here every night."

Millicent smiled, busying herself by helping bring in the suitcases. Her heart beat rapidly, but she tried to ignore the building anxiety, tried to calm it with conscious breathing: *in, hold three counts, out.*

The driver came in with the last two cases and joined Millicent at the elevator. "You must have been gone a while," he said, pointing to the luggage.

"Yes." Millicent tried not to be annoyed. The man was just being friendly. Still, she pushed the already lit elevator button again and then reached for her wallet. "Thank you," she said, handing the driver the fare plus a generous tip.

His eyes widened when he saw three Benjamins. Looking at Millicent with dreamy eyes, the driver responded in what was his attempt at sexy. "No, baby doll, thank *you!*"

Is he trying to flirt? He had no idea how not the one she was. She was *so* not the one. One of the last men to do that had ended up being stalked by a crazed woman in a wedding gown! For the first time, Millicent almost smiled at the thought.

The elevator doors opened, and she and the driver began placing the bags inside. "You need help up with these?" he asked, obviously wanting to prolong their encounter.

"No, thank you, I've got it from here." She was saved from further questioning by the elevator door closing in his face.

Millicent slowly moved the bags from the elevator to her front door. She paused, took a deep breath, and placed the key in the lock. As she opened the door and walked inside, she closed her eyes on the tears that threatened, then opened them again. A bit of a sting, but easier than she'd thought it would be. The impersonality of the place helped. Jenny had removed all of the more personal touches, photographs and other identifying belongings, and placed them in storage before renting the condo out. And now the place belonged to someone else. One more step in starting over.

One by one, Millicent brought her suitcases inside. Once they were in, she closed the door and again looked around. She walked into the kitchen, the dining room. She walked to the bathroom and stopped. This had been one of her favorite places, a bit harder to face now. So many dreams she'd created while soaking in the Jacuzzi tub, dreams that had floated away, disappeared down the drain, like the bathwater. Before the tears could gather, she walked briskly back into her bedroom, picked up the briefcase containing her laptop, and walked to the desk. *Stay focused, Millicent. Guard your thoughts.* Millicent sat and redirected her energy to preparing the condo for its new owner, looking at the potential homes Jenny had selected for her, and drafting a marketing outline for her new boss. The time for dreams was gone. With steely resolve, Millicent focused on her reality.

4

That's What Friends Are For

Vivian Montgomery waited at the predesignated meeting point, tapping her foot impatiently. Her children, nine-year-old Derrick Jr. and his seven-year-old sister, Elisia, were getting perilously close to failing their lesson on responsibility. She'd clearly told them to meet her by the Starbucks in Barnes & Noble in exactly one hour, and she'd made sure her and her son's cell phone alarms were set. The children were young, but she liked to loosen the reins every now and then, give them some independence. Plus, their neighbor's son, Chris, was with them, and he was eleven. She felt okay with them on their own at the Westside Pavilion, but one more minute, and—

"Hello? Yes, you'd better be on your way. I didn't tell you to call me in an hour, I told you to meet me in an hour. Bye." Letting out the worried breath she'd refused to acknowledge she'd been holding, Vivian strolled down the aisles, casually scanning the book covers. Just as she heard Elisia's high-pitched laugh, she glimpsed the store's CD section.

"I told them, Mama, I told them to come on," Elisia said as she ran to Vivian.

"No, she didn't. She was too busy playing to even listen to me tell her it was time to go," D-2 countered.

"Uh-uh. I told you, I said let's go 'cause Mama said one hour—"

"You a lie! You—"

"Enough," Vivian said in a low tone that brooked no argument. "Both of you were irresponsible. You need to understand that a big part of responsibility," she said, dragging out the word for emphasis, "is being able to follow through when a direction is given. Especially when it's your mama's direction, and especially when that one direction may decide whether you get to follow through on any further such directions."

Silence.

"Now, calling was good, Derrick; it let me know that you were all right. But being where I told you *when* I told you would have been better." She looked at Chris, who'd become extremely preoccupied with the pattern on the floor. "And what do you have to say, young man? You're the oldest of this bunch."

"Uh, I was so busy making sure no one bothered Elisia that I, uh, lost track of time."

"I see," Vivian said with exaggerated slowness. "You got some oceanfront property in Nevada you want to sell me, too?"

"Ma'am?"

So now he was going to act like he was deaf or confused. "You heard me," she said seriously, while mussing his curly dark hair. "Come on, let's go look at CDs. I need to get some music."

Vivian reached the CD aisle and began to browse.

"Mama, can we go look at our music?"

"Yes, D-2. Elisia, stay with me." She walked over to the R & B section, looking for the artist Tai had babbled nonstop about since his debut years earlier. *He sounds like Al Jarreau, but with his own style. And he's a Hershey, honey. . . .* One thing about Tai, she'd never let the fact that she was first lady of a large Baptist church get in the way of her love for R & B.

Vivian quickly found the CDs Tai had recommended,

Kemistry and Album II, then strolled further, stopping at the oldies compilations. "Do you think Aunt Tai will like some oldies music, Lis?"

"Yes. She always listens to that old stuff."

Vivian smiled, remembering when she thought people in their thirties and forties were ancient. Now, nearing forty, she knew they were barely middle-aged.

Vivian had just reached for an "80s Gold" anthology when her cell phone rang. . . . "Hello?"

"You're not going to believe who's back in town," Tai said without a greeting.

Vivian didn't answer immediately. From the sound of Tai's voice, whoever it was wasn't someone she welcomed. Vivian asked anyway, not knowing if she wanted to hear the answer. "Who?"

"Tootie."

"Tootie?" Would the drama never end? Tai and King's marriage had just gotten back on track following King's last infidelity. And now Tootie, his schoolboy crush, was back in town? Vivian motioned to the boys and headed to the counter, Elisia following her. "Look, I'm in a store. Let me call you when I get to the car."

"As soon as you can," Tai said, exasperated.

"On second thought, I've got the kids. I'll call when I get home."

Vivian tried to remain calm as she waited in line. No need to get upset before hearing the details. But what did Tai know that had upset her so? Then again, just the mention of Rita "Tootie" Smith's name could be enough.

Vivian was thankful for the kids' mindless chatter on the way home. That and the smooth sounds of the newly purchased Kem CD she'd placed in the stereo before starting the car. She only half listened, however, her mind wandering from thoughts of Tai to the Sanctity of Sisterhood seminars she'd been moderating. Thankfully, traffic was light and soon she was turning into her driveway.

The tires had barely stopped rolling before the kids rushed out of the car. Kathy, Chris's mom, was just running by, at the end of her afternoon jog. Chris ran up and showed her his namesake Chris Brown CD.

"Yes, Kathy, you can thank me for the noise you'll hear later," Vivian said as her neighbor trotted up the drive. "It's the radio-edit version, but you still might want to have a listen."

"Gee, Viv, thanks a lot. I really needed to hear more hippity-hop in my house."

"Hip-hop, Mom," Chris groaned, the expected reaction and exact reason his mother had mispronounced the term.

"Hey, man, let's ball," D-2 suggested, inviting himself over to the half-court basketball asphalt in Chris's backyard. He and Chris began walking toward the Winters' home.

"Derrick, don't lose that CD I just bought you," Vivian directed at his back.

"You can lose yours, Chris," Kathy added. Both women laughed. "See you later, Viv."

Vivian ejected the Kem CD, placed it in its case, and retrieved the shopping bags. Once inside her home, she put down her purchases and quickly looked through the mail on the foyer table. "Change your clothes before going out to play, Elisia," she said to her daughter, who was headed up the stairs. "I need to make an important call. Only disturb if it's an emergency, okay?"

"Yes, Mama," Elisia answered.

Vivian watched her rapidly growing daughter bounce up the stairs. *Lord, please help her not grow up too soon.* She lay down the mail, walked into the kitchen, and took marinating chicken breast fillets out of the refrigerator. After placing them in the oven and setting the other dinner preparations on the counter, she headed to her office and called Kansas City.

Tai picked up on the second ring. "I thought you said you'd call right back."

"This is right back. I had to start dinner. So what's up with Tootie being back in town? How long has it been, ten, fifteen years?"

Tai's voice dripped with sarcasm. "Janeé, she goes by Janeé now."

"Tootie is Ja-nay?" Sometimes an upset Tai was hard to follow.

"Yeah, I guess the name *Tootie* didn't look so good in lights. Remember she moved to Germany, did some recording? She was pretty popular from what I hear, starred in musicals, recorded a couple albums. What was that one hit song of hers? 'Heat' or 'Hot' or something? Anyway, I haven't heard anything about her in a minute. . . ." Tai's voice trailed off.

"So what is she doing back in Kansas City?"

"Her mother's sick. In the back of my mind I just knew that would bring Tootie's ass back here. I prayed it wouldn't, but I just knew . . ."

Vivian was all too aware of how Tootie used to be Tai's nemesis, continuing to see King while he and Tai were dating, and having an affair with him after they married. She remembered how relieved Tai had been when right after her second child, Princess, was born, Tootie moved from the Midwest, swearing never to return. But that was a long time ago. Everyone was older, wiser, and Tai and King's marriage was on solid ground. Vivian wasn't going to make a mountain out of a molehill.

"Okay, wait a minute, Tai. Why are we going here? Why are you making a big deal of this? Of course she'd come back to care for her mother."

Vivian continued, determined to make Tai focus on what was really important. "You and King are back on track, tighter than ever. He loves *you*. He's committed to *you*. So, Tootie's back in town—Tootie, Janay, whatever her name is. So what? What has that got to do with you?"

"Everything. One of the first people she asked about was King. That's how I found out she was back."

"Well, good. He told you."

"That's the other thing. King didn't tell me. Mama Max did."

Vivian wished it had been King instead of his mother, but she still wasn't going to help her friend trip.

"When did Mama Max tell you?"

"Earlier today. Sistah Stokes ran into Tootie at the store. Tootie asked about King. Sistah Stokes called Mama from Albertsons parking lot." Sistah Stokes, a longtime church member, knew of King's affair with Tootie and had believed a warning was warranted.

Vivian let out a chagrined breath. That's how stuff got started. "You just found this out? So how do you even know King knows she's back, Tai?"

A pause on the other end, and then, "I guess I don't."

"See? And you're getting all worked up, letting your imagination take you where you shouldn't want to go, over nothing."

"You're right. You're absolutely right, Viv. I guess I'm still a little paranoid."

"A little?" Vivian teased her friend.

"Okay," Tai said, laughing. "Your sistah's trippin'. But King's past infidelities aren't easy to forget."

"Nobody says you have to. Just remember, the operative word in that sentence is *past*. We're living in the now, and right now, you and King have never been better."

The conversation drifted to other things until Vivian noticed the smell of teriyaki chicken floating under the office door. "Listen, I need to finish dinner. Call you later?"

"Sure. And Vivian?"

"Uh-huh?"

"Thanks."

Vivian smiled, glad to hear the relief in Tai's voice. "Don't mention it, sistah. That's what friends are for."

5

Tootie Says Hi

Even though it was Saturday, the parking lot next to the main edifice of Mount Zion Progressive Baptist Church was almost full. Meetings, rehearsals, classes, and Sunday service preparations were in full swing. A slight flurry of snow began to fall as King navigated the suburban streets of Overland Park, Kansas. On one such street, the buildings of Mount Zion Progressive Baptist Church, its offices, youth center, and fellowship hall now took up the entire block. He eyed the surroundings dispassionately, critically evaluating size, layout. And even though they'd just finished a major one, he was considering possibilities for a greater expansion. The membership was growing in record numbers, and plans were on the drawing board for a preschool and private K–8 learning academy, within five years.

King consciously stopped that train of thought as he eased into the reserved spot directly in front of the door that led to his office. There would be plenty of time to consider those projects later. Presently, his focus was on the meeting with his new media staff, and the television broadcast that was being taped the next day. There had been much deliberation before King had decided to go on the air. He'd gotten requests for years, and had done a brief stint on the local cable channel several years back. But the Total Truth Association had linked up

with MLM, a cutting-edge broadcast network based in Atlanta, which aggressively pursued a handful of ministers with
progressive, contemporary messages to fill their Sunday morning time slots. It had taken several months to find and hire a
media director, get the equipment in place, construct a pro-
duction/media room for the actual taping of the services, and
train volunteers to man the various cameras and production
equipment. Today's meeting would be about confirming that
everything was in order to shoot tomorrow's eleven A.M. services. The crew would later do a quick run-through while he
moved on to a meeting with the deacons.

His assistant, Joseph, met him as soon as he stepped into his
office. "Afternoon, boss."

"Good afternoon, Joseph. You order this weather, brothah?"

"Hey, I'm from down south; I'm probably never going to
get used to these Kansas winters."

King placed his coat on the rack, took the scarf from
around his neck, and placed it over the coat hook. He looked
at the stack of phone messages centered neatly on his desk,
next to the one-page report of scheduled activities and ap-
pointments that his multitasking, multicapable assistant provided daily. He sat down and began going through the messages.
"Besides the media project, how's it looking today?"

"I kept it light today, boss. Knew the television taping was
the main focus. Darius made it in from LA. He and his band
will be coming by later to do a sound check." Darius Crenshaw and his gospel band, otherwise known as D & C, for Darius & Company, were in demand at churches all over the
country. King had had to pull some strings with Darius to
book them as special guests for this, his first taping for a national audience.

"Oh, and Deacon Nash called," Joseph continued. "He's
feeling under the weather. So if you'd like to reschedule the
deacons' meeting, there's time for me to do that."

"No, let's keep it, but no more than an hour. Von here yet?"

"On his way. He called earlier, too."

Lavon Chapman was the new media director for Mount Zion. He'd been working for another ministry in Minneapolis when King's church recruited him.

Joseph answered a knock at the door and welcomed Lavon inside. He entered like a snowstorm, powerful and heavy.

"Man, it's cold outside. Hope this snow don't fall all day." Lavon walked over to the desk and extended his hand. "What up, Preach?" He sat down opposite King.

It had been that way from the first time they met, a respectful yet informal quality to their relationship. Most of the staff addressed King as Pastor King or Minister Brook, but somewhere in between the two-hour interview process and the last erected tripod, "Pastor King" had become "Preach," and from Von, it was okay.

"You tell me," King responded casually, noting Lavon's muscles flex through the sweatshirt he wore over jeans. Being around Lavon made King want to join a gym, lift some weights. He resisted the urge to do a curl and check the state of his own biceps.

"It's all good. Met with Bryan last night. He's going to be a good right-hand man," Lavon said, referring to his assistant director.

"So, who all's in this meeting?" King asked.

"The entire media staff," Von responded. "That's Bryan, the program manager, technical directors, sound engineers, camera crews, grips, shaders, tape operators, and a few floaters for whatever miscellaneous needs arise."

"Good, good," King said, rubbing his newly grown goatee. He loved efficiency, made it his mission to surround himself with capable staff.

Joseph's phone rang. "Hello? Oh yes, I've got that for you, hold up." He walked out of the office and to his desk.

The door had barely closed when Von leaned forward. "Guess what, Preach? Turns out I know an old friend of yours."

King leaned back. Never having spent time in Minnesota, he had no idea who that could be. "Who?" he asked.

"Janeé Petersen."

"Janeé Petersen." King thought for a moment and then shook his head. "No, the name's not familiar. Where am I supposed to know her from?"

"She said you wouldn't know her by that name. But that y'all go way back. Said she used to live here, and to tell you Tootie said hi."

Just then he remembered Janeé was Tootie's middle name. King sat forward, on high alert. "Tootie? Tootie Smith? You have *got* to be kidding me! She lives in Minnesota?"

"No, she lives in Germany, but I ran into her a few blocks from here."

King was even more confused. *Minnesota, Germany, and now Tootie's here, in Kansas?* "Is that so?" he said, slowly. Then he remembered the news about Miss Smith. "I know her mother's been sick. She must really not be doing well for Tootie to come back here."

"She's not," Lavon answered. "She's got to have open-heart surgery."

King wrote a quick note to have Joseph schedule a hospital visit. Then he asked in what he hoped was a casual tone, "How do you know, uh, Janeé?"

"I met her a couple years back, at a hotel in Minneapolis. You know she had that hit, back in the early nineties. I guess she's still doing her thang in Europe. Anyway, some of my buddies and I checked her out and stayed to meet her afterward. I know Germany pretty well from my army days, so we struck up a friendship. I contacted her when I was in Hamburg last year. We went out for dinner. I was just as shocked as you seem right now when I saw her down the street. Small world."

Small world indeed. Too small. "Wonder what she's doing over this way?" King pondered. Neither her mother's house nor the hospital was in the area. Was she on her way to the church?

"I don't know. I was so surprised to see her I didn't ask. We talked for a few minutes, exchanged phone numbers, and when I told her I had to get to the church, she asked if I knew you. I told her yes. She asked all these questions about you, and said to tell you hi."

Questions? What kind of questions? What would his first lay, his steady from back in the day, want to know about him? Regardless, his heart warmed with memories. "How's she doing?" King responded with a query of his own. "She must be married. Her last name used to be Smith and now it's . . . ?" He waited for Lavon to fill in the blank.

"Petersen. Yeah, she's doing grand. Husband is an investment banker or something."

"Hmm," King said.

"Yeah, they got a couple kids, the whole nine."

King raised his brows. The Tootie he used to know and "mother" was a tight fit in the same sentence. But people change. *Tootie, Tootie, with the big boo*—King shook his head. That was one memory lane he need not go down. He turned businesslike. "Well, I'll be sure and pray for Miss Smith. And for Tootie, I mean, Janeé," he corrected. "I know what it's like to be worried about your mother's health." And then an abrupt change of subject: "Did you say your church used five or six cameras?"

Lavon didn't miss the quick change in King's demeanor, or in the subject matter. "We used five there. Here, we'll use six, an additional hand-held for special shots." And then, because he couldn't resist, "I'm not trying to be out of line, Preach, but is she an old flame or something? She was looking all nostalgic when talking about you. I mean, I'm just asking. She said y'all hadn't seen each other in years."

She was right. It had been a long time. Every now and then he'd wondered if she still lived overseas and how she was doing. Tootie had been a wildcat back in the day; that "cat" had gotten him in trouble more than once. That girl did everything, was a real daredevil. He and his friends used to compare notes afterward.

Lavon watched King try and remain impassive. But he was convinced some past passion lay just beneath the facade.

King was just about to respond to Von's question when Joseph stuck his head in the doorway. "Everyone's gathered in the conference room. Should I tell them we're ready to begin?"

King was up and out of his seat in a flash, reaching for the suit coat he'd removed earlier. He was glad for the interruption, so the conversation about Tootie could come to an end. Relieved to not have to ponder the feelings that the mention of her name evoked. With determination, he channeled his thoughts to the tasks at hand—running Mount Zion Progressive, a million-dollar corporation, for the Lord.

6

Mercy . . . Peace . . . Love . . .

Millicent stopped working and stretched. She grabbed the arm of her chair with both hands and twisted her back, grabbed the other chair arm and repeated the motion. She still felt tight. Looking at her watch, she understood why. Where had the time gone? It was almost two o'clock in the afternoon and she'd been hard at work, barely moving from her computer, since before eight. *It's time for a break,* she thought, saving her work and punching in the code that sent her phone calls to the company's answering system.

"Back in an hour," she said cheerfully to the receptionist.

"Oh my goodness, you're just now getting out for lunch?" the receptionist asked. "And it's such a beautiful day!"

"I've barely looked up from the computer long enough to notice, but you're right." Millicent quickly checked her mail slot and added, "I might make it an hour and a half."

"There you go, you deserve it. You've been working non-stop."

Millicent smiled and headed for the door. Her therapist was right. Getting back to work had been helpful. The workplace had always been an area where she felt in control, and here was no different. The long hours and hard work had been therapeutic, and productive. She'd already made big strides toward Innovative Design's new marketing direction.

Millicent stepped out into a typically beautiful February afternoon in California. The sky was a brilliant blue and, after the rains of earlier in the week, crystal clear. She greeted two of her colleagues as they passed her on their way back into the office, hopped into her Infiniti coupe, and quickly maneuvered out of the parking lot. But instead of taking a left toward her usual lunch locale, a quaint shopping center a few blocks down, she took a right and decided to drive toward the ocean. Maybe she could enjoy a quick stroll and a sandwich. Yes, the beach sounded like a great choice.

San Diego was growing on her, and she'd already fallen in love with her condo in La Jolla. She'd initially balked at the large purchase. The housing market had grown absolutely ridiculous in the five years since she'd purchased her last abode, and she'd felt reluctant to take on such a huge debt. But in the end, she'd figured that not only was the condo a good investment, but it allowed her to live as she desired, in an affluent neighborhood. Her new complex boasted every amenity, including swimming pools, three hot tubs, an exercise room, sauna, doorman, lounge with a pool table and big screen TV, and an exquisitely designed club house for parties and other social functions. Fortunately her good credit, and her ability to place a large down payment with some of the profit from her previous condo sale, allowed her to get a good interest rate, reasonable terms, and a manageable mortgage. She was also glad she'd decided to sell her old furniture and start fresh with her new home's decor. The only things she'd kept were her personal accessories and artwork, including the prized Henry Tanner original, *The Annunciation*.

Millicent was still becoming familiar with the streets of San Diego, so it was a half hour before she found what she was looking for, a small strip of shops next to the ocean. She pulled into a parking lot and stopped by the attendant's booth. Within minutes, she was following the bike path several yards from the water. She'd removed her suit jacket and was sorely tempted to take off her shoes, but refrained. Just seeing and hearing the water was enough. There was something immensely soothing about the waves ebbing and tiding against the shore. She'd walked for less than ten minutes when she could resist no more. She eased out of her two-inch-heeled sandals and cautiously stepped into the sand. The ocean seemed to call her, and she obeyed the urge to move closer, let the water touch her feet. For several moments she stood there, head tilted up slightly, eyes closed, breathing in deep breaths of the moist, sea air. Opening her eyes, she gazed out to the ocean's edge, a mirage, of course, because the ocean went on forever, past the Hawaiian Islands, past Japan, beyond China, and on until it joined quietly, seamlessly, with the Arabian Sea.

There was such gratitude pouring from her heart in this moment. No one could have convinced her she'd ever live in California again, much less be working and enjoying it. From the beginning, Innovative Designs had made it clear that they wanted her to come on full-time, and now she was actually considering their offer. It was a great group of people—less than twenty made up the whole company—and it had a decidedly family feel. She'd objected adamantly at first but Bob, the brilliantly charming president, was slowly wearing down her resolve. The near six-figure salary he'd waved in front of her was part of the company's attraction as well.

There was yet another attraction. Working at Innovative Designs kept Millicent's mind off Cy, at least what had been daily, continuous thoughts of him. Since beginning her work there, she'd actually experienced twenty-four-hour periods when she didn't think of Cy at all. She still dreamed of him, but not as often. And yes, a part of her heart still ached for him, still loved him. Millicent didn't know if that would ever go away.

She wondered if he and Hope were married yet. That had

been one of her worst days, when Alison had phoned her with the news that Cy was engaged. In a last, desperate act, she'd dialed him as soon as she hung up from Alison. All of his numbers, home, office and cell, had been changed. His engagement told the world what Millicent couldn't tell herself: she and Cy would not be together. *But why couldn't it have been me, God? Why did another woman's dreams come true?* But they had. Cy had Hope, but ironically, Millicent's hope of having Cy was gone.

Millicent sighed, breathed deeply, and then turned back toward the bike path and the small outdoor café she'd passed on the way. Once back on the sidewalk, she was reminded why she hadn't wanted to take her shoes off in the first place. She stopped and tried unsuccessfully to wipe the sand off her feet. She slipped back into her sandals and covered the short distance to the café. Only one of the six or so tables was occupied. She ordered a fish sandwich with fries and an iced tea, chose a table a safe distance from the other lone diner, and took a seat. Trying to recapture her former light mood, she reached for her iPod. She'd just slipped on her headphones and punched in Beethoven's Sixth Symphony in F Major when a shadow came over the table. She didn't look up, thought it was the waiter again.

"Good afternoon." The voice was deep, melodious.

Millicent looked up into blue eyes and a sincere smile. "Good afternoon," she replied, with no enthusiasm.

"I don't mean to bother you, but would you mind terribly if I sat with you a few moments?"

Millicent did mind; she was in no mood for company, especially of the male variety. She looked around pointedly at the other empty tables and noted that the man before her was from the table that had been occupied when she'd arrived. Putting down her earphones and picking up her Blackberry, she said, "I'm a bit busy, on my lunch hour—"

"I promise to not take more than two minutes of your

time," the stranger interrupted, his hand already on the chair opposite her. Still, he waited.

"I guess I can spare two minutes," Millicent said, reluctantly but not unkind. She looked at her watch to indicate the seriousness of her intent to hold him to the time limit.

The stranger smiled. He had bright, even teeth in a slightly tanned face. His windblown hair was sandy blond streaked with lighter, almost white highlights, making his a distinguished yet playful look. His face looked young, very few lines, but when he smiled, faint crow's feet appeared at the corners of his eyes. "Jack Kirtz," he offered, his hand outstretched.

"Millicent Sims," she responded, shaking his hand lightly.

He pulled out the chair, talking as he did so. "I saw you walking along the beach, enjoying the view." Jack had enjoyed the view also, only he hadn't been looking at the ocean. He decided to keep the conversation official, however, and not verbalize his attraction to this tantalizing stranger. "It's rare I get a chance to do this," he continued, "take time off in the middle of the day. Good to do though, take a moment and enjoy God's creation. I've been making a point to try and do it more often."

Millicent nodded, but remained silent. His opening lines had taken up almost thirty seconds.

"Listen, I stopped because I'm a pastor and, believe it or not, this is not something I get to do often, but I'd like to invite you to services this Sunday." He reached into his shirt pocket and pulled out a business card. "Do you live in the area?"

"La Jolla," Millicent said, scanning the card.

"Oh, nice, very nice. So you must work around here then?"

Millicent was not up for twenty questions, especially from this ministerial stranger. She'd made it a point to stay busy and focus only on work and keeping spiritually fed through tapes and television. Her dear friend, Alison, sent what she thought were inspirational, uplifting messages regularly, messages she thought Millicent would enjoy. And they talked every week. There were only two topics off-limits: Cy and Kingdom Citizens.

And then there was the fact that this man was a pastor. The thought of going into anyone's sanctuary elicited an involuntary twitch in her stomach. Her mom's small Methodist church had been different, perhaps because her mom had been there. The congregation was barely a hundred people, most over sixty years of age. But the thought of seeing someone she knew, especially someone who knew about "the incident," had been a motivating factor in her relocating almost two hours away from LA. She wondered if even that were far enough away. Sister Vivian had called a few times when Millicent first arrived in Portland, but Millicent had asked her mom to politely dissuade the calls. She truly loved her, but First Lady Montgomery was too close to all that she was trying to forget. Millicent had rediscovered herself in Portland, and realized that as busy as she'd been with KCCC, a solitary life was sometimes okay. Now was one of those times.

These thoughts quickly ran through her mind, one right after the other. And then the waiter brought her food, steaming hot and smelling delicious. Perfect timing for the dismissal that was about to take place.

"It was nice to meet you, Mr. Kirtz; thanks for the invitation," Millicent said, dropping his business card into her purse and picking up a fry. "Now, if you'll excuse me, I'd rather enjoy my lunch alone." She smiled briefly to show there were no hard feelings.

Jack got the message and stood up. "Jack, please, call me Jack. Whenever you could come by, we'd love to have you. Ours is a small congregation, but we're serious about spreading God's love. Enjoy your meal, and the day." With that he flashed another smile, turned, and walked toward the bicycle path she'd taken earlier.

After he was well out of sight and she'd eaten half of the sandwich and fries, Millicent reached into her purse and retrieved the business card. "Open Arms Ministries" was centered in bold, with "T. Jackson Kirtz, Pastor," underneath. The contact information filled the bottom of the card, just above a line of scripture: "Mercy unto you, and peace and love be multiplied. Jude 1:2."

Millicent stared at the card a moment before dropping it on the table. She shrugged, as if dismissing the entire episode. But the words of the scripture repeated themselves in her head, and were soothing in a distant, mellow sort of way. She finished her sandwich and pushed the rest of the fries aside. Swallowing the last bit of tea, she stood, put on her jacket, and grabbed her purse. Another cursory glance at the card and then she turned and walked purposefully up the walk and away from Jack's outreach efforts. She'd appreciated the scripture though, and thought to write it in her journal when she got home. God knew she could use His mercy and peace, and love, for the time being from Him alone. *Or from Cy Taylor.* "No, God's love is enough," Millicent said aloud. But was it?

1

It's Still Good

"I just have one question," King whispered, as he drew lazy circles around Tai's cinnamon-colored nipple. He bent down and licked it lightly, causing an involuntary shiver down her spine.

"What's that?" Tai turned her head and looked at King.

"Is it still good to you?"

Tai smiled, and continued the familiar Ashford and Simpson tune. "Yes," she said, kissing his soft, full lips, and kissing them again. "And it feels more than alright."

Her body was still vibrating, singing the praises of his lovemaking skills. They were spending a rare Saturday morning alone, and making the most of it.

"I think it gets better with time, baby."

"I think you're right."

Tai ran her hands up and down King's back, which was still slightly moist from their zealous coupling. She agreed with what he said. Lately, their sex was some of the best they'd ever had. She turned and snuggled her back against King's body, spoon style. He rocked up against her, brushed his hand over her still throbbing pussy, and pulled her closer. Tai closed her eyes, a smile dancing across her lips. She'd thanked Vivian more than once for calming her down last month, preventing her from blowing Tootie's return out of proportion. Especially since, when King returned from his meetings at the church that day, he'd asked if Tai knew about Tootie being in town to care for her mother. Tai had watched King's face as he delivered the news, had looked for signs of she knew not what exactly. But he'd seemed pretty casual about it and she'd responded in kind, even encouraged him to go to the hospital and pray for Miss Smith.

Even with her rush to judgment about Tootie's return, Tai had matured in both her marriage and her faith in God. Realizing she was only being human, she forgave herself for her initial reaction. The memories of King's past behavior were fading, but not gone. God was still a miracle worker, because if anyone had told her a few months ago she'd be contently snuggled up in King's arms, she would have asked what drugs they were using. A few months ago, she'd contemplated divorcing King, leaving the church and the city. A few months ago, she'd felt worlds apart from her husband, unable to reach him. And she had been. A woman named April had been in the way.

Tai read a book once that suggested there was a blessing in everything, that one just had to look for it. Who would have thought that out of an extramarital affair would emerge a union that was closer, stronger, better than it had ever been?

Reconnecting after the last affair hadn't been easy for either of them. King had to get over his guilt and Tai had to lose her anger. Both had to forgive, each other and themselves. They'd had to learn to love each other all over again, make their relationship fresh and new. They'd implemented "date night," where once or twice a month they let Mama Max watch the kids while they went out to dinner, the theater, a concert, or a movie. Sometimes they'd pass a nice hotel and spend the night, adding some scenic variety to their renewed romance. Tai had taken Vivian's advice on how to spice up the marriage, and one day, when King came home late, it was to a woman in a bustier, garter belt, fishnet hose, high heels, and a waist-length, blond wig. King had been shocked, and delighted. The firecrackers had popped that night!

Tai looked and felt better than ever. Thanks to the Full Workout Fitness Center, she had gotten her "sexy" back. Not only was she thirty pounds lighter, but according to her annual medical checkup, healthier, too. Her blood pressure and cholesterol were low, and her heart beat a steady, healthy rhythm. The cardiovascular routine on the bikes and treadmills had paid off, and the twice-weekly aerobic dance workouts and weight-lifting exercises had toned up her abdomen, buttocks, and thighs.

Now, she was considering a breast augmentation to firm up her four-kids-later set of low riders. Despite all of her efforts, the sagginess of her breasts continued to plague her. King assured her they were fine with him, but ever since a woman at the gym had proudly showed off her new "birthday tits," the thought of implants had remained firmly in the front of her mind.

A gentle snore sounded behind her. Tai chuckled softly. *Yes, baby needs to rest a little longer after our sexcapades, but a brothah can still "make it do what it do."* Things had gotten even more fun after Tai ordered a *Pleasurable Sex* DVD she'd seen advertised on late night television. At first, King had balked and said, "I don't need nobody telling me how to love my woman." But after she began playing the DVD one night, and the host started suggesting various positions to try, he'd changed his tune. Now, she had to tell *him* to turn the thing off. He'd counter that he was "just studying." And indeed they had learned a couple new positions, laughing heartily as they'd tried to become human pretzels. Tai had finally admitted it was going to take more than aerobics to get her in that upside-down, legs over the head position. Who did those video instructors think she was, Nadia Comaneci?

The telephone rang. Tai glanced at the clock and was surprised to see it was almost eleven. She rolled away from King and grabbed the receiver. "Hey, Mama Max," she said, yawning.

"Don't tell me y'all still in the bed! Lord have mercy, I don't know what I'm gonna do with you lovebirds. You betta' be careful, else y'all be saying hello to number five."

Tai had never told her mother-in-law that King had had a vasectomy. Guess he hadn't either. "Now, Mama Max, don't worry yourself."

Tai swung her legs over the side of the bed and stood. Donning her robe, she padded down the stairs to the kitchen and the coffee machine. It was definitely that time. "What are the kids doing?"

"The twins are outside, running around like chickens with their heads cut off. Princess is on that datgum cell phone. You'd think that thang grew out her ears long as she stays on it."

"I told her about that. Let me talk to her. She's at your house and should be visiting with you!"

"Ah, don't bother that child. She alright, helped me fix breakfast this morning. We had a nice little chat. She's a sweet baby, growing up though. Pretty soon she'll be grown and gone just like her big brother, Timothy. You'll have two in college."

"Don't remind me. The boys are circling like bees to honey."

"Well, just watch and make sure that none of 'em sting."

Tai jumped as King lightly patted her booty. She'd not heard a sound as he walked up. "You scared me!"

"That's what I intended." King reached for the phone. "Is that Mama?"

"I'll be over in a couple hours, Mama. Here's your son." She pressed the speaker phone button, noticing King was dressed to go out into Kansas's winter chill. He looked impressive in his double-breasted, knee-length cashmere wool. "You're not eating?" Tai asked.

"Hey, Mama," King spoke into the phone and then over to Tai, "No time, baby. I'll grab something on the way."

Tai shook her head. Right after she and King picked up the pieces from his last affair, he'd cut back on work considerably. Slowly but surely, however, the workaholic was heading back to a full, hectic schedule.

"Look Mama, I gotta go, I gotta go, now," King said hurriedly when after a few pleasantries Mama Max started grilling him about his heavy workload.

"Uh-huh, such a hurry to get off the phone since she's getting in your business," Tai said, laughing at the easy repartee in which King and his mom communicated. It was good to hear; their relationship had suffered during his affair with April.

King promised his mother a visit, ended the call, kissed Tai lightly on the forehead and headed toward the front door. Tai could see it in his demeanor; he was already making the mental switch from husband to pastor/company president.

"I'll call you later." And he was out the door.

"Things still fine with Tootie back?" Mama Max asked.

"Yes," Tai replied. "King sees her when he visits Miss Smith in the hospital. You know she just had surgery. Deacon Nash visits her often, too, prays and reads the Bible with her."

"That's good. Nancy will appreciate having Deke there. They've known each other for years." Mama Max appreciated Deacon Nash being there regularly, too, instead of King, but she kept her concerns about King and Tootie to herself. She prayed the years apart had cooled the once unquenchable ardor between them. "You have any problems with King being at the hospital?"

"Not anymore," Tai answered. "I'm not going to let something that happened so long ago worry me now."

"That's exactly right, baby. Let bygones stay gone. Who knows? She might even come to church."

Tai didn't know how she felt about that. "Well, hopefully not in one of her cat suits."

Both Mama and Tai remembered the sinfully tight outfits Tootie had brazenly worn to the Lord's house.

"Oh, chile, she probably can't fit into those anymore."

Tai tried to squelch her strong desire for Tootie to have aged badly. "I pray everything turns out okay with her mom," she said, with compassion. While not extremely close to her, Tai couldn't imagine life without her mother, or her mother-in-law. "Thank God for you, Mama."

"Think nothing of it, baby."

"Hey," Tai said, wanting to change the subject and lighten the mood, "you want to work out today? You haven't been in what, about two weeks now?"

"No, chile, these old knees been giving me trouble. Best I sit in this here house and act my age."

"I pray you never start doing that," Tai answered sincerely. "I told the kids I'd take them to the movies later. If you're feeling better, we can go see something for grown-ups while they watch what they want. That sound good?"

"Now that sounds like something I'll be able to handle. Can sit on my behind in their chairs as well as my own, I 'spect."

They finalized their plans. Tai would go to the gym and then head over to Mama's. Mama would make sure Princess and the twins were ready. Putting the omelet fixings back that she'd grabbed for her and King, Tai decided on two boiled eggs and toast instead. Better for her workout, the second one of the day. The first one had been with King and, yes, it was still good.

8

Big Booty Tootie

"I'm glad the men decided to play a few holes, give us some time to catch up," Tai said to Vivian, as they strolled leisurely to Vivian's Escalade.

"Me, too," Vivian replied.

They had just enjoyed a few jostled, crowded hours in LA's famous "garment district." Vivian usually didn't have the patience for the dense street vendors, or "The Alley's" rambunctious atmosphere, but on special occasions, such as when she had her best friend in tow, she braved the traffic and ventured into the masses. It had been worth it. There were a few upscale shops that sold her beloved designer suits at a third of what she'd pay for them elsewhere. Plus, the February day was perfect, not a cloud in the sky.

Vivian punched a button and heard the locks pop open. She and Tai placed their bags in the handy back compartment and carefully slid onto soft leather seats.

"You haven't been here since the summit," Vivian said, as she pulled away from the curb. "I can't believe you guys are flying back right after the wedding."

"You know King is not trying to miss a service," Tai answered, buckling her seatbelt. "At least he got a guest minister for the morning message. We'll take a morning flight out and be home by five."

King and Tai had arrived Friday, a little after nine A.M., to a sunny, warm day in Los Angeles. A car had picked them up and whisked them to Derrick and Vivian's, where Vivian had prepared a sumptuous breakfast of homemade waffles, fluffy scrambled eggs, turkey bacon, fresh fruit, coffee, and juice. They'd spent a couple hours relaxing by the pool, and then the boys had headed off to their newfound passion, the golf course. Derrick had taken it up a year ago with some men at KCCC, and had soon thrown down the "you-can't-play-golf-it's-a-thinking-man's-game" gauntlet to King. King had hit the greens shortly thereafter with the most unlikely of partners, his dad, the Reverend Doctor Pastor Bishop Overseer Mister Stanley Obadiah Meshach Brook Jr. Now, in between King's love of golf and his dad's love of fishing, they were spending more time together than ever before in their lives. Both Tai and Mama Max were glad for that.

"I can understand his being anxious to get back," Vivian said, as she turned onto Olympic Boulevard and drove away from the crowded downtown area, "especially with the success of your broadcast ministry. I know it's only been a month, and you guys are still working out the kinks, but it really is good, Tai. King's charisma comes right through the TV screen, and he always was an awesome orator. You guys may not get that five-year reprieve you wanted between major building projects."

"Tell me about it. We're already seeing the increase in attendance at services. Just slightly right now, thank God, but as the network opens up in more markets, and the word gets around Kansas City and the surrounding towns," Tai sighed, "I think things are really going to blow up."

Tai's sigh had not gone unnoticed. Vivian glanced over. "I understand, sistah, mega-congregations are a lot of work. *Any*

size congregation is a lot of work, for that matter, but once
they get over a thousand, and then two thousand, and on and
on . . . no joke."

"Yeah, King's already talking about adding a second morning service, and I never dreamed we'd have to do that."

"Can you believe it, Tai? Did you have any idea when you
were in high school and declared to me that King was going to
be your husband, that your life would be anything like this?"

"Be careful what you pray for, is all I can say," Tai said drily.

Vivian knew that Tai's concerns were not limited to the
size of the congregation. She herself had had to deal with
more than one overly zealous churchgoing female trying to
get her hands on her husband. "I'm glad the air cleared about
Tootie being back," Vivian segued smoothly.

"I am, too," Tai agreed.

"You still haven't seen her?"

"No, and honestly, that's fine with me." Tai no longer felt
threatened but there was no love lost for the ex-girlfriend; the
farther the distance between them, the better.

"According to Mama Max, she's at the hospital mostly. You
know Mama and Miss Smith have known each other forever.
She's been to see her quite a bit." Tai looked at the foreign
signs as they passed through Koreatown. "Mama Max says she
looks good, says Germany must agree with her."

"Speaking of Germany, you and King still going on that
second honeymoon for your twentieth anniversary?" Vivian
segued again, flowing as easily as her Escalade through traffic.

Tai blushed. The past two months had felt like a honeymoon. "That's the plan. Don't know where, though."

"There are so many beautiful places: the islands, Hawaii,
Mexico, Europe. I saw a brochure on Madagascar the other
day. It's beautiful."

"Mada-who? I'm not going any place I can't spell or pro-
nounce, trust."

Vivian laughed. "Don't put off the planning too long. You know how time flies. And I didn't miss that blush, sistah. King must be, uh, taking care of business."

Tai's smile was proof enough that King was being *quite* the businessman.

"Aw, man, that shot wasn't nothin' but luck." King shook his head as he walked over and got a different iron. "Ain't no way you'd make that shot again."

Derrick smiled broadly and then agreed. "You're probably right."

King and Derrick had chosen a rather easy course, not far from Derrick's home. Their camaraderie was the main enjoyment, the golf was gravy.

"So man, I know you've seen Tootie a few times. How's she look?" Vivian had told Derrick about this thorn returning to Tai's side.

"Fine as ever." King putted.

Derrick eyed his friend a moment. King and Tootie had been quite the item back in the day. But that was a long time ago. "Tootie, Tootie, with the big—"

"Booty, booty," they both finished together.

"You're crazy, man." King laughed, even as a clear memory of Tootie's young, tight, upturned rear end floated into his mind's eye. "That's the first thing I thought, too, when Von told me she was in town."

"How's her mother doing?"

"A little better, according to Mama. I went to see her right before she had the operation, and again just before I came here." King watched Derrick choose an iron, practice swing, and then choose another. "You know Deacon Nash is a good friend of the family. He's been there regularly on the church's behalf."

Probably best, is what Derrick thought. "It's good Miss

Smith has someone to lean on," is what he said, and then continued. "Where's Tootie's husband? Although I guess I should try and call her. What's her new name, Janet? Wonder where she got that name, anyway."

"Home, in Germany. And it's Janeé."

"Huh?"

"Tootie is using her middle name now. Her name is Rita Janeé. You don't remember?" King asked.

"I don't think I ever knew that."

"You knew her pretty well not to know that."

They picked up their clubs and walked to the next hole.

"You know she's got kids," King said.

Derrick paused in midstroke. "Kids? Tootie?"

"Yeah, she's got three."

Derrick shook his head. "I never imagined Tootie as a mother." He swung his club and frowned at the less than stellar shot. As King was getting ready to swing, Derrick commented, "Big booty Tootie."

King laughed again. "Man, will you cut that out! It's like you're seventeen again." He carefully lined up his club, shadowed the ball several times, and then hit it directly into a sand trap. "Ah, man!"

Derrick laughed, commiserating with his friend. Golf definitely wasn't as easy as it looked. They both reached for their water bottles.

"Life is full of surprises," Derrick said. "What's it been, fifteen, twenty years since you've seen her? Guess she finally realized she couldn't have you and moved on."

"Humph. Hear you tell it. Remember how she used to drive everybody crazy singing Whitney?"

"And Donna, Natalie, Aretha, Chaka—anybody who can blow."

"That girl was wild though, wasn't she?" King asked, capping his bottle and picking up his bag. He'd thought of their wild times more than once since he'd seen her. He and Tootie were careful not to bring up the past, but one look in her eyes, and he knew Tootie had been thinking about it, too.

Derrick placed his ball on the tee and lined up his shot. He smiled slightly as he watched his ball land about six feet from the hole.

"Another lucky shot, dog," King said, playfully taking his iron and faking a swing to Derrick's head.

"That's skill, my brothah. I got skills." And then, "Tootie was something else, a sex addict before they invented the term."

"Sure was. Always classy though," King responded. "Even though we all knew who was doing her, it wasn't like she was a ho, you know?"

"Yeah, Tootie had that way about her. And she was just like a man. She'd do the do and then beat you out of bed, shower, dress, and be ready to go home."

"True that. Messed with a brothah's ego a little bit, almost made *me* feel like the ho sometimes!"

Both of them knew that feeling. Derrick reflected on who he was then, and who he was now. "We were different men back then, young, foolish." He thought the same of Tootie— Janeé—who'd obviously changed more than her name. "And she's married? Is the man *German* German?"

"He's White, if that's what you're asking," King replied. "Supposed to have money, runs some financial company or something."

"How old are their kids?"

"I didn't ask all that. But you know, me and Tootie had a couple close calls. I even thought she had an abortion right before me and Tai got married. She denied it, but to this day I don't know for sure if at one time she didn't carry my child. We were, uh, very active let's say, but then again, she was active with a lot of dudes." King looked pointedly at Derrick.

"Guilty as charged," Derrick said, a bit of macho mixed in with guilt. Tootie had been a favorite notch on a young man's belt. "All of us were fortunate to not make a baby. I wasn't even thinking about protection back then."

"Nobody was, man, you kidding? I never liked putting the raincoat on. I'm pretty sure she was on the pill anyway, all the action she was getting."

"I know one thing, we better shift this conversation. All this talk of Tootie is messing up my swing, not to mention my trying to let old things that have passed away, stay away." Derrick swung his iron just over the ball, lining up with the hole, now barely five feet away. Taking a deep breath and settling into his stance, he lined up once more, swung, and sank the ball. He looked at King smugly. "Now, that's what I'm talking 'bout."

The conversation shifted to church matters, and their co-officiating plan for Hope's wedding ceremony. Both were glad the wedding would be short and simple. They joked about Cy's few remaining hours as a free man, but agreed he was a blessed man, too. King liked Hope, liked her spirit. Plus, she was fine. Cy had done alright for himself. An hour later, they neared the eighteenth hole. They finished without tallying scores; the game had been for the fun of it all.

Once in the parking lot, Derrick lifted his bag into the trunk of his pearl Jaguar. King followed suit. Derrick easily navigated the midday LA traffic as the two longtime friends enjoyed a companionable silence.

"I don't know about you," King said after a bit, "but all that walking worked up my appetite. I'm about ready for that steak place you've been bragging about." King's stomach growled as if to underscore the statement.

Derrick smiled, but said nothing. He was thinking about Tootie being back in Kansas, hoping King's passion for his old flame had truly burned out. Little did he know, but King was thinking about Tootie, too, about how on fire their sex was back in the day. But King knew the lesson of fire better than anyone: if you played with it, you could get burned.

9

Worth the Wait

It had arrived, February 14, Hope's wedding day. She lay staring at the ceiling, hardly able to believe that the moment was here. She yawned, stretched, ran her hand over Cy's empty pillow. Cy, his father, and her father had spent the night in Cy's cousin's suite at the Ritz-Carlton. They, along with a couple of Cy's business partners and classmates from Howard University, had held a bachelor party. She could only imagine what that crazy group had put together for him. Knowing the wild shenanigans that often took place, she'd had only one thing to say to him about it: "What happens at the bachelor party stays at the bachelor party." Cy had assured her nothing would happen that he couldn't share with her, or her mother for that matter. That had elicited a smile from the bride-to-be. Hope, her mother, Mrs. Jones, Frieda, Frieda's mother, and four of Hope's longtime friends from Oklahoma had enjoyed a bridal shower in the penthouse. They'd had it catered by P. F. Chang's, Hope's new Chinese food favorite, and amid great food and goofy presents, had laughed, cried, played games, and basked in Hope's contagious happiness.

Hope rolled over and gazed out the floor-to-ceiling bedroom windows. With no nearby buildings as tall, their penthouse allowed privacy without having to close out the stunning ocean view. It was early, the sky still holding hints of night. But as she continued to look out over the ocean, wisps of light blue, orange, and pink emerged. This was going to be a beautiful Valentine's Day.

After returning from the bathroom and morning ablutions, Hope picked up the poem she'd tweaked the night earlier. She sat on the bed and began reading it again, out loud:

> *"God's gift to me was you, His undeniable treasure,*
> *Your value beyond numbers anyone could measure,*
> *A blessing designed by Spirit, such an awesome wonder,*
> *What God has joined together, man can't put asunder,*
> *You're the one. . . ."*

A tear fell. And then another. Hope set down the poem and covered her eyes. *Thank you, Jesus, thank you, God,* she prayed inwardly. More tears fell, tears of thanksgiving, and relief. Over the years, when doubt crept in, she'd feared ending up old and alone in a quiet, one-bedroom senior's complex, playing backgammon and cards with the neighbors, two or three cats for company. She cried harder. It was happening! She was getting married!

Suddenly a pair of arms went around her. She relaxed immediately, smelling her mother's familiar perfume.

"Sh-h-h, now it's gonna be all right, baby," Mrs. Jones crooned softly. Hope leaned her head against her mom's shoulder, willing the tears to stop. "You can't believe it, can you?"

Hope shook her head no.

"God is faithful, Hope. I always told you that one of these days, when the time was right, he would come along. And now he's here. God is good."

This powerful truth made Hope start crying anew. She tried to talk through her tears. "I'm, j-j-just so t-t-thankful," she sobbed. "I can't believe I'm getting m-m-married." Hope had revved up into an all-out boo-hoo.

Frieda burst into the room. "What the hell, oops, excuse me, Aunt Pat. Girl, what is the matter witchu?" She sat down on the other side of Hope. "I guess you're trying to get your eyes all red and puffy so you can look like some kind of baboon up there at the altar, have Cy think Queen Kong is walking up to meet him; is that it?" Her words had the desired effect as Hope's sobs turned to laughter.

"No, fool!" Hope answered, grabbing a pillow and attempting to hit Frieda upside the head with it.

Frieda jumped up and grabbed another pillow. "No, you're the one who needs some whup'ass . . . in here crying like somebody died."

"You'd better not, you're gonna hit Mama!" Hope snuggled under her mom for protection.

Pat pushed her away, laughing. "Oh no, don't be trying to get me to protect you. Take yo' whuppin' like a woman, a soon-to-be married woman. In fact"—she reached over and grabbed a smaller, decorative pillow—"take two whuppin's."

Hope rolled to the other side of the bed, grabbed two small pillows, threw one at her mother and one at Frieda. Frieda ducked and it almost hit Jackie, Frieda's mother, who walked in at just that moment.

"What in the w—?"

"She's trying to hit you, Mom," Frieda warned, "said she was gonna get you back for beating her at bid whist last night."

"Ooh, Frieda," Hope said, in a menacing tone. "That's not true, Aunt Jackie. I'm trying to get at your crazy daughter." Hope ducked as Frieda threw the pillow back, and picked up another one to throw.

"Y'all stop," Pat scolded. "You both need Jesus."

"I need some breakfast, that's what I need," Frieda said, watching herself pose in the mirror. "And I need a man that can put me in a place with a view like this. Now, this is livin'. Hurry up and go on your honeymoon so I can come over here and get my groove on—I mean, so I can house-sit."

Three pairs of eyes gave her "the look."

"Just kidding," Frieda said sheepishly before flouncing out the room. A trio of laughter followed her out.

The day flowed seamlessly. After a hearty breakfast, Cy, Simeon, and the fellas had enjoyed a game of basketball. Hope and the women spent their morning being treated to a full body massage, manicure/pedicure, and an in-home hair stylist. The limo picked them up promptly at three. Hope, exquisite and serene, now sat in the boat's largest bedroom, waiting for the moment she became Cy's wife.

Cy and his cousin, Simeon, relaxed quietly at a table, enjoying the view of sparkling water and sailboats. Wisps of conversation floated around them from the thirty or so guests who mingled on the luxury yacht Cy had chartered. It would be their last moments with Cy as a single man.

"Well, cuz, the water isn't too deep here; still time to make the great escape."

Cy raised up a bit as if gauging his chances for a successful jump; then he smiled. "Even with a gun to my head, there's no way I'd leave. I've never been surer about any move I've ever made than I am now."

"You're a lucky man."

"I'm blessed, Simeon. Nobody but God put Hope and me together."

"Humph. You're talking about her behind her back and she ain't even yours yet." Hope's dad, Earl, punched Cy's arm playfully as he sat down. The three men could have graced the cover of *Elegant Man,* if there were such a magazine. Cy's tux fit flawlessly and Simeon's blue Kenneth Cole suit was equally stunning. Mr. Jones was dignity personified in a charcoal gray double-breasted suit, with silk blue shirt and complementing necktie. In fact, everyone on the boat looked quite refined.

Mr. Pheneas Taylor, Cy's father, joined them at the table.

An older, distinguishably handsome version of Cy, Mr. Taylor still turned the heads of women half his age. "Well, now that the *important* people are ready and on the scene," he said, pointing to himself, "the festivities can begin."

Earl's eyebrows rose at that comment. "Careful now, you're gonna be like that slave who showed up in the field with a tuxedo on, after a visit to the doctor's office."

"How you figure?" Pheneas asked with mock indignation.

"Well, when the other slaves asked him why he was in the field wearing a tuxedo, he told 'em," Earl continued in an exaggerated southern accent, " 'since the doctor say's I'se impotent, I'se might as well look impotent.' "

The men tried not to, but laughed anyway. Earl Jones was a character, one anybody would be hard-pressed not to like.

It was time. The guests lined the stern of the boat, leaving the middle empty. Three of the Musical Messengers, a guitarist, saxophonist, and keyboard player with drum machine, kept a low profile on the side. Soft sounds of smooth jazz emanated from their corner. Pastors Brook and Montgomery stood waiting with appropriate seriousness. King had chosen to wear a white pastor's robe, complete with scarf bearing a solid black cross and fringe at each end. Derrick had on a stellar black tux.

Mr. Jones waited in the back, talking quietly with Hope, whom her mother had finally summoned.

After the parents and guests had been seated, an imperceptible nod from Mrs. Jones signaled all was ready.

Pastor Derrick began. "Ladies and gentlemen, we are here to celebrate another love affair that God has designed. Let our hearts be filled with love as we surround this couple, here and now, at the beginning of the rest of their lives." With this, he and Pastor King moved to the side as Cy's classmate stepped up to sing "The Lord's Prayer" in a rich baritone.

Hope stood just outside the door, near the rear of the ship. She couldn't see anyone, but heard the wondrous melody float like waves across the boat, now anchored in the middle of the ocean, halfway between the marina and Catalina Island. She closed her eyes and leaned against her father, whose eyes were misty. He was losing his only daughter, albeit to a fine young man.

After the solo, Frieda and Simeon took their places. Cy came next. The keyboardist began playing Hope's instrumental wedding march, Luther Vandross's "Wait for Love." When the saxophone joined in with the melody, Hope, led by her father, came around the side of the boat. She was radiant. Every eye was on her. Her eyes were on Cy. A solitary tear slid down her face as he stood beaming.

After Mr. Jones had escorted his daughter to the front, he joined his ex-wife. Having a child together created a lifetime bond, and both had put differences aside, even if temporarily, to be united in this moment. Cy reached for Hope's hand and held it gently as her poem, "The One," was read by a child-hood friend. They turned and looked into each other's eyes as Eric Benet's duet with Tamia, "Spend My Life," was performed with enchanting loveliness:

> *"Can I just see you every morning when I open my eyes?*
> *Can I just feel your heart beating beside me every night?*
> *Can we just feel this way together till the end of all time?"*

In these moments, Cy's only thoughts were for the ceremony to be over, the guests to be gone, and Hope to be in his arms. Hope was thinking the exact same thing. The rest of the ceremony went by in a longing-induced fog, repeating the vows, the ring, the kiss, purposely chaste so as not to fan the already searing flames of desire.

And then it was official. Cy and Hope were pronounced man and wife. Bubbles were blown as the couple walked around the boat lined with guests, hugging and thanking each one for their presence. While this was happening, the caterers sat up a sumptuous feast of tenderloin steak, baked chicken, and fish, a roasted vegetable medley, and rice pilaf. Simeon toasted the couple, who in turn toasted the guests with their choice of either Krug's Clos du Mesnil champagne or sparkling juice. Once the bubbly started flowing, the evening began in earnest. By the time the almond-vanilla frosted carrot cake had been eaten, toasts made, dances danced, and the boat finished sailing around the marina and docked outside the Ritz-Carlton, folks were speculating on who could get married next so they could have an excuse to enjoy such fun all over again.

Cy and Hope faced each other in the middle of the king-sized bed. Maria, Cy's housekeeper, had cleaned up the day's mess and, with Frieda's help, had set a romantic stage in the bedroom, with candles, orchid petals, and burning, scented oil. The newlyweds each held a glass of sparkling champagne with bobbing strawberries. Both were naked, having enjoyed a relaxing, sensual bath in the penthouse Jacuzzi. They'd explored and pleasured each other's bodies. Their senses heightened by months of agonizing celibacy, the first orgasms came quickly. It was just the beginning, though. Cy planned for Hope to be thoroughly satisfied from head to toe before the night was over. Hope had likewise secretly vowed to make her husband's pleasure her singular focus, believing that if she took care of his needs, she too would be satisfied.

"A toast to you, Mrs. Hope Taylor," Cy began, "the woman of my dreams." He reached out and gently pinched her nipple, which took notice immediately. Hope's quick intake of breath made him smile. He leaned over, nipped it, licked it, and continued. "It will be my life's mission to make you happy, woman, to satisfy you in every possible way. I'm so happy you're in my life, baby, and I will spend a lifetime trying to repay you for how happy you've made me."

Hope drank in his words of love. She tried not to cry—there had been enough tears for the day. But she was so happy, beyond her wildest imaginings. She took a breath and returned a toast of her own. "When I prayed to God for a husband, it was you I longed for in my heart. I didn't know your name, or what you looked like, but I knew how I'd feel when I was near you . . . like I do right now. I love you, baby."

They raised their glasses and toasted new love. Finishing quickly, they fed each other the strawberries, followed by passionate kisses. Hope felt desire pool in the pit of her stomach, and spiral lower. Cy moved over and placed Hope in the middle of the bed. He straddled her, lay full weight on her body. His shower of kisses began. He kissed her lavishly, their tongues dancing, dipping, the heat rising. He kissed her eyes, ears, neck, before lifting up a bit to move down farther. He grabbed her perfect breasts in his hands, tasted and blew on them softly. A quiet moan escaped from between his lips as he eyed the feast that had been set before him. Hope writhed beneath him, her hands in his hair. His exploration continued as he kissed her stomach, her navel. He nipped her hips playfully, causing bubbling laughter from his bride. "Ooh, that tickles, Cy."

"Hmmm . . ." was his quiet reply as he continued his journey, down into the valley of her paradise. He sighed softly. He would especially savor this moment. Placing soft kisses into her furry mound, he gently spread her legs. Hope was beside herself with anticipation. For so long she'd waited, dreamed, desired, yearned for her man. Cy took his time, honoring every crevice with skilled finesse. It had been a long time, but just like riding a bicycle . . . He alternately licked and kissed her inner walls, flicking her love button with his tongue. Hope's escalating moans assured him his skills had not diminished from lack of use. She tried to move from his sexual assault but he simply changed positions, placed her on her side, grasped and gently lifted her thigh, and licked a slow, wet journey down the crevice of her lush buttocks before thrusting his tongue deeper into her hot feminine flower. It was a delicious way of making love, the best Hope had experienced. She grabbed Cy's head, grinding her hips against his mouth, murmuring his name over and over. Her body shook with another release, and Cy drank her as he would the finest nectar.

Only after he was satisfied that Hope had reached multiple climaxes did he prepare for the next step in their love dance. He rolled over, preparing to position Hope on top of him. But before that happened, Hope had rolled over to begin her own kissing assault. Cy was pleased. He knew they were matched sexually, had the same tastes. *Yes*, he thought as Hope grabbed his manhood and lavished her praises. He sighed deeply as she rolled her tongue around the tip of his dick before taking him into her mouth, worshipping at Cy's penile paradise. Cy closed his eyes and smiled. *Yes,* he thought as Hope showed her love. *We are a perfect match.*

Their mating dance continued into the early morning hours. Cy took his time as he entered her, aware of his size and Hope's years without sex. Not until she was totally ready did he join them in divine union, complete oneness. Hope was not able to hold back the tears then, crying in ecstasy, holding Cy tightly. Cy was an exquisite lover, his long, thick manhood at times fast, forceful, and plunging, and then slow and steady. Their lovemaking took on a variety of rhythms, in a variety of positions. As streaks of dawn announced the coming day, Cy turned on his side, pulled Hope into his arms and held her firmly, possessively. Hope nestled back against the hard chest of her man, rested her arm on top of his. Mr. and Mrs. Cy Anthony Taylor had chosen to wait until marriage to experience this oneness. It had been worth the wait.

10

The Sanctity of Sisterhood

Millicent looked at Alison a long moment after they'd been seated at an ocean-view table. "It is really good to see you again," she said finally. "I'm glad you're here. Didn't realize how alone I'd been."

Unlike the many other times she'd suggested it, Millicent said yes when Alison invited herself to La Jolla. Funny thing was that in hindsight, Alison had needed it as much as Millicent, and shared this with her friend: "Like I said earlier, this is blessing me as much as it's blessing you."

Alison had moved from Los Angeles back to Clarkstown, New York, to take care of her mother. The transition was difficult. Her mother's condition wasn't good when Alison had arrived, and even with prayers, faith, and blessed oil, the Alzheimer's was getting worse.

Alison looked out over the ocean. "Be thankful for your mother every single day," she said, almost to herself. "Call her every day, love her every day, because when things change . . ."

Millicent reached over and took her friend's hand in silent sympathy. These past few months had shown her all too well the value and power of a mother's love.

"How is your mother?" Millicent asked.

Alison gave her an update. "I can't keep worrying about

Mama," she said after answering Millicent's question. "Her health is in God's hands now." The waiter brought tea, and Alison used that time to change the subject, as well as the mood. She was glad that Millicent seemed to have picked up the pieces of her life but concerned that she might have still carried a torch for Cy. Alison knew from experience that the best way to get over one man was with another. She intended to help her friend jump-start her love life, to truly move on. "Enough about me," she said. "What is going on with you? How's the job? It must be nice, surrounded by a group of successful bachelors."

Millicent deftly sidestepped talking about men and focused on the job itself. "I love what I'm doing. In fact, just this week I agreed to go full-time."

"That's excellent," Alison exclaimed. "You had said you were thinking about it. They must have agreed on the salary you wanted."

"And then some, plus the benefits are great—three week's vacation the first year. I don't know if I'll stay past the one-year contract though. Just trying to live in the moment, one day at a time."

"Is there any other way? One day is about all I can handle; tomorrow will take care of itself."

Alison continued to listen as Millicent went on about her job. That's all she talked about. As Alison suspected, Millicent wasn't seeing anyone. If she had been, either an e-mail, a phone call, or something in the conversation so far would have at least alluded to it.

The forbidden topic, Cy Taylor, was on both their minds. Millicent wanted to ask about him and Alison wanted to acknowledge him as the proverbial elephant in the room. She decided to plunge in.

"Have you heard from—?"

"So what's new at—?" They both spoke at once and laughed.

"No, you first," Alison offered.

"Well," Millicent began again. "I was just wondering if you'd heard from anybody: Sister Vivian, the S.O.S. Summit women, or anyone from Kingdom Citizens. I miss the women's fellowships, and especially the conferences."

Arriving at Cy by way of Kingdom Citizens was fine by Alison. "I haven't talked to Sister Vivian," she replied, "but I have talked to a couple of Kingdom members. Ladies First is planning another Sanctity of Sisterhood Summit."

Alison and Millicent recapped some of their favorite points of last year's conference, which Vivian had called a summit to signify the place godly women should occupy in the scheme of life, the very top.

"Do you remember the slogan we all learned at the end?" Alison asked.

"Of course," Millicent replied confidently. Alison remembered it, too. They recited it together:

"I'm uncommon. I'm unusual. I am not the status quo.
Set apart, an earthly treasure—'cause my Father deemed
    it so.
Yes, I am my sister's keeper, and it should be understood,
That today we stand united, the Sanctity of Sisterhood!"

Reaching across the table to high five, they laughed at how their voices had unconsciously raised as the words flowed. Fortunately, there weren't many in the restaurant; the ones who were just turned and smiled politely.

"Wow, I can't wait—" Millicent began, and then caught herself. She wouldn't be going to the next S.O.S. Summit, or the one after that. The door on that part of her life was closed and locked.

"Hey, maybe you could start a side chapter, a smaller one, here in San Diego," Alison suggested, having correctly guessed the reason for Millicent's hesitation.

Millicent thought a moment. It sounded tempting but, no, she knew she couldn't do it. Seeing Alison was great, but she wasn't sure about reconnecting with Sister Vivian or anyone else from her former church life. Plus, the chances were too great that if a smaller conference was planned for San Diego, people from Los Angeles would hear about it and come down. The day would come when she'd have to confront her past, but she hoped that day was months, years in the future. "I'm not ready for that," she answered simply.

"Are you ready to talk about Cy?" Alison asked, in a smooth segue. She sat back and crossed her arms.

"It feels like I've never stopped talking about him," Millicent responded.

Alison didn't get it. "With whom?" she asked. Alison had gotten shot down so much that she'd finally stopped mentioning his name.

"My therapist. Things got a little tough for me after I got here. My doctor in Portland recommended a therapist here. I've been going twice a week for the past month."

Alison was taken aback; she thought Millicent's therapy sessions were over. *Lord, what is it going to take to get that man out of her system?*

"They're married, right?" Millicent asked, more a statement than a question.

"Yes."

"Yeah, I heard." Millicent had discussed Cy and Hope's impending marriage with her therapist, but somehow talking about it with her friend, someone who'd been there when she claimed Cy as her own husband, made it hurt more. But a masochistic side of her wanted to hear the details, wanted to know it all. "I guess the wedding was fabulous," she said sarcastically.

The wedding, and especially the onboard reception afterward, had been all the few chosen ones who got to go had talked about. But Alison wasn't going to be the one to provide a play-by-play. Instead she gave a brief, two-minute synopsis, trying to make it seem as boring as possible. She rolled her eyes as she wrapped it up, "You ask me, twenty-something people on a boat in the middle of nowhere isn't my idea of a wedding."

Millicent nodded. She'd get married in the middle of a muddy river if the man at her side was Cy. Besides, what Alison described sounded much too plain, especially for Cy. She was sure some details were being left out, but didn't push.Maybe it was best not to know.

The waiter brought their food and the women ate in silence. Millicent mostly picked at hers. Discussing Cy's marriage had put her in a dark mood. True, she'd known about it, had thought she was dealing with it. Obviously not, as tears began to silently cascade down her face.

Alison's heart ached at her friend's pain. "I'm sorry, Mill. I shouldn't have brought him up. Let's go." Alison met the waiter and paid the bill while Millicent left to give the valet her ticket. By the time Alison got outside, Millicent was in the car.

"I'm sorry," Alison said again.

Millicent was silent, gripping the wheel and driving a bit too fast for Alison's taste. Alison began praying under her breath.

After ten minutes of silence, Alison spoke. "I know it's probably the last thing you want to hear right now, but have you thought about getting back out there, dating again?"

Millicent's response was an unladylike snort.

Alison was undaunted. "There are plenty of good men out here, Millicent. I know God's got one for you."

"Don't talk to me about what God's got," Millicent said angrily. "Because the God who told me that Cy was my husband got it wrong!"

Alison didn't respond, didn't want to "go there," especially as long as Millicent was behind the wheel doing eighty miles an hour. But she wasn't going to give up. A friend sometimes had to tell it like it was, even if the other person didn't want to hear it. Millicent could blame God for what happened to her all she wanted. But Millicent was the one who'd created the madness. The only one to blame was herself.

II

One Way or Another

Pastor Derrick Montgomery entered the pulpit amid the joyous sounds of the Kingdom Citizens' Chorale, led by Stellar Award–winning minister of music, Darius Crenshaw. Darius had done the church proud a year earlier, when he'd performed "God, My Jehovah," the hit single from his debut CD, at the televised BET awards. Now the follow-up CD, *Timeless Love,* was ready for release, and rumor had it the title song had secular record execs chomping at the bit.

Derrick thought of that BET evening as he watched Darius simultaneously direct the choir and play piano, a perfected series of head nods, one-handed cues, and an occasional one-word verbal directive. Derrick hadn't missed Darius's increasing popularity, or how the choir had added a host of sopranos and altos to its ranks. Darius seemed to take it all in stride. He'd stayed pretty low-key in the dating department since his wife had divorced him a couple years back. Guess divorce took a while to get over, no matter what the situation. In Darius's case, he'd come home one day to find his wife in bed with another man. But looking at him now, the picture of poise and confidence, none would imagine his past pain.

Darius's mind wandered as his hands glided across the

piano keys. He tried to focus on the instrumental but was in auto-mode, the past night's events drifting in and out of his consciousness. He'd never experienced love as he had with this newfound romance, had never basked in the feeling of sheer bliss. As he closed his eyes to take in the music, a pair of luscious brown ones with long, curly eyelashes gazed back at him from his mental screen. A flashback of lips, full and sensual, floated to the forefront of his mind. He remembered the heady kisses and smiled. He opened his eyes and saw Stacy smiling back at him. *Not you*, he thought. Not any of them in the choir, or in the church. He'd found something special where he'd least expected it, and felt as if he was walking on a cloud.

Stacy's soprano got a little brighter with Darius's smile. Figuring she needed a change of pace and a chance to hear Pastor Montgomery's sermons again, she'd resigned from the youth ministry and joined the choir. Singing had always been a favorite pastime, and she was glad to be surrounded by the harmonious sounds of the chorale. One could think she was most glad to be around Darius on a more consistent basis, and she wouldn't have denied it. She'd sat back for months waiting for him to make a move, given many hints that she was interested. Not overtly, of course; she was trying to be a lady. But she knew he knew because Tanya, his sister and her best friend, had told him. She'd berated her at the time, but afterward, was glad the truth was out.

Excited at first, she'd gotten frustrated when nothing beyond polite hellos and brief conversations followed Tanya's letting the cat out of the bag. The closest Stacy had come to hanging out with him was when he'd dropped by his sister's unexpectedly while she was there. He'd been cordial as Tanya, on Stacy's behalf, had coaxed him into staying for dinner.

Stacy hadn't gotten much out of him that evening. His monosyllable answers had quickly dashed her hopes of finding out more concerning the breakup of his marriage, but he loosened up when she turned the conversation to a safer topic, their mutually beloved Lakers. He was impressed that she knew other players' names besides Kobe's, could quote stats, and followed the progress of other teams as well. She'd flirted a little, threw in some innuendos. Feeling more comfortable, he'd flirted back. She'd given him her phone number, unsolicited, suggesting that they take in a game together sometime. He'd hugged her upon leaving and said he'd call. He hadn't. She'd thought about getting tickets and inviting him to the Staples Center. But since all she could afford were the nose-bleed seats, that idea died a quick death. Still, she was determined to up her game off the court.

Vivian watched Stacy watch Darius. *It never ends,* she thought. The chase was always on, and more and more, it was the females leading the charge. Times had changed, and Vivian couldn't say she wouldn't have done the same thing had she been single. Of course, it had been so long since that was the case, she could hardly imagine it. She looked at Derrick and was glad God had blessed her when He did. These days, the field of romance seemed a much trickier one to navigate. As if feeling her thoughts, Derrick turned and gave her a look that only she could interpret. He raised his brows slightly, licked his lips slowly, surreptitiously. She knew he was remembering last night, and the thought made her warm. She diverted her eyes to break the contact. It was as if he were mentally touching her, warming her more.

Derrick slowly shifted his gaze away from his wife. He still had it, could still melt Vivian with "the look." He smiled, remembering the first time it had happened. More than fifteen years ago at the Kewana Valley District's Baptist convention. He'd sensed fire underneath her conservative, understated ensemble, and he'd been right. He'd discreetly questioned his good friend, King Wesley Brook, as the offering was lifted. Vivian and Tai were best friends even back then, so King knew about her. He told Derrick her name was Vivian, that she was majoring in broadcast journalism, and was selective about who she dated. More than one of King's buddies had attempted a "get to know." But Vivian wasn't having it, had been all about business, until Derrick. The four had gone to dinner, Derrick had gotten her number, and just over a year later, she became Mrs. Montgomery.

Vivian was thinking about the same thing, about the start of their marriage. Those early years had been crazy. Vivian became an exemplary first lady, albeit kicking and screaming all the way. Her goal had been a broadcasting career. Right out of college, she landed a job as the weekend anchor on a cable station. She worked her way up to noonday anchor, Monday through Friday, at an ABC affiliate station, and then got hired as the prime-time, evening anchor in Birmingham, Alabama, an almost two-hour drive from Atlanta.

The commute worked okay for a while. Derrick was busy as an associate minister and realtor. Vivian stayed in Birmingham during the week, but was front-row center at the Sunday services. Dedicated to her job and often working ten- and twelve-hour days, however, she couldn't be as active in the church as Derrick would have liked.

But she was active at home. Their love sustained them. Vivian thoroughly enjoyed making their house Derrick's castle, and he loved watching her do it. They'd shop together on the weekends he was available, finding just the right piece of furniture, picture, or antique. Then they'd do dinner, catch a movie, and go home and make wild, passionate love. Vivian was totally uninhibited, which played to Derrick's adventurous side. Plus, she kept it exciting. She bought sexy lingerie and thought of imaginative places to reveal them to him. They made love in locations most people wouldn't dream of, and then swore each other to secrecy afterward. If the community only knew what their studious anchorwoman and the young, charismatic preacher were up to! From the beginning, Derrick had eyes only for Vivian. Sure, there were many fine honeys in

Atlanta, but how could he think of straying with such sweetness at home?

He got offered his first church, a traditional Baptist congregation of about a hundred people, in the small town of Lithonia, Georgia. That's when the tension started. Lithonia was about twenty miles east of Atlanta, even farther from where Vivian worked. Derrick wanted her to quit her job so she could assume the role of pastor's wife and all that position entailed. Vivian dearly loved Derrick and wanted to support him, but his suggestion was about as appealing to her as rotting cabbage. She held out for six months, ran herself ragged trying to juggle a full-time job with a full-time ministry. A conversation with one of the longtime members of the Pilgrims' Rest membership, Mrs. Faye Moseley, would set Vivian on a different course for the rest of her life.

It was early on a Saturday morning. Vivian had still been in bed, the covers pulled over her head, trying to catch up on the sleep she'd missed all week. Derrick had left earlier, on his way to the church to handle any number of issues continually cropping up in the small but growing spiritual family. The consistent ringing of the phone pulled her from a deep sleep. She looked at the clock, frowned, and decided not to answer. It went silent for a moment and then began ringing again. Whoever it was wasn't going to give up. Pre-caller ID, she'd had no choice but to answer, thinking it might be an emergency. Her frown returned when the cheery voice of Sister Moseley crackled through the line.

"How do, Miss Vivian. This here's Sister Moseley."

"Uh, good morning, Sister Moseley," Vivian croaked.

"I'm sorry, child, did I wake you?"

Thinking this was her opportunity to cut the conversation short, Vivian readily answered. "Yes, ma'am, I was in the middle of a *very* deep sleep."

"Well, I'm glad you're up now. Can you come to the church?

I want us to go have a little breakfast, more like brunch by the time you get here."

Did she not hear what I just said? Vivian held her impatience. "Is something wrong?"

"Not exactly, baby. I just need to talk to ya, is all. Round 'bout ten-thirty be all right?"

I guess it'll have to be, is what she thought. "Yes, ma'am," is what she said.

Vivian rolled into the tiny parking lot at a quarter past ten and was surprised to see Sister Moseley waiting on the sidewalk. Her face lit up as Vivian pulled to a stop, and before she could turn off the engine, Sister Moseley was opening the door to get into the car.

They engaged in small talk during the short ride to the Waffle House, a place Vivian later discovered was Sister Moseley's favorite restaurant for breakfast fare. As Vivian had anticipated, they got down to the heart of the matter once the orders had been taken and the coffee had arrived. Sister Moseley asked her how she liked the church, discussed being a pastor's wife, and took real interest in Vivian's descriptions of life as an anchorwoman. After she'd eloquently stated her very sound reasons for continuing to work in the highly competitive market in which she was blessed to have landed a job so quickly, even with her husband's promotion to his own church, Sister Moseley took her turn.

"Now this might sound like I'm getting in your business, but at my age, it's what I do—get in folks' business. You say you love your husband, right?"

Vivian got a bit perturbed. "Of course," she replied in a clipped tone.

"Uh-huh. And you want the marriage to last a long time, have babies, the whole thing?"

"Sister Moseley, I don't mean to be disrespectful, but my husband and I—"

"That Cook girl, the one that's so faithful, comes every time the church doors open. She's a pretty little thang, ain't she? Acts like she's got a few screws loose sometimes but pretty girl. What's her name, Robin? Yeah, I think that's her name."

This got Vivian's attention. "What about her?"

"Oh, nothing, just real dedicated to the ministry is all. Almost becoming your husband's right hand; she's got good . . . administrative skills, I hear."

The toasty pecan waffle with butter melting sat untouched in front of Vivian. Meanwhile, Sister Moseley was eating like there was no tomorrow.

Vivian crossed her arms. "Is something going on between this Robin and my husband, Sister Moseley?" She went straight to the point; no need to pussyfoot around.

"Nothing that I know of," Sister Moseley said calmly, wiping her mouth with a napkin and sipping freshly poured coffee. "But I've occupied many a church pew, more than twenty-five years of 'em at Pilgrims' Rest. I've see'd some thangs over the years, know how these women flock around the pastor. It's easier to do when the wife ain't around much."

Vivian was silent. Sister Moseley continued. "You're a bright girl. I can tell you're good at what you do. But sometimes in life, we have to decide what's really important to us. What's gon' matter in the long haul."

Vivian sat attentive, waiting.

"Now, that Derrick, he a fine man. I see great things happening for him. Y'all in this here small town right now, but ain't always gon' be this way. That preacher is going places. Mark my words. What you have to do is decide whether you want to be by his side when he gets to wherever place that is."

Sister Moseley gathered the last of her fried egg, waffle, and sausage onto her fork and downed the huge bite. She looked over at Vivian's still-untouched and now cold waffle. "Shame to waste that good food; ain't you gon' eat, girl?"

Vivian said she wasn't hungry. Sister Moseley promptly called the waitress over, asked for a doggy bag, paid the bill, and announced she was ready to get back to the church, that she was trying to get things prepared for the Lord's Supper the following day.

When Vivian arrived back at the church, she didn't drop Sister Moseley off. She parked and went inside. Laughter rang out from her husband's office, which was at the front of the cramped, four-room building. She opened the door without knocking and found Robin leaning over her husband, pointing at something on the computer screen.

Derrick had greeted her warmly. Robin's hello was as chilly as winter in Anchorage. Their laughter sounded comfortable and intimate, but Vivian neither felt nor saw any hanky-panky going on—not yet.

Vivian put in her two-week notice the following Monday. She asked Sister Moseley to help her, and over the next several months, learned the ropes of what it meant to be a first lady. She was young and, to her credit, wisely called on the older members of the church for their sage counsel. The church grew, and soon there was both a youth and adult choir, a thriving Sunday School, women's fellowship, and a well-attended BTU, Bible Training Union, which took place Sunday night. Wednesday night Bible study was a lively, interactive affair, where discussion and dissension was encouraged. Derrick's reputation grew quickly and before long, they were fellowshipping across a tristate area, with a few cross-country invitations. By the time Derrick accepted the offer to pastor Good Lord Baptist, five years later, which Derrick renamed Kingdom Citizens' Christian Center, both the Montgomery ministry and marriage were well-oiled machines. A handful of dedicated members went with the Montgomerys to California. Sister Moseley, who over the years became Mother Moseley, was among them. Unable to conceive for the first seven years of their marriage, another source of tension at times, Vivian carried Derrick Jr. in her womb as they celebrated their first pastor's anniversary in Los Angeles.

As Vivian finished reminiscing, she looked up to find Derrick's eyes fastened on her. *God has brought us from a mighty long way.*

Praise and worship was almost over. Darius and the band were playing their jazzy instrumental rendition of a gospel classic. The melodious sounds of the different instruments drifted over the audience. Eyes closed, some hands raised, others standing in the congregation, the words echoed in the minds of those who knew them as the instruments played: *Then sings my soul, my Savior God to Thee, How great Thou art . . .*

For a moment, almost everyone in the congregation was focused on Christ. Their deep, collective worship ushered in the sweet presence of the Holy Spirit. Doubts and fears eased, worries dissipated, sadness evaporated. The power of God blew into the sanctuary like a gentle breeze, wafted over the sounds of the saxophone, sat on the strings of the guitar, and perfumed the piano keys. As the chorus was played for the last time, Stacy was given the microphone to vocalize this declaration of the saints. *How great!* Her impassioned soprano took the worship up another level.

Yes, almost everyone was caught up in the glory of the promise—almost, but not quite. While most had their eye on Jesus, one woman had her eye on Derrick. *He looks so serene,* she mused, drinking him in like a cool glass of water in the desert heat. *I wonder if that's how he'll look while sleeping, after a night of loving me.* She had no doubt that that was how the story would end, with the highly esteemed man of God in her bed. She'd waited years, bided her time, but now she was ready to claim what was hers. Robin squirmed in her seat, the very thought making her salivate. She glanced over at her unknowing opponent, Vivian, standing with her arms lifted toward heaven, a tear rolling down her face. *Yeah, tramp, get your praise on now, 'cause you'll be singing a different song in a minute.* Her smile turned into a sneer as the music ended. She caught herself, and forced her eyes away from the woman who had what she wanted, who had what she deserved, who had what she was going to get—one way or another.

12

Open Arms

The pulsating jets of hot, steamy water pounded into Millicent's shoulders, neck, and back. *This is what's been missing.* Millicent, who'd exercised regularly in LA, had joined an upscale fitness club in La Jolla and adopted a strenuous workout schedule. It proved to be a great reliever not only of stress, but also of bad memories.

Weeks had passed since Alison's visit, but thinking of her friend's parting words still rankled. *Stop blaming God, Millicent. It was you who decided Cy was your husband, you who insisted on trying to force things to happen. That wasn't God's voice, it was yours. The sooner you accept responsibility for your actions, and the sooner you forgive yourself for what you did, the sooner you'll truly be able to put the past behind you and get on with your life.*

Alison's unsolicited advice echoed what her mother and her mother's pastor had told her: quit blaming God. If she did, they all admonished, she'd not only feel better, but she'd gain a new lease on life. But didn't she have that with her new job and home? The correct answer was no, because Cy still occupied her most important home, her heart, where love resided. But who wanted to pay attention to details like that? Certainly not Millicent. It was easier to act as if all was well, even when it wasn't.

Millicent stepped out of the shower and dressed quickly.

The day was young; she planned to take in a movie, maybe head to the beach. Her life was a mundane routine of home and work. She was amazed at how much KCCC had accounted for her social life back in LA. Without a church family, the weekends sometimes seemed to go on forever—and back at Kingdom Citizens that had never happened.

Reaching in her bag for the car keys as she rounded the corner, she didn't see the gentleman heading her way. "Oops, I'm sorry," she began as she bumped into him, looking up into sparkling blue eyes.

"Millicent?" the man asked. "Millicent Sims?"

Millicent's brow furrowed. The guy was handsome, well-built. He must have been about six feet tall and obviously worked out on a regular basis. The shorts and muscle shirt fit him well. "How do I know you?"

"Oh, I'm sorry," the stranger said, holding out his hand. Millicent took it, still looking into his eyes. "Jack, Jack Kirtz. I met you on the beach in San Diego."

That jogged Millicent's memory. It had been several weeks; she was surprised he remembered her name. She took a step back, then stopped herself from giving him a head-to-toe once over. On the beach that day, he'd worn casual slacks with a large pullover. He looked quite different in workout clothes! "Pastor Kirtz?" she asked.

"Only if you insist," he replied in a friendly manner, grabbing the towel around his neck with both hands. "For you, I'd prefer Jack."

Millicent was immediately on the defensive. "Why for me?"

"I don't know," Jack countered easily. "I'm casual like that, I guess."

What did that mean? She didn't know why Jack made her uncomfortable, but he did. The pastor title, maybe? If he'd been a regular guy, she may have been attracted. As uneasy as she felt, she'd checked, and found, no wedding ring. She started around him.

To her dismay, he turned and started walking beside her. "You come here often?"

Millicent started to lie but knew that could backfire, so she told the truth. "I just joined but yes, I'm here three to four times a week."

Jack whistled. "That's commitment." He refrained from blurting out what he was thinking: *and boy does it show!* He appreciated her lean, toned body with long waist and legs. Something about Millicent turned him on, ever since he'd seen her gazing out over the beach, a myriad of emotions playing across her face. The feeling hadn't diminished as she'd tried to brush him off at the sidewalk café. In fact, that had for some reason or other intensified his interest. "The offer I made you to visit our church, Open Arms, still stands," he said as they reached the parking lot.

"Thank you," Millicent said. She'd reached her Infiniti.

He stepped in front of her to open the door. "I'd really like to see you there," Jack continued. "Our church can use more women like you."

"You don't even know me," Millicent said flippantly, moving to get into her car.

"I don't, but God does," Jack replied. And with a wink, he was off.

Millicent watched Jack stride over to the fitness center entrance. His body was lean, calf muscles pronounced, buns tight. At the door to the club, he stopped and turned around. Millicent hurriedly closed the door and started the car, embarrassed he had caught her staring. *That's the last thing I need.* She further comforted herself with the fact that she'd thrown away his business card. She didn't even know where the church was. But the image of tight buns and friendly blue eyes stayed with her all afternoon.

13

Personal Matters

Cy sat back in Derrick's well-appointed pastor's suite. It was April, two months after the wedding, but it was still taking him a while to get back in the groove after his honeymoon. In fact, a part of him hadn't wanted to return to Kingdom Citizens at all. It wasn't the church itself. He enjoyed his role as associate minister and financial advisor. And he loved the brother on the other side of the desk, appreciated Derrick's spiritual depth and biblical intellect. It wasn't even the fact that this is where, almost a year later, he was still the brunt of "Millie gone mad" jokes regarding the Millicent debacle.

No, it wasn't any of those things. It was Hope. She'd reinvigorated him in ways he couldn't have imagined. He'd found his niche in California, found a wonderful spiritual family in Kingdom Citizens. But now he wanted something more, something different. The time he'd spent in the Cayman Islands had revived his love of travel, his desire to see every inch of the planet and make it a better place to live. Hope was just as adventurous, told him she'd be glad to traipse through the jungles of Africa, ride a rickshaw in China, or gaze upon the Taj Mahal. She'd not been able to travel as he had, and he wanted to be the one to introduce her to the world; he wanted to give her the world. Cy wasn't caught off guard often, but he'd had no idea he could be this happy.

"Well, why don't you take some time and think about it," Derrick responded to Cy's pondering a resignation. "You're all discombobulated right now, just months into marriage, not thinking straight."

"I can't disagree with you, man," Cy said with a laugh. "I still feel like I'm on my honeymoon."

"If things go well," Derrick said, leaning back in his leather swivel chair, "you'll still feel like that in fifteen, twenty years. It's not easy, but it's possible."

"I'll definitely work toward that," Cy answered. "The best thing about me and Hope is how well we communicate. I feel like I've known her all my life, can't remember life before she was in it."

"Man, you are gone!" Derrick said, laughing and shaking his head. "You are whipped, brothah, nose wide open!"

"No, no, no . . ."

"Don't even try to deny it. I've seen that look. I've *worn* that look. And I know what it's about! God sure is good, isn't He?" Derrick reached for the intercom button. "Yes?"

"Excuse me, Pastor, but it's Mrs. Reynolds again," Derrick's secretary, Angela, announced.

"Find out who she is and what she wants," Derrick countered.

"I asked," Angela responded. "She keeps saying hers is a personal matter."

"Take a message, Angela. Better yet, transfer her to Tamika." Tamika was Vivian's assistant. "Tell her that all personal matters from female congregants are discussed with my wife." Derrick stroked his mustache, a slight frown on his face.

"Problems?" Cy asked.

"Same old, same old," Derrick sighed. "You'll see. Don't think the fact that you've got a ring on your finger is gonna stop the women from coming at you. You might even see an increase."

"Unfortunately, I know you're right. It's already happened. And telling 'em you're married don't mean a thing."

"They make it hard for a brothah sometimes," Derrick continued. "The things some of the women have done in this church . . . man . . ."

"Vivian's a strong woman to be able to handle all that, year in and year out."

"Oh, she's strong, fearless; none of them want to go up against my wife."

Derrick and Cy's conversation drifted from their wives to the ministry to investments. Finally, Derrick turned to the Kingdom Citizens' Shopping Center and Business Complex—the shops, business offices, bookstore, and restaurant development in which Cy was his liaison. The entire project would take a good two years to complete. It was a lot to handle, made easier with Cy by his side. Derrick wouldn't try and talk him out of it if Cy was adamant, but he sure didn't want to see a brother resign.

"How's King doing?" Cy asked, gathering his things and preparing to leave. "Did you tell him I was sorry for not getting to hang out with him when he was here last?"

"He understood. You know you've got a standing invitation to go back and speak at his church. I think he wants to put together some type of economics seminar for his members. He's trying to change their mind-set about money, get them to start saving and investing. You know that seventy percent of Americans are two paychecks away from homelessness? It might be even higher in the Black community."

"Well, I'll be glad to help him. I'll give him a call a little later on."

"And we want you on the committee for the Brothers' Brigade Conference he and I are planning, along with some other ministers from Total Truth."

"Oh, yeah? When is that scheduled to happen?"

"We're planning it to run alongside Vivian's national S.O.S. conference, about eighteen months from now."

"I'll do all I can. Just let me know."

"Excellent. Thanks for all the good work, my man."

"Anytime," Cy said. He waved good-bye and left the office.

"Pastor," Angela beeped in again, "what should I tell Mrs. Reynolds? She's called twice since the last time I told her you were in a meeting."

Derrick's brows creased. *Mrs. Reynolds, Mrs. Reynolds . . .* The name didn't ring a bell. "Didn't you transfer her to Vivian's line?"

"I did, but she keeps calling back here."

Derrick sighed. This kind of stuff came with the territory but he didn't have to like it. "Thank you, Angela. I'm sorry that you're being harassed. Tell her she must speak with an associate minister, or my wife's office, end of story."

Derrick leaned back, thinking. It had been a long time since he'd been harassed. It definitely wasn't unusual, especially from strangers. While he didn't have a regular television broadcast, like King, he was seen frequently on Trinity Broadcasting Network and provided video feeds at the church's Web site. No telling who this Mrs. Reynolds was. And no telling what she wanted. The fact that she referred to herself as "Mrs." didn't dim his suspicions. Like he'd just told Cy, rings, and the vows they symbolized, didn't mean a thing to some people.

He reached for the phone. "Hey, baby."

"Hey," Vivian said, surprised. "I was just thinking about you."

"Hum, and what were you thinking?" Derrick asked in a sultry voice.

Vivian responded in an equally seductive manner. "You'll find out later tonight."

"Baby! That'll get a man riled up."

"I sure hope so." She paused. "So, what's up?"

"Besides me?" Derrick asked. "Hey, do you know anybody at the church named Reynolds, a Mrs. Reynolds?"

"What's her first name?"

"Don't know."

"Can't say I do, babe, but that doesn't mean she's not a member. Not like in the old days when we could do roll call from memory."

Derrick smiled. "Not quite, huh."

"What did she want?"

"Who?"

"Mrs. Reynolds."

"Ooh, sorry, baby. Your voice is distracting."

Vivian smiled.

Derrick could feel her smile through the phone. "She's been harassing Angela all afternoon. When asked why she's calling, she keeps saying it's a personal matter, whatever that means."

"Transfer her to my voice mail next time, baby," Vivian said easily. "I'll try and call her tomorrow."

"Tried that. She wants to talk to me."

Vivian understood. "Oh, one of those."

"Looks like it."

"Well, we have had a reprieve. Guess we couldn't think it would last forever."

"I was praying."

"You just shouldn't be so doggone fine, and intelligent, and sexy, and—"

"Stop it now. I've got a meeting in half an hour. You're going to make me cancel and come home early."

"It's all right, baby," Vivian said mischievously. "You can cum later." Chuckling, she hung up the phone.

Derrick smiled as he lowered the receiver. Mrs. Reynolds was forgotten, replaced by thoughts of Mrs. Vivian Stanford Montgomery, and what he'd do to her later that night.

14

Compromising Situations

Frieda winked as the doorman held the door open for her. "Here to see Mrs. Taylor?" he asked politely.

"The way y'all have this place on lockdown, you know good and well that's who I'm here to see," she responded candidly, but with a smile.

"A pretty girl like you, I'd let you in anytime," the older European man flirted.

"I'll keep that in mind," she cooed sweetly, as he walked with her to unlock the penthouse elevator button. "Bye-bye," she waved coyly as the doors closed.

"Ain't nothin' I want with an old ass man," she said to the mirrored walls as the elevator went up. "Not unless he's living *in* the villa, not working *at* the villa." *The nerve*, she thought as she reached Hope's floor.

"What are you frowning about?" Hope asked as she walked over to hug her cousin.

"Hope, you are glowing. That dick must be good!"

"Frieda!"

"Please, don't be trying to get all churchy on me. Ain't nothing wrong with enjoying yourself." She stood up and spoke dramatically. "You's married now, Miss Hope, you's married now."

They laughed, walked into the living room, and sat on the

couch. "Speaking of church, you want to come with us next Sunday?"

"I might."

"We can pick you up and everything."

"Okay, I'll call you when I know for sure."

Hope knew a dodge when she heard one. "Can I get you something?"

"No, I just came from having lunch with my crazy friend, Joe."

Hope's "male alert" antenna went up. "Your friend at work? I want *all* the details."

"And he wants *my* tail," Frieda quipped.

Hope raised her eyebrows. "Careful, Frieda, y'all just met."

"Oh, don't trip. Joe's my running buddy. I try not to mix business with pleasure. Break up with a nucka you work with, then have to see his ass every day? Not pleasant. He's taking me to a party tonight, some mansion in the Hollywood Hills."

"How well do you know this guy?" Hope asked, concerned. "You don't want to get yourself in a compromising situation, make me and Cy come and get you in the middle of the night."

"If my ass don't get in a compromising situation soon," Frieda countered, heading to the kitchen, "somebody gon' get shot. He assured me I'd have a good time. Y'all got any water?"

"Yes, and grab me one, please."

Frieda returned from the kitchen with two bottles of water. "Joe's cool, he really is. I can't say that for the rest of the stuffed shirts in the office. This one married dude is trying to talk to me though. I might let him hit it if he's got some money."

"You are not going to do that. You are not going to sell yourself for money."

"Please, child, don't you know? Everybody's selling it, eh-ver-ee-body. The price may be different but the bottom line is the same. You give 'em some pussy, they give you whatever."

Hope shook her head in frustration. "Frieda, that is not true."

"Is too," she replied. "You selling yours right now. I admit you got a good deal, a swanky home and a wedding ring, but pussy was still the means of exchange."

"What Cy and I are exchanging is love," Hope responded in annoyance. She caught herself. "Oh, why am I even trying to reason with you? You're going to think what you want anyway."

"Chill out, Sally . . . I know you're in love. It's all good. So," Frieda began again after a pause, "it's been what, two months now? You still happy?"

Hope leaned back against the sofa. "It is wonderful. I can't even believe it."

"So when are you going to start popping them babies out?"

"Believe it or not, Cy and I discussed that on the island. We don't want to wait too long, a year maybe."

"I'm still trying to get over the fact he owns an island!"

"Well, I tell you what. Cy and I will plan a party for a few friends and you can come see for yourself."

"Plenty of fine men over there, right?"

"I probably shouldn't tell you, but yes, they are a very attractive bunch of people. But ours is a private portion of the smaller island. You'll want to spend time in Grand Cayman."

Frieda was already figuring how much of her salary she could save per month, and who she could take with her. "That sounds wonderful, Hope. It's about time I take a trip outside this country."

"You'll love it," Hope answered.

After another hour, Frieda told Hope she had to go. She hugged her cousin and promised to do lunch soon. Back out in reality, the crazy California traffic, Frieda's mind was buzzing. She joked about it, but seeing Hope so happy had her thinking about finding a man, settling down. She was three years older than Hope, and while she'd never really considered it before, marriage had its benefits. She held no delusions about finding somebody like Cy—that didn't happen everyday. But a man who'd treat her right, someone to hang out with, help pay the bills . . . she could see some advantages.

As she turned the corner of her block, her "wanna-be gangsta" neighbors, Marlon and Blunt, were in the middle of the street doing God knew what. "Get out the street," she yelled, barely slowing down.

"Dang, girl, you high?" Marlon shouted.

"When you gon' let me get at that?" Blunt added.

Frieda pulled up to the curb and jumped out of the car. "Some other time, darlin's. Mommy gotta hot date tonight."

"Just my luck," Blunt said halfheartedly. "Somebody else gets to tap that ass."

Frieda had a window that faced Blunt's building and was well aware of the string of females going in and out, mostly to see him, but also to support his side business, selling weed. "Ah, you do all right," she said, heading inside. Their bantering was all in good fun. In fact, both men had helped her out a lot when she'd first moved in, adopted her in a way, kept the hard heads in check. As she opened her door, she thought of what to wear: something low, tight, F-me heels. A quick check of the voice mail and she jumped in the shower, still smiling at Blunt's constant bid to hit the kitty.

Frieda's eyes widened as Joe pulled into the sizeable parking lot next to the huge house. "You've got to be kidding me," she said incredulously. "We are *not* going in here."

Joe smiled. "Come on, my little pumpkin. This is exactly where we're going."

Frieda suddenly felt uneasy. She looked down at her outfit, tight black velvet pants, a low-plunging spring sweater with metallic threads running through it, and four-inch heels. She'd gone to the beauty shop first thing that morning, had her

short, flip hairstyle bumped to perfection. Her makeup was
flawless and the acrylic nails just the right length and color. So,
what was it? Normally she was confident, secure in her looks.
She knew she had what it took to turn a head or two. But
looking at this house, the size of an office building, made her
wonder if she was more than a little bit out of her element. "I
hope they've got something to drink in there," she said, trying
to sound nonchalant.

Joe put his arm around her as they walked inside. "Pumpkin, they've got anything you want!"

Frieda tried not to gape as they stepped into the foyer. The
mansion was quite simply gorgeous. A huge chandelier domi-
nated the entryway, its crystal reflecting off the gold accents on
the doors, walls, and ceiling. She'd never seen marble floors
throughout a house before. A bar was set up just inside the receiving room. She sauntered over, taking in the scenery.

"What will it be for you, pretty lady?" the jovial bartender
asked with flirty eyes.

"Are you on the menu?" she countered effortlessly.

"Uh, I can be, if you're ordering," he said with equal casu-
alness.

This broke the ice, and Frieda felt better. She should have
known, people were people, and men were men, wherever you
go. "Give me something high-class, to match my surroundings."

"What are you in the mood for?"

"You decide, but something relaxing, calm my nerves so I
can get my party on!" The sounds of dance music drifted from
the back of the house. "This is a big place."

"Yeah, well, the owner's got deep pockets. Here, this will
help you get in the mood." He gave her a double shot of Gold-
schläger, a cinnamon-flavored liqueur.

"What's this floating in it?"

"Pure gold, just like you."

"For real?"

The bartender nodded. "Drink up, and then I'll give you a glass of champagne to take along on your tour."

The shots worked miracles. Frieda soon lost Joe and made her way through the maze of people clustered in groups throughout the sprawling abode. Before long, she'd caught a few eyes here and there, made small talk. Mostly, she was just happy walking around a place right out of the movies, taking it all in. She went through a great room, past a dining room with a table that could sit at least twenty people, and into one of the dens. That's when she saw him, the man she determined on the spot was going to be her "compromising situation." He was leaning against the mantel of a huge fireplace, speaking intently to the brother next to him. The man next to him said something. Her man tilted back his head and laughed. She decided to check him out from the other side of the room first, finish her champagne.

Damn, he's fine. Frieda had sworn off pretty boys a thousand times but they were still her weakness. And this brother, oh-my-God. His bronzed skin was smooth and even, the perfect setting for his straight, white teeth. The close-cropped haircut showed off a perfectly shaped head. Frieda imagined running her hands over it in a moment of passion. His lips could have been sculpted by Michelangelo. They were perfectly shaped, evenly thick on top and bottom. She couldn't see his eyes that well, but based on everything else . . . my, my, my. He looked to be about six feet tall, and she hadn't seen anybody wear a pair of jeans that good in quite some time. The man he was talking to was fine, too, in a rugged sort of way. Dark-skinned, buffed, his posture was that of someone completely self-assured. He, too, wore his hair close-cropped, almost bald. He was about the same height as the other man, maybe twenty, thirty pounds heavier. As she stared, her man glanced around the room and she caught his sparkling brown eyes. They smiled at each other. *Hmm, I've got choices.* She determined that either one of these brothers would do just fine.

Pretty boy finished his drink. His friend did the same. They began walking toward the open doors on the other side of the den, casually speaking with two alluring women as they all exited. Frieda waited a moment. *Dang! Are they getting ready to do a foursome?* She didn't want to appear to be following, even though that was her purposeful intention. She grabbed another glass of champagne from a server and headed in the same direction her "situation" had gone. Turning the corner, she saw his back just before he disappeared up the stairs. She wished she'd gotten there a second sooner so she could see her competition, which woman was pretty boy's taste. She looked around to see if she could spot his friend. No, he was gone, too. She downed her champagne and set the glass on a nearby table. Having had nothing since lunch, she quickly felt the effects of the liquor, making her giddy and bold. She walked confidently to the stairs. The thought of breaking in on some wildly screwing couples was becoming exciting.

A handsome man with reddish brown hair and green eyes stopped her. "Looking for me?"

Frieda engaged in conversation for a brief moment, told him that maybe they could hook up later. Then she continued on her mission.

It was quiet, serene, on the second floor. There was a large open space at the top of the stairs where a few people stood around. Then there were halls on three sides, each with a series of closed doors. *Wow, this might get tricky.* Frieda had never been one to back down from a challenge, and the longer it took to find her temptation, the more she was determined to do so. She walked down the hall to the right, and quietly opened the first door. It was a nicely appointed bedroom, but empty. She opened a few more doors and had to apologize to a couple who were making full use of a guest room. A bathroom and large closet completed that hallway. In the next one, it was more of the same. She'd gotten the gist though, and started listening at the door before opening it. Hearing grunts and moans saved her a couple times. But not from the group doing lines of cocaine, a group of naked bathers in a Jacuzzi, and another group surrounding a woman holding tarot cards. She quickly was on to the third hall.

She stopped at the first door, listened. Hearing nothing, she eased the door open, stuck her head in, eased it open a bit more. This was a larger room, like a master suite. The door opened to a sitting area, the bed nowhere in sight. She was just about to close the door when she heard laughter, male laughter. She stopped. Silence. She slipped out of her heels and tiptoed across the carpeted bedroom, slid against the wall, and eased her head around the corner. Her heart pounded, she felt excited, a voyeur getting ready to observe someone doing the nasty. Slowly, she peeked into the sleeping area. *What?!*

On the bed lay her "compromising situation" and his friend, naked. Frieda closed her eyes. This could not be happening—those two fine brothers could not possibly be sweet. She looked again. "Buff" had rolled on top of "Pretty Boy" and was kissing him passionately. "Pretty Boy" was returning the kiss stroke for stroke. Each had the other's joystick in his hand, rubbing it like a good luck piece. She glanced around the room. Clothes had been hastily thrown over a chair near the bed. Frieda wanted to move but couldn't; she was mesmerized. Of course she knew about the lifestyle, and knew in LA to expect anything. But she still wasn't prepared for it straight up in her face. She stepped back and leaned against the wall. A lightheadedness came over her; she almost giggled. *I got to get out of here.* She peeked back one more time, watched as "Pretty Boy" got behind "Buff," joystick in hand, poised for entry. His eyes were closed in anticipated ecstasy. That was it, time to retreat. In her haste to leave, she turned the corner quickly and bumped a lamp on the table. She ran to the door, opened it as fast as she could, and held the knob so it would close quietly.

She ran down the hall and down the stairs, past reddish brown hair and surprised green eyes. She needed food, and fresh air, and not necessarily in that order.

Darius stopped, dick hard and pulsing. "Did you hear that, baby?"

Bo pushed back against Darius, eager for the coupling to begin. "What, I didn't hear anything."

"Sounded like a noise." Darius leaned over and kissed Bo's back, shoulders, neck, as he listened for additional sounds. Hearing none, he repositioned himself behind Bo. Time to finish what his beautiful lover had started.

Frieda sat back against the patio chair, staring out over the lights of Los Angeles and sipping sparkling water. Her appetite assuaged with king crab cakes and pasta, she calmly contemplated the scene she'd witnessed earlier. *It's a damn shame,* she thought, shaking her head. *For something that fine to not want me.* She sat her plate on the table and walked over to the stone wall surrounding the terrace. Leaning over it, she closed her eyes, took a deep breath of the night air. Two hard, tight asses popped into her mind. Frieda shouldn't have been surprised to catch them bumping booties. But she had been.

It was cool with her, though. She wasn't one to get in other folks' business. Her philosophy came from her beloved grandmother, who'd spouted it when Frieda had run in at the age of eight, with the gossip that the next-door neighbor was hugging someone else's wife. "Here's what you do," her grandmother had said calmly, while ironing clothes. "You take six months and tend to your business, and six months to leave others alone. Any months left? That's when you deal with other folks' business." Those words had stuck, and they played in her mind now as she thought of the two handsome brothers having sex upstairs. She thought of her friend, Joe. Maybe he was somewhere getting his groove on, too.

"Aha, I found you," a silky voice spoke against Frieda's ear.

She turned slightly and gazed into ambrosial green eyes, flecked with gold. "Was I lost?" She turned from the stunning city view and leaned against the stone wall to observe an equally stunning human one.

"Admit it, you tried to run away from me," the handsome stranger teased. "You came down those stairs like you'd seen a ghost."

Frieda had been too busy running to notice any onlookers witnessing her great escape. At any rate, what she'd seen had been all too real, live, and in living, buck-naked color. But she didn't want to get into that. "What's your name?"

The stranger smiled. "Gorgio."

"Ooh, sexy name. You're what, Italian?"

"On my mother's side. My father's Black."

"Well," Frieda said flirtatiously, revealing the hint of a smile, "remind me to thank your father *and* your mother the next time I see them."

Gorgio laughed and leaned against the stone wall next to Frieda. The conversation flowed smoothly, effortlessly. *Well, well, well,* Frieda speculated. *Looks like I might get compromised tonight after all.*

15

Precious Lord . . .

Darius reached for a helping of Bo's homemade vegetable-fried rice. He loved Bo's cooking, and had only snacked all day, in between the two church services and a last minute band rehearsal of that night's musical selections.

Bo placed a baked chicken breast on Darius's plate and one on his own. "So, how was church?" he asked.

"Long," Darius replied. "Wish you were there."

"Baby, I told you, I'm just not feeling that. I'd take one look at you up there stroking those keys? The next thing I know, I'd be down on my knees." Bo paused for effect. "And I'm not talking about praying."

Darius was flattered. Bo did this for him. Made him feel good, appreciated, loved—something no woman had ever done—certainly not Gwen, his ex-wife. It's not that he hadn't tried, to love women, that is. Growing up in a small Arkansas town, he'd learned at an early age that being attracted to other boys was not the thing to do. Or it was not the thing to admit.

He remembered the first time it happened. He was about six years old, in gym class. He had a big crush on Bobby, a gangly, big-lipped seven-year-old, who was great at anything athletic. They were playing on the playground, wrestling. Bobby got him in a headlock. Darius wrestled back, enjoying the contact. And then for him, it turned into something else. He got the incredible urge to kiss Bobby. And he did. He went home with a loose tooth and black eye.

Then there were the fire and brimstone sermons he heard, both from the grandmother who raised him and the pastor of their Pentecostal church. Darius's mother had abandoned him before his fourth birthday, and he'd never known his father. So, sitting with his grandmother on the first or second pew, he'd imagine the fiery hell that was every Sunday's focus, feel the accusatory scriptures on unnatural desires, hurled out like daggers aimed at his young heart, and fear the Sodom and Gomorrah story that emphasized God's anger and veiled His love. The preacher would mention the big ones: adultery, killing, stealing, and of course, homosexuality. But Darius noticed how other sins, such as judging, gossiping, lying, backbiting, were ignored. He remembered how he'd hear old man Johnson, his grandmother's neighbor, come over after Darius had gone to bed. His grandmother would reach into the top cupboard, above the refrigerator, and pull out the scotch. They'd get to talking, then whispering, and then the next thing Darius heard were her bedsprings creaking. They didn't know he knew. He was only seven, eight years old at the time. But Darius heard, and he knew.

When he was about ten years old a new boy, Frankie, moved to the neighborhood. Frankie was an outsider, a loner, from somewhere in the Midwest, Nebraska, if Darius remembered correctly. He was quiet, shy, and Darius could relate to him. Darius's secret had made him an outsider, too, in the span of four years. So he befriended Frankie, invited him over to his house. They did the typical boy stuff: playing catch outside, ripping and running, digging for worms, and video games. Then one day, Darius invited Frankie to his room to look at his comic book collection. They were sitting on the bed, close together, looking at the pages. He doesn't remember whose suggestion it was, but the comic books were soon covering ex-

posed penises, penises that were each held by the other boy. It
was Darius's first erection, and the first time he'd met somebody like him. In a careless moment, one of them suggested
pulling down their pants for better access. That's how his
grandmother found them when she came back from the store.
Frankie scrambled out of the house, barely able to get his pants
up, and Darius got a beating he would never forget. His grandmother had whipped and lectured him for half an hour, saying
how she wasn't going to raise no fags or sissies in her house.
She tried to literally beat the hell out of him, calling down fire
and brimstone. She told Darius she'd rather see him dead than
turn into "one of them kind of men." She'd warned him that if
he ever did anything like that again, she'd put him out of her
house.

Darius got scared straight, for a while. His grandmother
made him go to church with her almost every day—said she
was going to "cure" him. He'd always been musically gifted,
and she made him start playing for the church. He enjoyed
this, and tried to lose himself in the music. He repeated the
rhetoric that he'd heard in church to himself: how he was bad,
evil, a stench in God's nostrils. His self-esteem plummeted, but
his musical gift soared.

He promised himself he would not touch his penis again.
He prayed, begged, pleaded with God to change him. He tried
not to look at boys, tried not to have the feelings about them
that would rise, unbidden. As he entered his teens and his
friends started talking about girls, he'd join in, mimic what
they were saying about what they liked, and why.

When he was fifteen, he lost his virginity. She was seventeen, and invited him to a house party. She led him to one of
the bedrooms, pulled up her skirt. He tried to get an erection,
tried to recapture the feelings he'd experienced when Frankie
touched his penis. She laughed at him, told him he was scared.
Then she'd unbuttoned her blouse, exposed her young, pert
breasts. Darius had closed his eyes, thought of Frankie. As he

did so, he became aroused. She jumped on it and within five minutes the deed was done. But at least he'd done it. He'd no longer have to lie about having been with a woman.

When he was sixteen, he fell in love. He and his grandmother had traveled to Dallas, to a convention of big-time preachers and gospel choirs from all over the country. It had been six years since the incident with Frankie, and while he was still attracted to men, he had never again acted it out physically. The first night in Dallas, he'd met an eighteen-year-old musician who could play the piano as if he'd invented it. Darius had watched, mesmerized, as this kid commanded the attention of the entire arena, had them eating out of his hand and shouting like crazy. After the service, he'd run up to the platform, in speechless awe. The boy, Robert, had tossed him a crooked smile, looked him up and down. "I can teach you how to play like that," he said.

They went back to where Darius's grandmother was sitting. She was thrilled to meet Robert, told him how "blessed of the Lord" he was, how he was a gift from heaven, a gift from God. When Darius asked if he could stay in Robert's room and learn some new chords, his grandmother didn't hesitate to say yes, smiling broadly as she waved them off. She was already envisioning Darius on the stage, doing what Robert had done. Like him, her grandson was going to be a star!

They went back to Robert's room, stopped to get something to eat on the way, and discussed music over burgers and fries. Robert looked at him a couple times. Their eyes held a little too long for friendship, more like the length for lovers. Darius's heart skipped a beat. When finished eating, they went over to the portable keyboard that was set up in a corner of the room. Robert suggested Darius sit down, show him what he could do. Darius started with a simple run up the keys, then started playing "Precious Lord." Somewhere between "When my way grows drear" and "precious Lord lingers near" Robert reached over and rubbed Darius's neck. Darius kept playing, thinking maybe it had been an accidental brush. Robert sat down then, placed his arm around Darius's shoulder. Darius kept playing, the music speeding up with his heartbeat. Robert began rubbing Darius's arm, up and down. He was looking at him again, with the long, lover stare. Darius stopped playing. He turned and looked at Robert, in his eyes, at his lips. They kissed. Tentatively at first and then with passion, tongues swirling, arms entwined. Darius experienced his first male lover. And he knew in that moment that his life would never be the same.

"Hey, lover boy, where'd you go?" Bo looked at Darius, a bit concerned. Darius hadn't realized he'd eaten his entire plate of stir-fry without saying a word. "You were a million miles away."

"I was thinking," Darius said, getting up and taking his and Bo's plates to the sink.

"About what?"

"About how unfair life is. How I want to be with you but everybody else wants me to be with Stacy."

"Is that poodle still hounding you?"

"Please, she's even enlisted Tanya to plead her case. Got my sis asking all kinds of questions about why I don't take Stacy out, and when am I going to get remarried, and how nice she is, and how good a wife she'd make."

Bo started rinsing dishes, placing them in the dishwasher. "I told you we should get out of this town, go to San Francisco, or Seattle. I've got great connections there. We could have a wonderful life."

Darius leaned on the counter, watching Bo at the sink. "I've got to do something, because I sure don't want to go through the motions of being married again." He walked over and began to massage Bo's shoulders. "Unless it's to you."

16

The Man of Her Dreams

"Husband, come to me!" Millicent commanded.

Cy looked at her and was up in an instant. "Yes, darling, I'm coming. It is our time. I want you, and only you, to be my wife."

Millicent waited as he crossed the room, her heart bursting with love. The congregation cheered as Cy reached her side, took her hand, and pulled her close. Derrick and Vivian stood in the pulpit, two proud parents cheering them on. This moment was everything she'd ever envisioned. She couldn't be happier. She was marrying the man of her dreams.

And then they were dancing: down the aisles, out the door, across the parking lot, and through a meadow filled with flowers. The well-wishing cheers of the congregation, who'd followed them out to the parking lot, dimmed as they moved farther and farther away. Suddenly, they were alone, the sound of classical music surrounding them.

Cy pulled Millicent to his chest and kissed her passionately. "I can't wait any longer," he said, panting. "I want you, I want you now!"

"Yes, take me, take me!" Millicent replied. She began tearing off her Dolce and Gabbana suit, its worth nothing compared to the treasure in front of her. "I'm yours darling, I'm yours!"

The music got louder. Cy stepped back to drink in Millicent's beauty. He reached for his tie and slowly loosened it. Then one by one, he unbuttoned his shirt and took it off. His chest was model perfect. A faint line of hair from his chest disappeared into his waistband. Milli- cent couldn't wait to follow that trail.

Barely breathing, she watched as he took off his shirt and threw it in the grass. Next, he took off his shoes, unbuckled his belt, and re- moved his pants, throwing them into the growing pile of discarded gar- ments.

The music got louder, still. Millicent's heart beat wildly. She stared at the bulge pressing against the black silk Calvin Klein boxers. Her mouth watered. She looked up at Cy's face. He was smiling at her, dazzling white teeth in a face that made her warm all over.

"Do you want me?" Cy asked, teasing.

"Yes, yes!" Millicent replied. To prove her point, she grabbed the boxers and yanked them down. Cy's penis jumped out, large and lively, with a life of its own.

The music reached a crescendo. Millicent dropped to her knees, ready to show her appreciation. She opened her eyes to guide the mas- sive head into her mouth. But something was wrong. The tip of Cy's dick didn't look right. It looked like it had a face. Yes, there was defi- nitely a face on the head of his dick. Mesmerized, Millicent looked closer to make out the features, and stared into the eyes of . . . Hope Jones!

Millicent's heart pounded as she sat straight up in bed. Her nightgown, drenched in sweat, was tangled around her long legs. The music from her dream still reached her ears. She looked around, confused, until it registered that the sound was her radio, the alarm having been set to *radio wake up.* Millicent shook her head, trying to clear it. The dream had seemed so real. Only it hadn't been a dream, but a nightmare. She never should have eaten jalapeño peppers before going to bed.

Maybe if I could see him again, talk to him, apologize. Maybe the abrupt way their friendship ended was why Cy continued to haunt Millicent, even in her dreams. But how could she get to him without Hope finding out? Millicent felt her dream might symbolize just how tightly Hope was guarding Cy's penis!

"Forget him!" Millicent said, almost screamed, to the empty room. Her current train of thought was leading nowhere. *I've got to keep my mind occupied.* She peeled off her nightgown and stepped in the shower, letting the water, almost cold, bring her fully awake. Once out, she dried off and dressed quickly. Less than fifteen minutes after waking up, Millicent was in her car, headed to wherever.

Millicent stopped at the Starbucks just down the street from her home. She needed to be around people. As usual, this popular coffee haunt was crowded. For once, Millicent didn't mind. After ordering a soy chai latte and blueberry muffin, she took the morning paper to an outside table. She bypassed news, sports, and want ads, and scanned the arts and sales sections. Nothing could transport Millicent to a better mood faster than a great museum or art exhibit. She noted an art show happening in San Diego, and finishing the last of her muffin, headed for Interstate 5.

Three hours later, Millicent got back in her car, pleased with her purchases of an abstract painting for her dining room, a small waterfall just right for her patio, and a figurine urn that would occupy an empty corner in her living room. The art show had been wonderful, featuring several local as well as national and international artists and sculptors. There had also been food stands, juice bars, and live music. The atmosphere had certainly helped to lighten her mood.

But she wasn't ready to go home and face the ghosts she'd left there. Instead, Millicent decided to continue shopping. Next on her list was either an ottoman or side table for the overstuffed armchair she'd purchased to complement her sleek, suede couch. But where to look? Millicent wished she'd browsed the furniture ads before she'd left Starbucks.

Just as she was about to give up the search and enter the freeway on-ramp toward La Jolla, Millicent spotted a strip mall with the word "Furniture" on the tenant sign. Instead of the highway, she got into the left-hand lane and swung into the parking lot.

My, she thought after having to park several businesses down from the furniture store, *this is a busy place.* It didn't matter. The June sun was out, the temperature lovely, and Millicent had nothing but time.

As she neared the buildings, the faint sounds of beautiful music floated out with the gentle breeze. *Is that a harp?* Millicent walked toward the sound of the music and found herself in front of the double doors of the corner building. She looked up, but saw no sign. She heard the music though, and it was enchanting, indeed a harp. It had been a long time since she'd heard this instrument played live. Millicent opened the doors and went inside.

Upon entering the building, Millicent was greeted by two pleasantly smiling women. One, a cute brunette with caring brown eyes, dressed casually in jeans and a floral blouse, smiled broadly. "Good afternoon!"

"Good afternoon," Millicent replied. "I heard the music and had to come in. It's lovely."

"Go right in," the pretty blonde next to her encouraged. "Elena is quite an accomplished harpist. Her music will bless your soul."

Millicent was sure of that; it was soothing her soul already. But had the woman said "bless"? Was this a religious concert? Millicent fought the fear that rose up quickly. What did it matter if it was? Didn't she love the Lord? If this was a concert featuring Christian music, it was time for her to face whatever crazy fears she had about sitting among the saints. And what a great place to do it. The atmosphere was casual, the setting equally so, and there was beautiful music. What more could she ask for?

With a steely resolve, she reached for the doors and stepped inside. There was nothing religious-looking about the unadorned space. The gathering was small, only a couple hundred or so. They were seated in a circular fashion, with the stage directly in front of her. There was no usher, so she quickly found a seat. As the harpist strummed fluidly over the strings, she closed her eyes and gave in to the peace the music evoked. When the song ended, Millicent opened her eyes and smiled. The unfamiliar melody had felt like worship. It had felt incredible; she was suffused with the presence of God in an instant, and the last traces of her dream about Cy were washed away.

The woman next to her smiled. "Wasn't that beautiful?"

Millicent could only nod as tears formed in her eyes. She felt if she opened her mouth, an emotional dam would burst.

The woman seemed to understand and gently squeezed her arm. "That was 'You'll Never Walk Alone,' one of my favorites. But, my dear sister, I think God had Elena play that just for you." And then, as an afterthought, the woman added, "Welcome, welcome to Open Arms."

17

The Past Is Back

"Sleep well, Mom," Janeé said, kissing her mother on the forehead. "I'll be back in the morning."

Janeé turned off lights as she walked through her mother's quiet home. She rubbed her shoulders, tight from pent-up stress. Her mother was improving every day, but still Janeé worried. She'd barely known her father. Miss Smith was her only anchor to the past. Almost.

Closing and locking the door behind her, Janeé walked toward her rental car. Hans had suggested she purchase a preowned one, but Janeé had balked. That felt too permanent, too settled. Janeé wanted to return to Germany as soon as she could. Before returning, however, she would go to Los Angeles and visit her son, Kelvin. He was nearing the end of his second year at a prestigious private school in Santa Barbara and had just gotten a summer job in a town near the campus. Even though Kelvin was mature for his age and loved staying with Hans's family, especially his same-aged cousins, Janeé worried about him being so far from her, for many reasons. She looked forward to visiting him before they left the states, and to his rejoining the family in Germany during the holidays.

Janeé called Hans to let him know she was on her way. He'd insisted on bringing the family over once it became clear that Janeé would be in Kansas a while. He was at the hotel waiting for her, protective as always. She hung up the phone smiling, thinking of how lucky she'd been to meet and marry this man more than twelve years ago.

They'd met in Frankfurt during a convention. He'd been the guest of honor, she the singer hired to entertain the crowd of financiers. She'd flirted with him all evening, even sitting on his lap during one of her songs. Afterward, she'd received a note in her dressing room, an invite to dinner. They'd gone out once, twice, and before long, were an item—meeting between her singing engagements and his international travel. Ten years older, he was steady, attentive, and sincere. She was drawn to the security he brought to her life, providing shadows of a father figure she'd never enjoyed. What had melted her heart the most was his treatment of then four-year-old Kelvin. He'd embraced the child immediately, comfortable in his interactions with him, patient with instructions. Kelvin had warmed to him also, and by the time they married, two years later, her son was calling Hans "Da."

Hans as "Da" had sufficed until Kelvin turned thirteen. That's when he'd come home one day and out of the blue, asked about his real father. It was a question Janeé had anticipated, and dreaded. She'd kept the conversation short, told him that his dad was an old friend with whom she'd shared a casual relationship. She had moved to Germany shortly after he was born and had never told the man he had a child. At the time, she'd thought it best. Why further complicate an already messy situation?

Kelvin had listened attentively, asked understandable questions, which she patiently answered.

"Did you love him?"

"Yes."

"Did he love you?"

Pause. "Yes."

"Why didn't he want me?"

"He doesn't know about you. I was young, thought I was doing the right thing. I started to tell him, many times, but then my career took off and I never went back home. When Hans adopted you, became the father you needed, I thought everything had worked out perfectly. Hans has been a good father, no?"

"Yes."

"You know Hans loves you like his own child."

Pause, nod. "Do I look like my real dad?"

"Yes."

"Can I meet him someday?"

"We'll see."

Now, three short years later, someday was here. Janeé still didn't know what she should do, how to handle it. It wasn't just about her and Kelvin. There were other people involved, other spouses, other children. It was complicated. But was it wise to deny her child the right to know his father? She'd purposely not revealed the father's identity to her mother, but now the words Miss Smith had somberly stated shortly after Kelvin was born rang in her ears: "What's done in darkness always comes to light." Her mom was right.

And what of her lifelong love for King? She could tell he was avoiding her, had limited theirs to small talk when they'd seen each other at the hospital. It was just as well. One would think that time, and Hans, would have dimmed the flame that burned in her heart for him. But it hadn't. If he but said the word, she'd stoke the flames and in no time have them burning bright, and hot, all over again.

Robin Reynolds perched on the edge of her chair, drinking coffee and reading the paper in her friend's modest apartment. Or trying to. She'd been staring at the same ad for five minutes. Her mind was preoccupied with the reason for her trip to Los Angeles—Derrick Montgomery.

Coming to LA had been an impulsive decision, one made after seeing on television the man she'd lusted after years before, and being unable to talk to him over the phone. And now she was second-guessing all she'd done to be here. Having been dumped by her husband, and fired from her job, she had no ties to Florida. But she had no money either, not much anyway. She'd be through her severance check in no time. And she was almost out of Peridol, her anti-psychotic medication. Robin's friend had said she could stay with her as long as she liked, but how long could she share a two-bedroom apartment with three bad ass kids?

Even being here, there was no guarantee anything would happen between her and Derrick. And what did she want to happen? After seeing him at church service, she knew that for starters she wanted him to make something happen between her legs.

If they'd just let me talk to him, I wouldn't have had to come. The curiosity of how and what he'd been doing was innocent, initially. While flipping the channels one afternoon, she'd been pleasantly surprised to recognize Derrick being interviewed on a Christian television station. He was looking fit and fine all these years later. She'd watched the entire exchange and learned that he pastored a megachurch on the West Coast. Afterward, she'd gone on-line and checked out the church's Web site. That's where she'd seen he was still married to Vivian and learned they had two children. Without really knowing why, she'd called the number listed for those wanting more information on the ministry. That's when her frustration had started.

Why couldn't they just let her talk to him? She'd called every day, several times a day, for a solid week, and the closest she'd gotten to Derrick was Angela, his assistant. She'd thought about confiding in Angela, telling her who she was. But she was afraid Angela wouldn't put the call through. So she kept calling, and the more she tried, and the more she'd been denied, the more determined she became. The determination to

talk on the phone became a determination to reestablish physical contact. Their rules to keep Derrick isolated from female
congregants turned into a challenge for her to break through.
Vivian had won all those years ago. Wasn't it Robin's turn for a
victory?

As she sat and stewed in Florida, delusional memories of
Derrick's first months at Pilgrims' Rest caused Robin to con-
clude she had a right to see him, that she'd been wronged, that
he owed her. That, and years of getting the short end of the
stick, or at least of the dick, when it came to relationships, was
further incentive to not back down.

Robin recalled with fondness when Derrick first came to
the small congregation in which she was a member. She had
grown up in the church, and provided invaluable information
and assistance to the young preacher. She set up the church fil-
ing system, organized his calendar, and typed his correspon-
dence. They enjoyed a wonderful camaraderie, and more than
once, he voiced his appreciation of her assistance. Robin knew
he was married from the beginning, had watched Vivian prance
in on Sunday mornings in all her righteous glory. She fumed as
Vivian was handled with deference, was given a seat in the
front row and fussed over by the church mothers.

Robin decided to be patient. With Vivian's dedication to
her job as news anchor in Birmingham, she knew it was just a
matter of time before the marriage collapsed. In the meantime,
she strove to make herself even more invaluable to Derrick by
typing his sermons and transferring data from paper files to
computer when the new system arrived. She stepped up her
game then, went by the church almost every day. She never
missed a Bible study, never missed a service. Anytime the church
door opened and Derrick was preaching, she was there. No
one could preach the word like Mr. Montgomery and she told
him so, every chance she got. Her plan was to become invaluable to the ministry, then become equally so to the man.

But then, just like that, it was over. One Monday evening,

she walked into the office to find Derrick and Vivian huddled together. Vivian was sitting at the computer and Derrick was leaning over her, showing her the data file Robin had set up! Vivian turned and smiled politely, informed her that she'd quit her job in order to help her husband full-time. She complimented Robin on her work, told her the transition would be easier because of all she'd done. Then, to add insult to injury, Derrick gave Robin a list of churches and names, stating that he agreed with Vivian's suggestion that Robin coordinate the regional prayer circle, that she was the perfect person for the job. They teamed her up with Sister Moseley to work out the details, including topics to be prayed for and coordinating monthly prayer shut-ins. They needed someone like her, he'd continued, someone faithful and devoted.

"You've definitely shown those qualities," Vivian asserted. Whether it was true or not, Robin heard sarcasm and insincerity dripping from the statement. Jealousy turned to hate in that instant. *Prayer circle!* The last thing Robin wanted was to be stuck in a room with some old biddies, beseeching God on other people's behalf. She had her own problems; let whoever had theirs handle them on their own. She'd taken the list, acted equally sincere in seeing Vivian take her "rightful place" beside her husband, and agreed to start calling people that evening. And she had. She determined to beat Vivian at her own game.

Over the next two weeks, she called every person on the list, including Sister Moseley, her prayer partner and the old biddy she most despised. She always seemed to be around when Robin went to Derrick's office, and if Vivian was out running errands, made excuses to stay in there with them until Robin left. Robin couldn't make a move on Derrick if she tried. But that hadn't worried her. Robin was a persevering woman, and she was biding her time for just the right opportunity to connect with those soft lips, emphasized by a well-kempt mustache.

But her determination didn't last. Robin couldn't keep up

the facade. Vivian jumped head first into the activities at Pilgrims' Rest. She was there every day. Robin couldn't take it. After a couple months, she found another church, in Atlanta. The church was okay, but it wasn't the same. She didn't know the members, didn't feel the same ownership she had at Pilgrims' Rest. Slowly, church began taking a backseat to other activities in Atlanta. First, she stopped going to night services, then Wednesday prayer meetings, then only attended service every other Sunday. By the time she'd met the man with whom she moved to Florida, she'd all but stopped thinking about church, and Derrick. Not to mention the rocky relationships that followed, or the husband who'd left her for a firmer pair of thighs a year ago.

When Robin planned her trip to California, she'd told herself the reason for going was to see an old friend, a woman who'd worked at the plant with her before following a nucka to California and having three of his babies. Unfortunately, he'd made the bad career choice of committing an armed robbery while an off-duty officer shopped for groceries, and was now doing ten to fifteen. Her friend was struggling in costly LA with three children. Maybe she could help her out. And Derrick? Well, she was just curious, wanted to see him in person after all these years, see how he and the ministry had grown.

She had told herself these things, almost believing them. But the more she'd visited the web site, sneering at the "one big happy family" portrait of the Montgomerys, the more she admitted she wanted to go to California and see if she could shake things up a bit. Maybe Derrick was tired of Vivian after all these years, was staying with her for the sake of the ministry. Theirs might be a marriage in name only. No matter what anybody else said, Derrick Montgomery was *her* man. He probably wouldn't even be where he was today if she hadn't been there to help in the beginning!

But how would she do it, how could she finagle her way

into his life, into his arms? It would definitely be easier if the marriage had problems. But how could she find that out? Maybe Angela was the key; she had seemed kind and sympathetic each time Robin called.

One thing was sure. Nothing was going to get done inside her friend's musty, shabby apartment in which she now sat. She appreciated that the woman had agreed to let her stay there as long as she needed for free, but Robin felt with kids, cramped quarters, and a lumpy couch for a bed, free was a high price.

It was time for Robin to make something happen. She grabbed the sale papers and the large, freeway map. She would need a suit, shoes, pantyhose. She prayed to run into a clearance rack somewhere, but the purchases would have to be made. It was time for a "Sunday go to meeting" outfit, time to go to church again, and most crucially, time to reconnect with Derrick.

18

Manly Men

"Why do we have to sit all the way down front?" Frieda was already regretting that she'd agreed to go to Sunday night services with Hope. The main reason she had was because Hope had said it was a baptism so there would be only music, no preaching. And because she hoped it would get Hope off her back about attending. Hadn't the girl heard her when she said Christmas and Easter were her dates with the Lord?

"C'mon, girl, it's not gonna kill you. If this was Jay-Z, or your favorite girl, Fantasia, you'd be running to the front row," Hope pointed out, nodding at a few of the acquaintances she'd made in her short time as a member of KCCC.

"But it ain't them," Frieda argued as the usher stopped at the second row and stepped aside for them to sit down. She dropped her voice to a whisper and added, "And if I don't see some fine brothahs sitting close enough to flirt, I'm gon' be running right for the exit!"

"Relax," Hope whispered back, "and just keep your eyes on the Lord."

"Where he at?" Frieda asked jokingly.

Hope poked Frieda's arm and rolled her eyes. Frieda settled into the row, annoyed because she couldn't take a look at the male menu. That's why she'd wanted to sit toward the back. Because then, all the possibilities would be in front of her.

In reality, she was just talking. Frieda's new friend, Gorgio, was keeping her quite satisfied. She smiled, thinking of how pleasantly surprised she'd been when he had called like he said he would, the day after the Hollywood Hills party. They'd hooked up the next night and had gone out frequently. Both had decided to hang loose, go with the flow, and not try to put a definition on the relationship. Frieda was especially not trying to get in deep emotionally. She'd had her heart broken by more than one pretty-boy nucka who'd promised the world but only delivered a whirl, mostly between the sheets. Gorgio was upfront and honest, which she liked, and a good lover. What he lacked in size, he more than made up for in enthusiasm, and stamina. And the things that man's tongue could do to her va-jay-jay . . .

The rumbling sounds of the keyboard interrupted Frieda's train of thought. Just in time, too, because the memory lane she was going down was probably not the right one to indulge in here in the second pew of the sanctuary. She refocused her thoughts by listening to the band, who were now playing a gospel tune that had many people standing and clapping. They were jammin', just like Hope had promised they would.

Dang, wish I could see the band. Frieda had always liked musicians, especially drummers. Something about them and those sticks. . . . "I wish I could see the band," she said, leaning over to Hope, who was enjoying a head-bob, hand-clap kind of rhythm.

"Stand up," Hope suggested.

Frieda looked around and saw other congregants on their feet, clapping and swaying to the beat. She stood and joined them, now able to see the band on the slightly raised, temporary platform they played from when the baptismal pool was being used.

Now, this is better. There was the drummer, stocky, not really good-looking but sexy in his own way, especially how his head bounced, eyes closed, to the rhythm. *Nice shoulders,* she thought as he went for the snares, the bass, and a cymbal here and there. The lead guitarist was also handsome. *I like the way he's fingering those strings.* The intro was over and now the choir joined in. More people stood up and joined in the stomp-clap-clap, rhythm done in unity across the congregation.

Frieda turned to the singers. The choir loft was on a raised platform behind the pulpit. In their purple and gold robes, they indeed looked angelic. They were leading the stomp-clap-clap; some with subdued moves, others with flamboyance. *Hmm, a few cuties in the choir stand!* Especially the lead singer, who stepped away from the others and ad-libbed between the chorus. After a few rounds of that, it was time for the key-boardist's solo. Frieda turned back to the band as the beautiful melody bounced off the ivories. She shifted to get a look at the player, partially blocked by the man on saxophone. He stepped back momentarily, grabbing a reed or something from his case.

Frieda stopped stomping. She stopped clapping, too. Instead, she stood there with her mouth open, but only for a second. She pulled hard on Hope's arm. Hope looked at her questioningly. Frieda pulled harder and sat down, taking Hope with her.

"Girl, what is it?" The music was so loud they could talk rather freely.

"Oh-my-God," was all Frieda said, her eyes big as saucers as she stared her cousin down.

"What?" Hope said again. This girl was always trippin' about something!

"That boy on the piano, the organ or whatever, he's the one!"

"The one what?"

"Remember the two dudes doing the nasty at the party where I met Gorgio?"

Hope remembered, but had no idea what that story was doing in these pews. "Yes?" she said with a question mark in the tone.

"That man on the keyboards," Frieda said, leaning over and dropping her voice an octave, "he's the one who was getting ready to . . . well . . . It's him, girl. He's got a booty buddy!"

"Darius?" Hope exclaimed. She didn't know that much about him, nothing really, but she was having a hard time believing he was gay. She always saw women around him. She tried to blow it off. "No, he probably just reminds you of the man you saw."

"You think I'd forget the characters in a movie like that?" Frieda asked, her voice getting a bit loud before she toned down again. "I'd bet my next paycheck your boy is gay or at least bi. I'd already checked him out real good, that's why I'd followed him up the stairs, remember? It's him, Hope!"

Hope looked at Frieda and then stood back up. She wanted to see Darius, see if she could wrap what Frieda had said around him. Leaning forward, as if into the music, she stared at Darius as he effortlessly directed the choir and played the keys. He was as handsome as ever, and as manly. Looking closer, she wouldn't even give him the "pretty boy" label. He had gorgeous eyes and long eyelashes, but his close-cropped haircut and slight facial hair gave him a rugged look. He had a nice, toned build. And there had never been anything in his mannerisms to suggest he might be gay—not that mannerisms a gay man made. She couldn't detect a clue anywhere. She'd talked to Darius recently, when she and Cy were the Montgomerys dinner guests. Come to think of it, he'd had a date with him that night. She sat down and relayed this to Frieda, as the choir bumped the song up a notch.

"No," Hope said. "I remember now, he had a date when we had dinner at the Montgomerys."

"And?"

"And, he's not gay. He's got a girlfriend."

"Humph. She might be a decoy, so he can be with his boy toy."

Hope knew there would be no convincing Frieda, at least not before the benediction that evening. "Frieda, let it go, girl. Mind your own business." She stood up and tried, unsuccessfully, to get back into praise. But even an hour and a half later, as the associate ministers were baptizing the last candidate, Hope's mind was still on Darius. And the booty-bumping episode Frieda had relayed in graphic detail the day after the party.

At home that evening, Darius was still on Hope's mind. She didn't know why; it really wasn't her concern. Hope knew there were gays in church, plenty of them. It wasn't something that was talked about—not unless somebody was condemning them to hell. But many knew that homosexuals were and had long been a part of the church community, especially when it came to the music. And now with Frieda having pricked her curiosity, she wanted to see what she could find out.

"Hey you," she said as she kissed her man, looking sexy and scrumptious sprawled across the couch, watching television.

"How was it?" Cy asked, grabbing Hope and pulling her toward him.

She relaxed in his arms, taking off her shoes in the process. "It was nice," she answered. "The music was excellent, and there is always something special about seeing someone get baptized."

"Well, I'm glad you enjoyed it," Cy mumbled, nibbling on her ear. When Hope didn't respond, he looked up to see she was deep in thought.

"Cy, I have a question." She turned to him slightly and blurted it out. "Is Darius gay?"

"Darius?" Cy thought for a moment. "I don't think so. Why do you ask?"

Hope told Cy about what Frieda had supposedly seen and how adamant she was that it had been Darius. "I tried to tell her he had a girlfriend, but she wasn't hearing me."

"Darius doesn't have a girlfriend."

"What about that girl who was at Pastor's house?"

"No, she's connected to his music business somehow. They're not dating."

"Oh."

"I have heard rumors."

Hope turned fully toward Cy. "That he's gay?"

Cy nodded. "But those may have been generated by player-hating females. I know for a fact he was married, went through a messy divorce. That may be why he's been rather cool on the dating scene."

"Oh, so he *was* married?"

"Yeah, until he caught his wife at home with some dude."

"Really? Wow . . ."

"Speaking of gay, did you see this?" Cy began surfing the channels, stopping on a movie channel. *Brokeback Mountain,* a love story about two gay cowboys, was just beginning.

"I've been meaning to watch this," Cy said. "There was so much hype when it came out."

Hope snuggled up to her honey, prepared to find out what all the hype was about. But as she watched Jake Gyllenhaal and Heath Ledger cavort over the Wyoming plains, it was "Brokeback Ministries, starring Darius Crenshaw," and not the Oscar-winning blockbuster, that was on her mind.

19

Just Bring You

Darius knew it was too late to act as though he hadn't seen her. They were in the same aisle at Best Buy, both looking at flat screens.

"Hey, cutie," Stacy said, approaching Darius with a big smile.

"Hey, yourself," Darius responded easily. He liked Stacy, thought she was a fine, intelligent woman. Just not for him.

"Looking for flat screens, huh?" she asked.

"They're nice, aren't they?"

"Yeah, still so expensive, though. But I'm doing some redecorating, want to update some things. I'll invite you over for dinner when I get everything done."

Darius had no plans to ever visit Stacy's home, for any reason. "Sure, just let me know."

This was the closest Stacy had come to Darius actually agreeing to get together with her, privately, datelike. She wasn't going to squander the opportunity.

"Look, Darius, we don't have to wait until I redecorate. You know I like you. And I'd really like to get to know you better, even as friends, if that's what you want. I mean, we've known each other for a couple of years, working together at church. We're both single, why can't we just hang out?"

Because I'm in love with Bo! "We can, it's just, you know how busy my schedule is, between work at the church, touring, and my music projects."

"All the more reason you should take time to relax," Stacy said, standing her ground. "Why don't we set a date right now, just something casual? You come over, I fix burgers, dogs, or something. Watch a movie, play some games. I've got the latest Xbox, and can probably kick yo' behind a time or two."

Actually, Stacy wasn't much into video games. Her brother had purchased the system when he stayed with her briefly, before getting called back to Iraq for army duty. She'd played a few times but couldn't get into what her brother liked, all the shooting, killing, and violence. She couldn't get into him going to Iraq for the real deal regarding violence and killing, either, but that was another story. She relayed none of this to Darius, however. She knew if anything could act as an incentive to join her for dinner, the new Xbox could.

Darius considered his options. Stacy had been after him for a while. Maybe if he went out with her, gave her a little attention, it would be better for everybody. Some of the other females might back off if they thought Stacy was his woman, and that would quiet some of the rumors he'd heard cropping up in the music world. He made a snap decision. "Oh, you've got the latest version? You know how to get me, don't you?"

Stacy laughed. "I sure hope so."

"Okay, when?"

Stacy would forever be indebted to Darius's sister, Tanya, who'd given her a Best Buy gift card for her birthday. That's the only reason she was in the store. "Next Friday night?"

The more Darius thought about it, the more he believed that this setup might work. If he and Stacy could become good, platonic buddies, this might not be so bad.

"Naw, I'm going out of town the next two weekends. It'll have to be the Friday after that," Darius answered.

Stacy didn't want to wait, but at least she had a date she could circle on the calendar. "Okay, week after next."

Darius nodded. "I look forward to it."

Stacy smiled coyly. "Me, too. Hey, let's trade numbers, just in case."

Darius felt just a twinge of something—was it guilt?—as he exchanged telephone numbers with Stacy. As if he'd conjured him up, his phone rang—Bo.

"Alright then," he said, walking away from Stacy. "Next Friday." Then into the phone, his voice lowered, "I just did something stupid."

"What?"

"Made a date with Stacy."

"Stop playing." Bo thought Darius could be so silly at times.

"It seemed like a good idea when I was saying it." There was no humor in Darius's voice.

"Okay, back up. You serious?"

"Wait," Darius said, walking toward the exit. He didn't want to be overheard. Once outside, he stated his position. "Remember how we were just talking about Smooth trying to out me so I'll go out with him?"

"Yeah, but what's that got to do with Stacy?"

"I'm thinking if I can be with her in the minds of the public, the men and the women trying to swing on my jock will leave me alone."

No comment from the other end.

"Bo, you there?"

Still silent.

"Bo?"

"I don't like it. I don't like this shit at all."

"Baby, baby, don't act like that. You know you're the only

one for me. I'm going to stop on the way home and get your favorite ice cream. Do you want a quart or a pint?"

"A gallon," Bo said, a pout in his voice.

Darius laughed. "Baby, I'll bring you the five-gallon drum. I'll bring you the store!"

"I didn't ask for all that. Just bring me you."

20

Chocolate Cake, Anyone?

It reminded her of Kingdom Citizens' Christian Center. Not the surroundings, the surroundings were, blessedly, totally different. But the camaraderie, the warmth, the shared laughter and sense of belonging—Millicent felt all these things as she sat in Leah Chandler's living room, along with a dozen other women from Open Arms. It hadn't been easy for Leah to convince Millicent to come to her Saturday tea. But slowly, since the morning she had sat next to her at the harp concert, Leah had gently but continually encouraged Millicent to become a part of their congregation and more specifically, the women's group. And on this bright, beautiful Saturday afternoon, surrounded by the scent of herbal drinks and platters of tea sandwiches and scones, Millicent was glad she'd ignored her initial reluctance and accepted Leah's invitation.

Millicent had visited Open Arms several times since stumbling into the unconventional worship facility located in a strip mall. Pastor Jack—which Millicent insisted on calling him though many members used his first name—had made attending services a refreshing experience. The membership was small and, indeed, casual. Most times Pastor Jack wore jeans, mirroring the congregation. His were more talks than sermons, and he often used popular culture, commercials, or news headlines to illustrate scripture. And since going to the church, her dreams about Cy had ceased.

Seeing how casually Pastor Jack interacted with the other members caused Millicent to loosen up. He was jovial and friendly with everyone, genuinely concerned with each person's well-being. While not seeking her out, he always made a point to speak to her when she attended, with light, general conversation. The intimate size of the Sunday congregation made this easy to do. That and the fact that at least a dozen people usually stopped Millicent to chat, comment on an outfit, or make some other friendly remark. A couple times she'd been invited to brunch, but declined. So today was significant; she was back in a church group, and once again in the nurturing company of sisters.

"I was not aggressive. I was assertive," Leah said with a laugh, responding to a comment from one of the ladies who claimed to have seen her push another customer to get to the last roasted chicken at their favorite deli. "Besides, after working a ten-hour day, there was no way I was cooking when I got home!"

"My goodness, Leah," Debbi responded. Debbi was the one who'd witnessed the incident firsthand. "It's not like there wasn't a KFC down the street."

"But have you tasted Fred's chicken?" Leah said in mock amazement. "The colonel can't compare to Fred!"

"I haven't tasted Fred's chicken," Millicent chimed in easily. "But this chicken salad is delicious."

"Point made," Leah replied, nodding at Millicent and giving an I-told-you-so look to Debbi. "*That* is Fred's chicken!"

The ladies laughed and reached for more sandwich slices simultaneously. Leah turned to Millicent. "I want to hear more about the women's group you were a part of, Sisterhood or something?"

Millicent finished the bite of sandwich she was eating before responding. "The group was Ladies First, a group of pastor's wives. I helped coordinate a conference called S.O.S., the Sanctity of Sisterhood."

"Well, Open Arms doesn't even have a first lady; so that will obviously not be our group's makeup." Leah had shared with Millicent that Jack had lost his wife to breast cancer and was raising two children alone. "But doesn't that sound good, y'all; our meeting once a month in order to tackle various women's issues?"

Some of the women nodded, others listened for more information. "What kind of issues did the group address?" Debbi, who was sitting next to Millicent, asked.

Millicent shared the S.O.S. topics, from Spiritually Speaking to Sanctified Sex.

"Wow," Debbi said, after Millicent had finished. "That sounds like some summit, very timely though. Have you guys watched MTV and some of the other cable shows? I've already got parental control, but I think my kids know how to unblock it. As much as I'd miss the variety, I'm seriously thinking about going back to local channels only!"

"The thing is," Leah said, "we can't shield our children from all the sex and violence that's out there. That's a fact. These ladies had the right idea. We have to counter what they see with what we know. We've all been where they are now."

"Gosh, but it's so much more graphic now," Debbi said. "Sure, it was out there in our time but you had to look for it a little bit, had to sneak the adult magazines or racy novels or whatever. Today, we've got *Girls Gone Wild* being advertised as spring break fun! It's all so typical these days, so accepted."

Leah looked at Millicent. "Do you think you could help us do some type of seminar for our teens, our girls?"

Millicent wasn't surprised at the request. A part of her welcomed it, relished the chance to get back in a spiritually supportive environment, and the organizational work she so enjoyed. She had all the materials from S.O.S. It would be easy to put an afternoon agenda together out of the work that had spanned four Saturdays.

Millicent felt this was something she wanted, no, needed to do. "I'd have to work it into a rather busy schedule, but I'd love to."

"Oh, that's great," Leah gushed. She reached over and hugged Millicent. "So that's it, ladies, we have our next project. A sex seminar for our girls."

"I'm not sure we should describe it like that exactly," Millicent said.

"I don't know why not," Leah countered, her voice chipper. "If we put out a flyer advertising a sex seminar, I'm sure we'd get a full house."

"But who would be in the house is the question," one of the women said.

"Probably pervs, molesters, dominatrix fans, just the folk we need to talk to."

"Oh my goodness," Millicent responded with a smile. "Then we'd really better be specific. Because I know I can't teach what the crowd you've listed would want to know. The only thing I'm dominating right now is the rower machine at my gym."

"Oh, who wants to hear about your tight abs," Leah said with feigned disgust. To further bring home the point she went into the kitchen and brought out a tray. "Chocolate cake, anyone?"

Later, Millicent enjoyed Leah's quiet camaraderie as they cleaned the kitchen. Socializing had been nice, and Millicent wasn't ready for her home's solitude. She walked over to the table. "I think I'll have a slice of this cake now. Do you mind if I stay a minute? I mean do you have plans?"

Leah rolled her eyes. "Are you kidding me? I haven't had plans for Saturday night since John Travolta wore the white suit."

"Well, in that case . . ."Teasing, Millicent made an exaggerated move to take the whole cake. Instead, she cut a small slice. "Um, this is good."

"I try."

"You made this?"

"Yes. I'm a closet baker. That's my passion, but the travel agency pays the mortgage."

"You work for a travel agency?"

"Yes, Exquisite Journeys."

"I've heard of you guys! You have clients from all over the world. I'm told the packages you guys put together are amazing."

"They are, and the rub is I could never afford to go on the very vacations I create for others. You have to be rolling in the dough to go Exquisite."

"I bet your clientele list is stunning."

"It's confidential but, yeah, we do alright. Just last week we received a request from a man in Los Angeles, an investor I think, who wants to take his new bride on a special holiday, to this exclusive part of Mexico. Even as great as the dollar is in that country, with the type of accommodations and plans he's making, he'll easily spend six figures."

Millicent hadn't heard much past LA, investor, and new bride. She tried to remain calm, thinking there was no way . . . or was there? "Funny," she said, trying to be casual and cutting another piece of cake just for something to do. "A friend of mine's cousin just got married. He works in investments and lives in LA. But, no, I'm sure it's not him. His name is Cy."

"You're kidding. That's—" Leah caught herself before she exposed her confidential client.

Millicent pounced. "Cy? Are you making plans for Cy and his new wife?"

Leah told Millicent she couldn't reveal names. But the red creeping up from her neck and fanning out over her cheeks told Millicent all she needed to know. Mexico, around the holidays. *Hmm, I wonder . . .* Even as warning bells, and her therapist's voice, rang in her ears, and months of therapy went out the window, Millicent's mind was racing with how to get her hands on the information she needed, so she could plan her trip.

21

In the Name of Jesus

"How do?" Mama Max queried as she stepped into Tai's SUV. Mama Max looked younger than her sixty-plus years in bright red warm-ups and white Nikes. Her perfectly coiffed hair was in a tidy bun on top of her head and bright red nail polish glistened off manicured fingers. She threw a bag with towel and water bottle in the backseat and climbed in front.

"So what do you feel like today, the bikes or the treadmill?"

"Uh-huh," Mama Max said slowly, staring out the window.

"That was an either-or question. Mama, which one?"

"Oh, treadmill I guess."

Tai glanced at her mother-in-law. "Everything all right?"

That's what Mama Max wanted to know. And she wasn't sure how to go about finding out. But something had been bugging her ever since she'd talked with Tootie a few days ago. She'd tried to let it pass but there it was, sticking in her craw. And when things stuck in Mama's craw, there was usually a reason.

"Mama," Tai said, sounding concerned, "what is it?"

"Oh, nothing really," Mama answered. "I was just talking to Nancy when you pulled up. Guess I'm worried about her."

Mama Max wasn't ready to tell her that Miss Smith's daughter was really the one on her mind.

"How is Miss Smith? She's back home now, right?"

"Yes, she's out of the hospital again, but she's still a sick woman." There'd been complications about a month after Miss Smith's open-heart surgery. A second surgery had been necessary to remove a buildup of fluids from around her heart. "Thank God for Tootie. Those sons of Nancy's live right there in St. Louis and barely been up at all. She die, they'll cry the loudest."

"Something about daughters," Tai said. "We're the caretakers."

"Uh-huh." Mama Max hummed softly, looking out the window. She recalled when Tootie first came back, almost six months ago. They'd talked off and on, briefly, whenever they ran into each other at the hospital. It hadn't been a problem. Mama Max had known Tootie since she was born, and had forgiven her for the affair she'd had with King. She'd felt even more comfortable after meeting Hans, Tootie's husband, and the two youngest kids when they came over. It seemed Tootie had done well for herself.

Mama Max had met the children and thought they were adorable. She'd been surprised, however, to learn there was a third, older child. She'd seen Tootie when she'd returned briefly to the states about fifteen years ago, and there had been no mention of a son. But the boy had been a year old then.

Then Mama Max had asked to see a picture of him. Tootie had hesitated and then said she didn't have one. That's when the "thing" first pricked. What mother doesn't have pictures of all her kids? She'd asked the child's age and that's when the "prick" became a "stick." The child was sixteen, the same age as Princess. It was just about sixteen years ago that the affair happened, and Tootie had disappeared shortly after it ended. Everyone knew she'd wanted to sing, and hearing about her career, everyone assumed that is what kept her away. Miss Smith went to Germany every summer, so there really was no reason for Tootie to come home. So why couldn't Mama leave this alone? It wasn't her business who the daddy was. Lord knows Tootie used to get around. But Mama Max couldn't stop the thoughts. She knew how hot and heavy Tootie and King were, for years. She sure hoped . . .

"Oh, Lord," Mama Max said heavily.

Tai reached over and gently squeezed Mama Max's arm. "God is able, Mama," she said softly. "Miss Smith is well on the road to recovery. She'll be okay."

"In the name of Jesus, she'll be okay," Mama Max repeated. *But will you?*

22

A Pentecostal Handshake

It was the first Sunday, and one of the rare occasions when Pastor Derrick and Sister Vivian stood at the church steps and greeted the members as they streamed out of the sanctuary. In the beginning, they'd done this almost every Sunday. But as the membership grew, along with their responsibilities, the ritual had been reduced to once a month, to once every two months, to now, about every quarter. The day was cooperating, clear blue skies, breeze gentle and light. Conversations and laughter could be heard among the colorfully dressed church-goers, waiting patiently in line to say hello and shake the pastor and first lady's hand. The mood was jubilant, thanks no doubt to Pastor's fiery morning message that asked the question: Who's the most powerful nation? The answer had been inspiring: God's nation! His foundational scripture had been Genesis 12:2, when God spoke to Abraham and said: "And I will make of thee a great nation, and I will bless thee and make thy name great, and thou shall be a blessing." All of God's children basked in the glory of the day, feeling blessed and joyful.

Robin stood patiently. She'd waited for this moment a long time, and while calm on the outside, she was a bundle of nerves inside. She'd plotted thoroughly, planned carefully. This was a golden opportunity that didn't happen often. And as soon as she'd heard the announcement that the pastor and first lady would be greeting members outside the church, she prepared to make the best of it. Her mind had instantly gone into action, and as she stood in line waiting for her turn to greet the pastor, she was ready.

Her dress could not have been more appropriate, excellent for blending in. The suit was simple, a classic navy blue, double-breasted jacket with straight skirt that hit midcalf. Her heels were low, and as if fate were on her side, she'd found a medium-brimmed straw hat the same color as the suit, with light meshing over the eyes. Perfect.

I wonder if he'll remember me. Robin had gained almost forty pounds since she'd last seen Derrick and her then-black hair was now a reddish blond.

Memories of a distant past swirled through her head, of another church, in another town. Dreams and laughter shared in a small Baptist edifice that would fit well inside KCCC's parking lot. It had been far too long since she'd hugged Derrick, touched him. She wanted to throw her arms around him and declare her love. She wanted to push Vivian out of the way and take her rightful place by his side.

Yes, she and Derrick belonged together. The more she'd thought about it the past week, the more she knew it was true. Maybe this could be more than a fling. *Relax, stay calm, don't mess this up!* These words played in her head. There were now only five people in front of her. Her heartbeat quickened with each step. Was it warmer all of a sudden? Or was it the heat between her and Derrick? She resisted a strong urge to fan herself. Four people. She diverted her attention by looking at but not really reading the program. *Will he recognize me? Will he see the love in my eyes?* Three people.

Robin scoped Vivian from the corner of her eye. She'd hardly changed a bit—still gorgeous—but Robin wouldn't dare admit that. *Her dress is rather frumpy.* Actually, it was a perfectly fitting floral-printed Dior, with a wide leather belt and matching shoes. Vivian was letting her hair grow out, and it swung softly below her shoulders, sleeked back away from her face. Her makeup was simple as was her single piece of jewelry: the stunning pink diamond ring Derrick had given her on their tenth wedding anniversary. For all of her frumpiness, Robin didn't miss that touch of class. *She doesn't deserve it! But no, don't think of that. . . .* Two people.

Please don't let them hear my heart. It was racing. She stuffed the program in her purse, pulled out what she'd prepared for Derrick. God, she hoped the sun hadn't oiled up her skin. It was too late to pull out a compact. *It's okay, you just checked your makeup before you came outside, remember?* Yes, she remembered.

One person . . .

She took a deep breath. It was like a dream. Derrick Montgomery, close enough to reach out and touch.

"Bless you, sister." Derrick smiled and reached out his hand.

"Oh, Pastor Montgomery," Robin said, staring deep into his eyes. "I so enjoyed that sermon today. Thank you." She grabbed his hand and shook it, placing her other hand on top and pressing something into his palm.

Derrick noticed something vaguely familiar about the woman. But he saw so many people every Sunday, familiarity was not unusual. The woman clung to his hand. "Well, bless the Lord, sister, that's where the Word comes from. What is your name?"

Robin thought quickly. "Brown," she said, reverting to her mother's maiden name. *Robin* may have been a red flag, and with her incessant phone calling, *Reynolds* was definitely one. "Ms. Brown." That was general enough.

Vivian, who'd been speaking to the person in front of her, turned on that note. "Welcome, Ms. Brown," she said genuinely. "We're so glad you joined us today."

Robin's smile could have come from the Wax Museum. "It's"—Robin resisted the urge to jerk her hand back—"it's good to be here." *Good to be standing next to my man!*

Vivian was unaware of the storm swirling around her. "And may I say you look wonderful in that outfit. I love the hat."

Robin simply nodded. She couldn't see past the haze of green that temporarily blocked Vivian from view. She thought she mumbled something or nodded her head or grunted; seconds later she couldn't remember. It had all happened so fast. Just a touch, a touch of his hand is all she got! And then it was over. It was time for him to greet the next person in the still-long line.

You've got him now but not for long, she thought, smiling about the note she'd folded inside a twenty-dollar bill. *My waiting days are over. Derrick will be mine.*

Derrick looked briefly as the woman in blue elegantly descended the stairs. He smiled at her "Pentecostal hand-shake," a long-held tradition of pressing a blessing into the preacher's hand. He pocketed the money, looked at Vivian, and smiled again. Then he turned back to the next member and continued the ritual that went on for more than an hour.

Finally, he and Vivian left the crowd and stepped inside his cool suite of offices. Vivian immediately took off her heels. "My goodness, I thought the line would never end."

"It didn't end," Associate Minister Allen Anderson responded with a chuckle. "We did."

"More like my feet did," Vivian said, rubbing her toes as she perched on the loveseat.

"Don't complain, baby," Derrick enjoined, taking off his suit jacket and joining Vivian on the loveseat. "I remember the day we would have finished that line in fifteen minutes."

"More like ten," Vivian replied with a smile.

"More like five," Derrick countered, taking Vivian's foot in his lap and rubbing it. "What's for dinner, babe? I'm starved."

"I have no idea. I turned the reins and our household over to Mother Moseley. She and some other sisters left after the early morning service and headed to the house. Something fattening, I'm sure, but we'll both be surprised. Speaking of which," Vivian said, rising from the couch and putting on her shoes, "I probably should head over there, make sure they don't need any help. You coming?"

"Go ahead," Derrick replied. "I need to speak with my ministers about the service tonight."

He gave Viv a peck on the lips and she was out the door before he sat down at his desk. "Allen, would you gather the men?" The faster Derrick began the meeting, the faster he could go home and attend to more urgent matters. Like his appetite.

Derrick sat back waiting for the men to arrive. Remembering the "handshake," he reached in his pocket. Andrew Jackson's profile told him he'd been handed a twenty-dollar bill. He was about to place the money back in his pocket when he felt it again, felt that it was thicker than a single bill. He unfolded the bill and saw the note inside. *Oh, so that's what this is.* He debated on whether or not to even read the note. There were so many different ways women tried to come at him. And she had stared at him rather intently. Still, she hadn't acted flirtatious, but genuinely touched by the day's message. Maybe it was a prayer request. Or maybe it was a question about the Word, or the ministry. Curiosity won out. He unfolded the paper and leaned back in his chair.

Dear Derrick,

It is so good to see you again. I didn't want to bother you today, but would love to meet you, catch up on all the years since Pilgrims' Rest. I won't be in town long. Please call me.

Robin

Robin? Pilgrims' Rest? It took Derrick a minute to remember the young woman who'd helped him immensely when he first took over the little church in Lithonia. She'd encouraged him during bouts of self-doubt regarding his ability to lead a congregation who for the most part were at least a decade older than him. He'd shared his fears with her, and she'd shared her confidence in his abilities to do the job. Derrick remembered she'd been willing to share more than encouragement. They'd flirted, but nothing serious, not even a kiss.

Why didn't she say who she was this afternoon? Shrugging, Derrick dismissed the question. It didn't matter. He decided it would be good to talk to Robin, to find out what she'd been up to all these years. After all, she was probably married with a few children, in town on vacation. He hadn't paid much attention, but she hadn't seemed to be with anyone in line. He shrugged again, and wrote a note for Angela to set up a meeting. The note said she'd only be in town a few days. Lunch for an old friend was the least he could do.

Vivian entered her house to the combined smells of frying chicken, frying steak, baking rolls, and some sweet dessert scent blending in underneath it all. A song from *The Best of the Winans* CD blasted from the stereo in the living room, and voices bobbed and weaved for attention in the verbal sparring match going on in the kitchen.

"I tell you that BeBe Winans wrote that song 'Stand.' I heard him sing it on *Oprah*." The KCCC church matron put her hands on her hips for added clout.

"I don't care if he sung it on the moon," Mother Moseley countered. "Donnie McClurkin wrote that song."

"Well, BeBe sings it better. Can't nobody sing like a Winans."

"Except a McClurkin," Mother Moseley rose up to defend

her favorite male singer. "That Donnie can croon the Lord's praises to me anytime. And anywhere," she added with a sparkle in her eye. "Hey, First Lady, you're finally here!"

"And just in time, I see," Vivian said, hugging Mother Moseley and the others in the kitchen. "Is there anything you didn't fry in here?"

"Oh, we thought of you," Cynthia answered. She and Vivian had become good friends during her year as a Ladies First member. "I think there are some sliced tomatoes in the fridge."

"Oh, nice," Vivian answered, playfully batting at Cynthia and picking up the woman's one-year-old son. "Your mother thinks she's a comedian," she cooed at a wide-eyed Judah. "Your mother thinks she's got jokes." She put the boy down and turned and looked around her. "You guys are cooking up a feast! And it smells delicious."

Mother Moseley provided the report. "We got fried chicken," she began, counting down on her fingers, "on account of it's Sunday and we Black folk."

"And at a preacher's house," Mary interrupted.

"That's right," Mother Moseley agreed. "If it's Sunday and you're Black, at a preacher's house, ya gotta serve fried chicken." Everyone laughed. They all knew it wasn't true, but they also knew no one in their right mind turned down a perfectly seasoned crisp wing, thigh, or drumstick, no matter what day it was.

"So, we've got the chicken," Mother continued, "greens, green beans, mashed potatoes, swimmin' in real butter," she added, throwing a sideways glance at Vivian. Vivian just licked her lips.

"And," Mother went on, "we got mac and cheese, some candied yams, and a big pound cake with chocolate icing—from scratch. Ain't no boxes in here; real cooks are up in this house."

Vivian shook her head as she hugged Mother Moseley again. In many ways, she felt as close to her as she did her own mother. She felt blessed to have her around. "You've outdone yourself," she said genuinely. "And even though I gained five pounds just from you quoting the menu, I'm gonna roll up these designer sleeves and throw down y'all."

High fives went around on that note. Everybody had to let their health-conscious hair down once in a while.

"I probably shouldn't go over to Miss Smith's house again," King mused out loud. "The thoughts running through my mind after I saw Tootie the last time, well, they won't preach on Sunday morning." As hard as he'd tried, the name Janeé wouldn't stick. Tootie had always been, well, Tootie.

Tootie had initiated the thoughts with a single glance, a pointed stare at his crotch. King's manhood had raised its interested head immediately. The low-cut top and tight pants she'd been wearing hadn't helped matters. Not where staying away from her was concerned, at any rate. He told Derrick this as well.

"You're doing the right thing," Derrick encouraged his friend. "You did your part. It looks like Miss Smith is finally out of the woods. Let your deacon handle things from here on out."

"Maybe dinner wouldn't hurt," King continued. He wanted to see more of Tootie, and as a married man, much more than he should.

"No, King, not dinner, not even lunch." Derrick spoke firmly, even as he had his own news to share. They hadn't talked about it but they didn't have to. King and Tootie should not hang out. "And speaking of lunch," he said in ironic similarity, "guess who I'm inviting over next week?"

"Who?"

"Robin, an old friend and former member from my early days at Pilgrims' Rest." Derrick chuckled. "This must be the season for old friend reunions."

King's ears perked up. An old friend? King could count on one hand the names of females with whom Derrick had been seriously involved. The name Robin was not among them. "Who's Robin?"

"I guess you could say she was my assistant, unofficially, when I first started in the ministry, back in Georgia. Helped me a lot before Vivian quit working to join me full-time."

King remembered all the different ways Tootie had helped him, ministry aside. "What kind of help?"

"Not the kind you're thinking, brother," Derrick said. "She must be here on vacation, decided to look me up. That's only natural. I must admit, I'm curious to talk to her as well, find out what she and other members she may still be in contact with have been up to."

It sounded innocent enough. But with women, one never could tell. "Is Vivian going to be there? I mean, you never know what could be on this woman's mind, calling you out of the blue."

Derrick hadn't thought about that, but it wasn't a bad idea. "I'll make sure and invite her." His cell phone rang. "Speaking of, she's calling me now. Take care, man."

Derrick flipped open his phone. "Yeah, baby, the meeting's over. I just got held up with a phone call, that's all. I'm on my way."

"Well, I hope you bring an appetite. Mother Moseley and these sistahs cooked up enough to feed an army. And they're all your favorites."

"No, you're my favorite," Derrick answered, grabbing his keys and walking out into the warm, summer sunshine.

"Well, all the dishes besides me," Vivian cooed. "I'll see you shortly?"

"I'm already there." Derrick unlocked the door and started his Jag. It purred its greeting. As he left the church parking lot, drove down the crowded boulevard, and turned onto the highway, he thought of Robin. Mother Moseley had told him years ago that Robin had a huge crush on him. At the time, he'd laughed it off. But now, he wondered. What had brought Robin to Los Angeles, and more importantly, after all these years, to Kingdom Citizens' Christian Center?

23

Mama's Got a Feelin' . . .

"Why are you telling me this, Mama?" King paced his mother's living room floor, peered at the ceiling, paced again.

"Because keeping these suspicions to myself ain't setting well with me. I've been feeling funny ever since that girl wouldn't show me a picture."

"But you know how loose Tootie was. Maybe she just doesn't want anyone here to know who the daddy is."

Mama Max stared silently, her lips pursed. *Nucka, please,* is the phrase her countenance expressed.

"Why do you think he's *my* son?"

Mama Max went over to King and spoke calmly. She knew he had every right to be upset. "Believe me, son, I'm hoping, praying, it ain't yours. But you know your mama can sense thangs, and something ain't adding up when it comes to Tootie's tight mouth and that near-grown son."

King sat down heavily. Just when he'd decided to distance himself from seeing the woman, this news comes. As nerve-racking as it was, however, and with its potential implications, he was glad his mother had shared her concerns. Because if there was any chance he had another child, that Tootie's oldest boy was his . . .

What did he mean, if there was a chance? There was more

than a chance. If Mama was right, Tootie was pregnant when she left Kansas, only a few weeks after he ended the affair. He'd never questioned why she left so quickly, had assumed she needed her space, a chance to start over. He'd never given the illusion that he'd leave Tai, had always told Tootie that while hers was a special place in his heart, she could never replace his wife. He and Tootie had messed around for years, off and on since they were teenagers in high school. To this day, he'd never had better sex. That's basically what the relationship had been about, s-e-x.

He tried to retrieve the past in his mind, tried to recreate those years around Tootie's leaving. "Remember when she came back, what, fifteen years or so ago? That last time? Do you remember her looking different? Like she'd had a baby?"

Mama Max clearly remembered when Tootie had come back, had spent time with her through the relationship with her mother, Miss Smith. "I absolutely remember it, and that girl was as skinny as she always was. I remember commenting on it, teasing her about what kind of food they ate in Germany."

"Right, and she'd already had the baby then."

"That's right. And Miss Smith never said a word. I've known that woman for going on forty years, and she never said a word about that child." Mama Max started thinking back . . . visits to the Smith home, dinners, shopping sprees. "Come to think of it, there's not a picture of that boy in the house, not that I've seen anyway. Then again, I could have been looking at that child for years and not known."

Both she and King thought the same thing, at the same time. That it was time for Mama Max to visit Miss Smith.

"Yes, I need to check on her." Mama Max smiled. "She's up and walking around real good now, might want some help around the house, somebody to dust, around pictures and whatnot. . . ."

King laughed, thankful his mother could find humor almost anywhere. "Thanks, Mama."

"So not to talk nothing up but, what in the world are you going to tell Tai?"

"Nothing! Please, Mama, say you haven't men—"

"Well, give me some credit. If I ain't got nothing else, I've got common sense. Of course I haven't said anything, wanted to talk with you first. I tell you what, though, the next time I see Nancy, I'm gonna ask a thang or two about Tootie's boy. I need answers. I'll start with Nancy, and if she won't talk about it . . ."

"Mama, no."

"Look, if I have a grandchild out there somewhere, it is my right to know about it. I will ask Tootie to look me in the eye and say that ain't my grandbaby."

"Can you believe it? She's been here all this time and I just ran into them? The whole family, in the mall, husband, kids, everybody." Tai checked her feelings as she said this; she still felt fine.

"You know life, it had to happen. So, was it as bad, or awkward, as you thought it would be?" Vivian knew with God anything was possible, but she was talking to Tai about Tootie, after all.

"You know what? God can really do a work in people. Because believe it or not, it was almost cordial. She noticed me first. I was walking with the twins, and felt these eyes on me. I looked over just as we passed the food court, and Janeé, her husband, Hans, and their two children were sitting at a table. It was as if God planned it to happen just that way, so I'd have to stop. There was no way I could have acted like I didn't see them, and I didn't see them until I was right by the table!

"Looking back, it was almost surreal, as if I watched myself interact with her. She said hello; I stopped and answered. Now, it wasn't hugs and kisses, but I didn't pimp-slap her either.

"Then she introduced me to her family. They've got two girls, cute as can be. Her husband is very distinguished-looking as well. I introduced her to the twins, asked about her mom; it was a very sensible, almost amiable conversation."

Both women reflected on the power of God's grace. Then Vivian remembered a conversation she'd had with Derrick, right after Hope's wedding. He'd shared some of the conversation King and he had on the golf course. She'd forgotten all about it until now.

"Wait, you said two girls. Doesn't she have three children?"

"I don't know; I only saw two. How would you know anyway?"

"I don't, just remembered Derrick mentioning that she had kids. He'd brought it up because of how unlikely it was, considering the woman he used to know."

"Two, three, it don't matter. I'm just glad I had a chance to talk with her," Tai said, "to see her with her family, and her *own* husband. Now I can honestly say I wish her well."

Vivian smiled as she listened to Tai comfortably discuss her former nemesis, the woman who at one time had been such a source of pain. She was reminded of a scripture that read: "He that began a good work . . . would finish it, complete it, perform it." As these friends laughingly went from talk of Tootie to church and other things, Vivian thanked God for His work.

"Mama Max thinks he's your son?"

King sat in his church office, where he'd gone after the conversation with his mother. "She doesn't want to think so," he said to Derrick, the first person he thought to call after hearing the news about Tootie's son. "But she says Tootie acts funny whenever she asks about her oldest child. Says she finally showed her an old picture where you could barely see the boy, and that Miss Smith is being tight-lipped, which is not like her at all, the way that woman gossips."

"Have you talked to Tootie?" As hard as they'd tried, no one had been able to stick with *Janeé* for long.

"No. I need to though, and quick. Looks like Miss Smith's health has finally stabilized. Mama said they're going back to Germany at the end of the month."

"Well, maybe that will be the end of it. Mama Max's imagination may be working overtime. I think that with the history between you two, Tootie would have said something."

That sounded rational. Why hadn't he thought of that? Of course Tootie would have told him. Mama Max had him trippin'. "You know what? You're right about that. I'm going to tell Mama to squash this nonsense the next time I see her. Why am I worrying about what probably exists only in Maxine Brook's imagination?"

"There you go, dog, keep your focus. We'll probably be laughing about this in a few days."

They said their good-byes, but as King hung up he couldn't find a damn thing funny.

24

Air for Breathing

"What's up with your brother, Tanya?" Stacy asked.

"What do you mean, what's up?" Tanya considered Stacy one of her best friends, but this obsession with Darius was getting on her nerves. Stacy had called almost every day this week.

"I mean, where's he at?" Stacy was leaving choir rehearsal, disappointed again. For the second straight week, the assistant director had been there instead of Darius. "We were supposed to hook up, and he keeps cancelling."

"They're probably still out of town. Did you call his cell?"

"All I get is voice mail. And who's 'they'?"

"Him and Bo. I think they went to New York for some kind of publicity or something, and probably stayed over for the Fourth of July holiday. You know Darius has friends all over the country." Too late, Tanya realized she probably shouldn't have added the last sentence.

Stacy immediately copped an attitude. Well aware of Darius's sex appeal and popularity with the females, she was ready to go toe to toe with any bee-atch who tried to come between her and her heaven. It had taken her two years just to get a date. Whoever this sistah was had met her even change.

"Hold up, wait a minute." Stacy threw her bag in the backseat of the car, started the engine, attached her Bluetooth headset, and headed out of the Kingdom Citizens parking lot. "Now, who's he with?"

"Calm down, Rock-aletta Balboa," Tanya said, laughing. "Bo is a friend of his, a *male* friend. He helps Darius out with marketing, PR, and stuff."

"Oh, okay." Stacy calmed down a little, but immediately wondered how quick she could get her marketing and PR skills up to speed. She wanted to be the one jetting around with Darius. "I don't think I've heard that name. Does he go to our church?"

"Uh-uh. But look, chickie, don't be trying to use me as your encyclopedia for all things Darius. I'm not about to get in the middle of y'all's budding romance. I am not my brother's keeper; if you have questions, ask him."

"I would if he would answer his phone."

Tanya rolled her eyes. She'd never told Stacy how many women questioned her about her brother, how many tried to befriend her in order to get a hookup. Besides being her friend, Stacy had been one of the saner ones, showing a casual interest in Darius without being overbearing. Until now. Since Darius had agreed to go out with her, he was all Stacy could talk about. It was getting old, and if their friendship was going to survive the courtship, she needed to speak her mind.

"Look, Stacy," Tanya said, her voice agitated, "you're my friend. So I'm going to give you some advice you didn't ask for. Chill the bump out. I know you like Darius and he knows you like him. But running after him and calling him over and over is just going to make you look like all the other girls trying to get in where they fit in. Obviously he's interested in you, or he wouldn't have agreed to go out. So stop acting all desperate, like he's your air for breathing.

"He's got an album to get done. He's dealing with the

record company, his band, their upcoming tour, and handling the music at Kingdom Citizens. The last thing he needs is another person bugging him."

Stacy remained silent. Tanya softened a bit.

"Play your cards right, is all I'm sayin'. You know you're my girl. I'd love to have you as family. But if you're acting like this now, and y'all haven't even gone out yet, how are you going to act when his record blows up and he's gone on tour?"

Stacy didn't know how she'd act. But Tanya was right. She needed to chill out. She'd waited this long to be with Darius and now she was getting ready to blow everything by being insecure.

"You know what, you're right," Stacy said, as she pulled into her driveway. "I do need to chill out. What God has for me, is for me. I need to trust that."

"Now you're talking like a friend with some sense."

They laughed. Stacy hung up the phone feeling better, with even more resolve. She and Darius were made for each other. There was no mountain high enough, no valley low enough. Nobody would come between her and Darius—nobody.

25

Enjoy Your Time at Kingdom Citizens

She'd only had a few days to plan things out, but Robin was ready. She'd done what she could. It would be tricky, but if everything worked out, she might once again get a chance with Mr. Derrick Montgomery. Maybe her last one. Because if things didn't work out . . . She didn't even want to think about it. Instead, she started thinking of what it would be like to talk to Derrick.

Derrick had wanted to meet Robin soon after she'd given him the note, believing what she'd said about only being there a few days. She'd just said that to speed things up, and was glad she'd been able to push back their lunch date. At any rate, she wasn't in a hurry to rush back to Florida. She wondered if she could live in LA, whether she should move there. No matter where she ended up, she knew she needed a job. The severance pay she'd gotten was almost gone and she'd taken her last pill days ago.

No time to think about that now, though. Robin needed to make the most of the time at hand. God knew she was ready for the lunch Derrick had arranged. She was starving, had barely eaten since she'd received Angela's phone call. Hoping to drop a pound or two, she'd gone to the store, bought a case of Slim-Fast, and had forced herself to stick to their ridiculous plan of two drinks and a meal to drop pounds quickly. As she slipped on her pants, however, she was pleased to see less rear end in the mirror when she turned around.

The shopping trip had been an experience in itself. Robin went back and forth on what to wear. Should she continue the conservative facade? Try for something flashier? Go ho? In the end she'd purchased what she hoped achieved a little of each idea: a black summer pantsuit with long jacket and a low-cut, floral shell. And her best find? Vida, the sister who'd hooked her hair up in the mall salon the day before. After telling a sob story about having to survive in a two-bedroom with three kids, Vida had cut her price in half. Robin had been professionally fried, dyed, and satisfied with a style she thought really complemented her face. Vida had added shoulder-length loosely curled extensions. It was not a style she or her hairdresser in Florida would have thought of. She was glad she'd followed her first instinct and gone inside Lady Locks.

Robin appraised herself in the mirror. She cocked her head this way and that. *You can do this, Robin.* She felt tense, needed to loosen up. She looked in the mirror again and gave herself a big smile. *You go, girl!* She reached into her suitcase, pulled out Flori Robert's Ashanti, her aromatic weapon, and after a liberal spray placed the bottle in her purse. There was only one thing left to do—make the phone calls. Her appointment was made easily. Now she could only hope everything would fall in her favor. With one last look in the mirror, she walked out the door.

"How's your day looking, baby?" It had been a crazy week. Vivian and Derrick passed like ships in the night, or day anyway. The nights had found them together, both too exhausted to do anything but sleep.

"I have a lunch today at one o'clock, an old friend from believe it or not, Pilgrims' Rest."

"Oh, that should be fun. Who is it?"

"Robin. Remember the assistant who used to work with me, left shortly after you started working with me full-time?"

Vivian did remember, all too well. "Oh, yes, I remember Robin." Before she could go there, Vivian pulled back. It had been years. She was now secure. "Well, baby, I hope you guys have a nice catch up. Speaking of, I have a one-thirty myself, that Mrs. Reynolds you told me about some time ago."

"What? She actually called you? Well, I can't wait to find out just what the personal business is she needed to discuss so desperately. That woman bugged Angela for a solid week or more."

"Looks like we're getting ready to find out. And it sounds serious. Tamika said the woman was almost hysterical when she thought I wouldn't be able to meet with her today."

"She'll be better after talking to you." Derrick's intercom blinked. "Okay, baby, gotta run. And remember I have the dinner meeting tonight about the business center. Don't wait up."

"Okay. Love you, baby." Vivian looked at her watch. She had some time before her appointment and decided to get a manicure before heading to the church.

Robin pulled up to the large, intimidating structure that was KCCC. She'd taken her friend to work that day and had the use of her filthy, beat-up Toyota. But she couldn't look a gift horse in the mouth. It didn't have air-conditioning, but it had gotten her there. Following Angela's instructions, she drove around from the main sanctuary to a parking lot in front of what looked like several small office buildings. She went through the door Angela had described, then through a foyer where, thankfully, she saw a human being.

"Hello, Kingdom Citizen," the receptionist greeted Robin cheerfully.

"Hello, uh, could you tell Angela that, um, Robin is here?"

Robin had handled a variety of tough encounters in her life-time. It took a lot to make her nervous, but here she was, stut-tering like a teenager.

"Sure, one moment please." The receptionist pushed a but-ton, spoke to Angela, and in what seemed less than a minute, Angela was coming through a side door.

"You must be Robin," she said cordially, extending her hand. "I'm Angela. Everything is set in our dining room. Just come with me."

Angela's down-home nature brought Robin the calm that had evaded her during the hour-long drive to the church. *No wonder road-rage is common on these highways,* she thought. Not only were there a zillion people traveling, but they all acted like they were the only ones on the road. It was during the drive that she'd made her decision. An affair with Derrick is all she could hope for, because she could never live with the crazy drivers in Los Angeles.

"Pastor says you're a former church member, from Geor-gia, right?" Angela waved to various workers as they crossed the parking lot and entered another building.

Trying to digest being described as a former church mem-ber, Robin didn't answer Angela immediately. *That's all? A former church member?* Pilgrims' Rest would not have moved forward had it not been for her administrative and organizational skills.

"Yes," she said, after a pause that elicited a curious look from Angela. "I was there when, uh, Pastor Montgomery's ministry began." She hoped she sounded conversational enough; inside she was steaming. "He's come a long way."

The building they entered was well appointed: soft, fabric-covered walls coupled with mahogany, deep-plied, light blue carpeting, brass handles. They passed a conference room, a li-brary, a few closed doors, and then went down a short hall that led to a great room filled with chairs, couches, coffee tables, and a plasma-screen television mounted on the wall. Delicious aromas assailed Robin's nose just before they turned another corner into the dining room.

The room Robin entered matched the taste and elegance of the rest of the building. She wondered if Vivian had worked with decorators and guessed she probably had. Robin had to admit that if the goal was to create an atmosphere of understated, comfortable elegance, they'd more than achieved it. Her surroundings were splendid.

"Oh, forgive me. I wasn't thinking. Pastor should be here in five or ten minutes, so if you'd like to freshen up, there's a ladies room just down the hall. Would you like that?"

If for no other reason than to still her nerves, she agreed. "I'd like that very much."

"Right this way please." They walked the short distance to the restroom. Again, it was first class, and opened into a powder room. Angela turned to Robin. "Can I get you anything else?"

"You've been very kind. Thank you, Angela."

"One of the staff will be ready to serve you as soon as you're back in the dining room. You saw it as we passed, right? Just two doors back?"

Robin nodded.

"I'm sure they've prepared a sumptuous meal for your luncheon. Enjoy your time at Kingdom Citizens."

Angela left, leaving Robin alone amid tastefully understated floral wallpaper, the fragrance of fresh flowers, and the beauty of a well-lit vanity accessorized in gold. Robin pulled out her compact and repowdered her sweaty face. She dabbed a touch of gloss over her lipstick, sprayed a touch of Ashanti between her breasts, and popped in a mint. She looked at her watch: 1:05. *This is it.* Grabbing the door handle, she walked out of the ladies room and almost ran over Derrick.

"Whoa, excuse me," Derrick said, grabbing Robin's arm.

"Oops, I'm sorry," Robin said at the same time, almost spitting her mint into Derrick's mustache.

"Are you okay?" they said in unison.

That broke the ice. Derrick looked at her, stepped back, looked again. "Robin?"

Robin was suddenly shy, but covered it with volume. She hoped she looked okay, hoped the mirror hadn't lied. "Derrick Montgomery! It's been a long time!" She grabbed Derrick and hugged him tight.

Derrick hugged her back. "Robin! It's good to see you." He began walking toward the dining room. "When I got your note, I couldn't believe it. I told Vivian I was having lunch with you. She would have joined us, but an emergency appointment came up. She sends her best."

They reached the dining room. Derrick pulled out Robin's chair and waited for her to be seated. He walked around to the other side of the table and sat down. Almost immediately, an older lady came out of a side door with a pitcher of lemony ice water.

"Good afternoon, Pastor," she said, pouring his water. "Good afternoon," she said to Robin as she filled her glass.

"Good afternoon, thank you," Robin replied. It was as though Derrick had his own personal maid service. She could get used to this.

Derrick looked at Robin with a big smile. It had been some time since he'd talked with anyone from Pilgrims' Rest besides Mother Moseley. He'd run into other members from time to time, in his travels, but none lately. Looking at Robin made him realize how good it was to reconnect with people who'd been a part of his life's journey.

"You look well, Robin," he said. "What a pleasant surprise to get your note. I didn't even recognize you that day, all clandestine in that hat and everything."

Robin took a sip of her water. "I started to say something, but the line was long and I really didn't want to bother you. That's why I wrote the note. Thought that if you had time, you'd call, but if you were too busy, or had other reasons . . ."

"Of course I'd call. It's been what, ten years or so?" The server came in with a bowl of rolls and two tossed salads. Derrick grabbed a roll immediately. "I see you've been at it again, Margaret. You and these homemade rolls are going to send a brother straight to the gym. Robin, this is Margaret. She's going to be one of our premiere bakers at Kingdom Citizens' new restaurant, Taste & See. Margaret, this is one of my former members from back in the day, from my very first ministry, Pilgrims' Rest Baptist Church." He said the last line with a southern preacher's flare, and proudly.

"Well, nice to meet you," Margaret said warmly. "Now, what y'all want to drink?" she asked.

Derrick looked at Robin, nodding at her to go first, and she said, "Oh, a cola is fine for me."

Margaret turned to Derrick. "I guess you'll have your usual? And as for those rolls, they aren't jumping in your mouth by themselves. I don't see a gun anywhere near your head, neither." She let the implication of those statements linger behind as she sashayed into the kitchen.

"You've got to try these rolls while they're warm. And here, she makes this honey butter to go on it. C'mon now, dig in!"

Robin's stomach chose that moment to growl. "Well, I guess I'd better!" she said, reaching for a roll and the butter knife.

"Oh, wait, we have to thank the Father first." Derrick said a quick prayer, closing with, "Amen!"

"Amen," Robin echoed mindlessly. She was looking at Derrick and thinking of something she'd like to eat beside Margaret's bread.

There was a moment of silence as both enjoyed the light and fluffy rolls and salad. Margaret came in with Robin's cola and Derrick's raspberry iced tea.

"So, Robin," Derrick began again, "how is it that you're in California, looking me up after all these years?"

The story Robin had concocted rolled off her tongue easily. "My job," she said, swallowing a mouthful of salad. "I'm overseeing a project here."

"What company do you work for?"

"IAC Products. It's a manufacturing plant in Tampa. We make the large bolts and other connecting devices that go into everything from bridges to airplanes." She felt there was enough truth in this to be safe. She'd worked for IAC long enough to talk about the company with a fair amount of intelligence.

"Hmm, that's an interesting career choice for you. How'd you get into that?"

"By accident. I moved to Tampa, and after a failed relationship, found myself in need of immediate work. They had an opening, I needed a job, and almost eight years later, here I am."

"You must enjoy it."

"It pays the bills."

"You mentioned a relationship. Are you married, children?"

Margaret interrupted them with aromatic plates of spicy sausage lasagna. Robin was thankful; she knew this subject would be trickier to navigate, especially with a pleasant face. Another server came in with more iced tea and a fresh cola. Robin looked at her watch: 1:20. She glanced at the door and at the table setup. Both she and Derrick's water glasses were still almost full.

"So, you're married, right? Kids?" Derrick repeated around a mouthful of lasagna. "Man, this is good!" he added.

"Actually, no," Robin said. "I'm divorced."

"Oh."

Robin took a bite of her lasagna and was silent. She glanced at her watch: 1:25.

★ ★ ★

"Hey, Sister Vivian," her assistant, Tamika, said as Vivian entered the office. "Ooh, you are rushing. Where's the fire?"

"I didn't think I'd make it in time for my appointment. I can never figure out why they decide to do road construction in the middle of the day. Traffic is congested enough as it is. But I'm here, praise God." Vivian placed her large Louis Vuitton bag and briefcase down and quickly scanned the phone messages. "Anything important in here?"

"Well, nothing except . . . hold on a moment." Tamika picked up the telephone. "Kingdom Citizens, Sister Vivian's office, this is Tamika."

Vivian picked up her purse and headed to her office behind Tamika's reception area.

Tamika stopped her. "That was for you, Lady Vee. Your husband wants you to come to the dining room."

"He does? He knows I have an appointment. What else did he say?"

"It wasn't Pastor Derrick, must have been one of his assistants."

"Angela?"

"No, I know Angela's voice. I'm sorry, I didn't ask."

"It's okay." Vivian looked at her watch. It was 1:30. "Has Mrs. Reynolds called?"

"No, not today. I'm surprised she's not here yet."

Vivian placed her belongings in her office and returned to Tamika's desk. "It's okay. Derrick's having lunch with an old church member, probably wants me to say hi. Look, I'll only be a minute. When Mrs. Reynolds comes, get her something to drink, make her comfortable. I should be back in no more than five, ten minutes."

"I still want children," Robin said, taking another bite of the lasagna. It was probably the best tasting food she'd ever had. She and Derrick had been chatting pleasantly all through lunch. She could already imagine this as a daily affair.

"Well, what are you, thirty-eight or nine; it's not too late," Derrick said. "Vivian was thirty when she had Derrick Jr., and we had Elisia two years later."

Robin looked as if she was listening, but her mind was on the ice water sitting on the table. She gauged its distance from there to Derrick's lap. He probably wouldn't be too happy about getting that debonair-looking suit wet but . . .

"Oh, that's right, you have two beautiful chi—" Robin began. She made a dramatic gesture of pointing to Derrick and knocked her glass of water over. It fell into Derrick's tea glass. The liquid from both glasses poured into Derrick's lap.

"Oh!" Derrick exclaimed, jumping up.

"Derrick!" Robin exclaimed at the same time, jumping up with her napkin and running around to his side of the table.

She took her napkin and began frantically wiping at the large stain on his shirt and pants. She rolled the napkin over his manhood. "Derrick," she said more softly.

Derrick backed up. "It's okay, Robin," he said, a slight frown on his face. He took another step backward.

But that's as far as he got. Robin pushed him up against the wall and began kissing him, touching him, trying to unbuckle his belt.

Derrick was so surprised that for a moment, he didn't move. *What is this woman doing?* Just as the answer began to dawn on him, two doors opened. One was the side door and Margaret. "Is everything all right Pas—"

The second was Vivian at the door to the dining room. "Hey, honey—"

Both women were shocked into silence by the sight they saw: Derrick and Robin making out in the dining room.

But only for a moment. Vivian recovered first as she saw Derrick struggling to disentangle himself from Robin's vise-like grip on his body. She yelled out to Margaret, "Call security!"

Margaret was gone before she finished the second word.

"Robin!" Vivian said, trying to grab Robin's arm and pull her away from Derrick.

"Don't touch me!" Robin said, pushing Vivian away. Vivian stumbled back into the dining room table.

"Hey, don't do that." Derrick had freed himself from Robin but now came toward her again.

Robin became indignant. "My God, you were all over me!" she scathed. Then she turned to Vivian. "He was trying to reach over the table for me and knocked over his water. I was just trying to help him clean it up when he grabbed me, pushed me up against the wall, and began, began, having his way with me!"

"Oh, baby, you can't believe that," Derrick said as two burly security guards burst into the room. One headed directly over to Robin. "Let's go, ma'am."

Robin was a stout woman, but no match for six-foot-one, two-hundred-fifty pounds of "get out." The other guard grabbed her purse as she was led out of the room.

"I can't believe you still want me after all these years, Derrick," she said as the guard half walked, half dragged her away. "Are you still remembering how good it was in the office at Pilgrims' Rest? Are you still remembering my good puss—"

That's the last Vivian, Derrick, and Margaret heard coherently, though the muffled shouting continued as she was taken out of the building, across the parking lot, and placed in her car. The three stared at the closed dining room door for minutes.

Margaret slowly walked over to the dining room table, picked up the two empty water glasses and Derrick's soggy plate. "Lord have mercy," is all she said as, shaking her head, she walked back into the kitchen.

Vivian turned and looked at Derrick. "What on earth just happened here?"

26

My Man's Bone

"You're not going to believe what happened." Vivian had told Tai that Derrick was meeting Robin for lunch, and couldn't wait to call her. She dialed her number as soon as she got home, figured she was too upset to talk on a cell phone in LA traffic.

"What?"

"Robin attacked Derrick!"

"What?"

"You heard me, that woman attacked my husband! Attacked him!"

Tai who had been in the middle of cleaning out her closet, sat down amid piles of clothes. "What happened?"

"Okay. Derrick says everything was fine at first. They met, were talking, Margaret starting serving them."

"Uh-huh."

"They continued talking, catching up, general chit-chat, right? Then all of a sudden, Robin *accidentally* knocks over her glass of water into Derrick's lap!"

"Why did you say it like that?" Tai repeated the exaggeration the way Vivian had done.

"Keep listening, I'll tell you. So water spilled all over Derrick's clothes. He jumped out of his chair. Then Robin jumped up and went around the table with her napkin. Derrick thought nothing of it until . . ." Vivian could barely go on. She was seething.

"Until what, girl?"

"Until she grabbed his dick!"

"What!" Tai guffawed. "You are not serious."

"Totally serious. He said she was wiping his shirt, and then his pants, and then she went there. She grabbed my man's bone, girl. . . ."

"Girl, stop!"

"He tried to push her off him but she backed him against the wall and started kissing him, feeling him up, trying to take off his clothes!"

Tai couldn't help it, she was cracking up laughing. "Okay, stop. I can't take any more of this madness. What are y'all putting in the water at that church, women acting all crazy?" Both women knew Tai was thinking about Millicent as well as Robin.

"It gets better. Because that exact moment is when I walked in."

Tai stopped laughing, her voice dropped to a whisper. "You caught them?"

"When I walked in, she was all over Derrick."

Tai gasped. "What did you do?"

"I was so shocked, at first I just stood there. Margaret must have heard the commotion because she came out of the kitchen at the exact same time. We both just stood there, mortified."

Tai waited, silently, but Vivian could feel her *and then what!* through the phone.

"Derrick was able to get some space between them, and I went over and tried to grab her arm, help him get away. Then she pushed me against the table."

Tai couldn't help herself. She started laughing again, rolling around in her piles of clothes. "Stop, I can't take it."

"This isn't funny, girl. I'm ready to kick somebody's crazy behind!"

"You're lying to me; you are making this story up." Tai tried to regain her composure, sound serious, but the story was straight-up comedy.

"This is the truth, the whole truth, so help me."

"So what did you do when she pushed you?"

"Nothing, security handled it. I'd told Margaret to call them as soon as I got there. They took her away, with her yelling about how Derrick wanted her and how they'd screwed in Georgia. Girl . . . it was absolutely insane."

The last sentence stopped Tai's laughter. Derrick and Vivian were married when they moved to Georgia.

"Oh my God, no, Vivian. Did they have an affair? I mean, I'm confused. I don't even remember your talking about this woman. Where did she come from?"

Vivian gave Tai the background story, realized she may have never mentioned Robin before. That's how far in the past Vivian had placed her. She assured Tai there had been no affair, that she'd quit her job and started working alongside Derrick just in time.

"Well, my history doesn't allow me to be as sure of that as you are. For a woman to come back after all these years? I'm not trying to start nothing, Viv, but—"

"Derrick says there was nothing between them, says I can ask Mother Moseley. She was there the whole time."

Maybe nothing but a dick, is what Tai thought. "Hmm," is all she said.

"I'm not going there, Tai," Vivian said, although her formerly made-up mind was already flip-flopping. *Could there have been an affair? Is it possible I've been wrong about Derrick always being faithful?* No, she would not doubt him, she wouldn't doubt *them.* Fifteen plus years of fidelity is something they both treasured. She changed the course of her thinking by continuing the story.

"Anyway, after she left, and Derrick and I had regained our composure, we went back to his office to discuss what had happened. Figured out that Robin was the Mrs. Reynolds who called his office incessantly about a month ago. She planned this whole thing, Tai. Accepted the lunch with Derrick, scheduled the appointment with me, as Mrs. Reynolds, and excused herself to call my office once she thought I was there. I must admit, it was very clever. But there were a few things she didn't count on.

"First, she didn't count on the fact that almost everything that is said in the dining room can be heard in the kitchen. Margaret and the other workers heard the whole thing. Second, she didn't count on my husband's strong resistance to her blatant come-on, and third, she didn't count on the fact that I trust my husband implicitly. It will take more than soggy pants and a crazy woman's accusations to shake my faith in Derrick's fidelity."

Vivian said that last sentence to herself as much as to Tai. And then she was almost sorry she'd said it, considering all the infidelity Tai had lived through. "I mean, you know what I'm saying," she added.

"You don't have to feel uncomfortable, Vivian. Ours have been very different marriages. But they are both still standing. Two couples, two journeys, one God. That could be our tagline; you two, and me and King. It's a great testimony, actually. How two very different marriages can stand the tests of time and get better, stronger, no matter what." They both thought on Tai's statement a moment, before she added, "I'm just glad nobody was hurt."

"I am, too. And it's just a shame because Derrick prides himself on being able to be open and available to all members, male and female. You know how hard I work to establish a strong sense of connection with all the female members, especially the singles. But stuff like this is exactly why Derrick no longer counsels women unless I've talked to them and okayed it."

"So what do you guys think? Do you think this was it, it's over? Girl, you never know. She might be a stalker."

"Ooh, Tai, don't say that, don't even think it! Fortunately, the office cameras caught her on tape. All the security and office people know what she looks like. Plus, we filed a police report and obtained a restraining order. I guess time will tell."

"I'm telling you, if Robin remembers us having sex, she's dreaming. There's been no one but Viv since we said 'I do.' Believe that." While Vivian was talking with Tai at their home, Derrick was in his church office talking to King.

"I believe you, dog. It's just crazy how messed up people can get in their thinking. I mean, you show a woman some kindness, maybe flirt a little bit, and they think you're ready to get married and father their children." King could definitely sympathize with his friend.

"I guess, man . . . anyway . . . knew you'd appreciate a good story. Especially since you're usually the one bringing the drama."

"Hold up, Dee. I've been good lately."

"That you have. I'm real proud of you, brothah, real proud."

"'Preciate that man. Oh, it looks like they're getting ready to board my flight." King nodded at Joseph, who'd motioned to him from the door of the airport's VIP lounge. "I'll be in California next month, a church over in Pasadena. Let's hook up."

"Bet. Have Joseph call with the exact dates. Hey, glad things went well in Texas."

"All right man, peace."

Robin was livid, shaking with rage. She'd successfully stopped smoking almost a year ago, but immediately after being thrown out of Kingdom Citizens, had pulled into the closest gas station and purchased two packs of Kool Menthol 100s. Now,

amid a haze of cigarette smoke and smoldering self-righteousness, she tried, unsuccessfully, to calm down.

She replayed the scenes over and over, scenes that had
warped and distorted during her frenzied drive back to her
friend's apartment. Derrick had tried to act like he didn't want
her. But she'd seen the lust in his eyes. He'd stared at her
breasts, then took a bite of food and claimed, "This is good."
Humph. She wasn't born yesterday. It was her, not a plate of
spicy-ass lasagna he'd wanted to bite into. And it would have
happened, too, if that sanctimonious witch Vivian hadn't
pranced her nosy ass in there like she was the Queen of Sheba.
She called security; the bitch actually called security on my ass! The
thought of how they'd physically removed her from the
premises started her shaking all over again. She pulled another
cigarette from the pack and lit it from the butt she was smoking. *Hell, I should file charges. They could have just asked me to leave
nicely.* Manhandling her, who did they think they were? *Well,*
Robin thought menacingly, *they're going to find out who I am. It
may take a year, it may take a lifetime, but they have messed with the
wrong muthafucka. Payback's comin'.*

27

Pastor Jack

Millicent bounced out of the locker room. She'd had a great workout, spent a half hour in the sauna, then relaxed in the whirlpool. Now that her plans were in motion, she'd stepped it up in the gym, wanted to look her very best when she ran into Cy and his bride in Mexico. Her very best.

Millicent was going to see Cy again. The more she thought of the idea, the more she felt it was the right thing to do, to co-incidentally bump into them while on vacation. It had taken a bit of detective work, and a bit of luck, to find the resort where the Taylors were staying. A year ago she would have given the credit to God, but she had purposely not sought his advice on the matter. She'd spoken with a wealthy ex-boyfriend who used to do business in Mexico, had asked him about the high-end resorts. Armed with that list, she'd researched each one, looking at their amenities and trying to figure out which had the ones that would suit Cy's taste. And finally, she'd worn Leah down, mentioning a couple of the resorts and dropping Cy's and Hope's names, acting like her friend had already told her. Leah confirmed that yes, the Taylors would bring in the New Year at the Rosewood Mayakobá Resorts in Riviera Maya, Mexico. "You didn't hear it from me," she had added.

"No matter," Millicent had responded. "I know where I'll be for New Year's . . . at Open Arms."

"Me, too," Leah agreed.

Millicent had already thought about it. Open Arms would be the perfect cover. No one would suspect a thing. *But the next day, I'll be on a plane.*

Millicent stood at the juice bar, viewing the healthy choices on the menu. They all sounded good. But she was hungry and decided to skip the smoothie and go for an all-out brunch somewhere by the ocean.

"Which one should I get?" Jack stood a foot or so behind Millicent, viewing the menu easily with his six-foot-three frame.

Millicent recognized that voice. Now a regular at Open Arms' Sunday service, she'd probably recognize Pastor Jack's deep tremor in a choir of hundreds.

"Hey, Pastor Jack!" Millicent had run into her pastor only occasionally since changing her workout from afternoons to mornings. But on this particular Saturday, she'd gotten a late start. It was now almost noon.

Jack rolled his eyes in mock chagrin. "When do I get to be just Jack with you, geez!"

"Old habits die hard," Millicent responded. "It's hard for me to call a pastor by his first name."

"But everybody does, except my kids, that is."

"I know, it's just awkward for me."

Pastor Jack motioned toward the juice bar menu. "So, what are you getting?"

"Nothing. I've changed my mind and decided to replace the calories I just worked off with a real meal."

"That sounds delicious," Jack said, thinking that Millicent's slender frame could handle several real meals. "Can I join you?"

Millicent eyed him critically. "It looks like you just got here."

"All the more reason for me to leave with you." They started walking toward the exit. "Besides, Leah's been telling me about the plans for our girls, the Divine Daughters Celebration. It sounds great, and I'd love to hear more about it."

Millicent was excited about her plans for the teen girls at Open Arms Church and agreed to lunch.

"You can follow me if you'd like," Jack said, after suggesting a seaside inn for their decadent dining getaway. He walked to his Navigator a few spaces away. "Don't worry, I'll go slow enough for you to keep up with me."

He jumped in his car before Millicent could respond to the jab. Within minutes, they'd left the main avenue and were twisting up a smaller, tree-lined road that bordered the ocean. Millicent tried to take in the scenic route as she easily kept up with Jack. Here, months after her spectacle at Kingdom Citizens, she was almost remembering what it felt like to be carefree. Millicent hadn't felt this way in a long, long time.

Jack slowed and they pulled into a small, beachfront property that looked to be a sixties throwback. It was quaint, brightly painted white and coral with a sea-blue-colored roof. The parking lot, which held no more than ten cars, was full. Jack pulled his Navigator past the lot to a small, grassy area just beyond it, where a couple other cars had squeezed in. He met Millicent at the door. She'd tried to hide it, but he caught the skepticism with which she surveyed the old, yet well-kept restaurant that resembled a small house.

"Take my word for it," he said, holding the door open for her, "you'll enjoy it."

They entered a small dining room with typical beachfront decor: weathered wood tables, snorkel gear and surfboards placed precariously around the room. Bright red life buoys hung from the ceiling. Pictures of former diners hung on one wall, next to a large window with a view of the ocean. As they neared it, Millicent noticed Jack's was one of the photos hanging.

"Well, look who we have here," she said, as the waitress came over with water and menus.

"So, Jack, what will we have?" the waitress asked, with a rough, smoky voice. "Your usual?"

"Sounds like a winner," Jack answered. He explained his usual to Millicent: two eggs sunny side up, a large pork chop, hash browns with onions, and toast.

"Oh, my," Millicent exclaimed. "You took me literally at the gym, huh?"

"Absolutely," Jack said, grinning. "Are you game? Can you handle it?" His piercing blue eyes sparkled.

"Absolutely," Millicent said, echoing Jack's answer. "Except," she paused, "half the order of potatoes and hard-boil my eggs."

"Hey, there's no grease on a hard-boiled yolk," Jack teased.

"I think the pork chop and hash browns will cover my grease quota, thank you."

"I think you're right." He turned to the waitress. "That's it, Tenny. And bring us two tall glasses of that deliciously fresh-squeezed citrus tree you have growing out back."

"Coming up, Captain." Tenny winked at Millicent before walking off.

Millicent watched the waitress slap the order down in front of the short-order cook, then walk around to a large refrigerator for the orange juice. "Did you say 'Tenny'? That's an interesting name."

"No one knows her real name. Everyone calls her Tenny because she comes from Tennessee. The menu is straight out of the hills of Nashville."

As Millicent listened, she did hear the strains of country music playing in the background. "Funny, I didn't take you for a country boy."

"I'm California born and bred, but spent many summer

nights at my grandparents' farm in Indiana. They'd settled there after trekking from South Carolina, brought the South to the Midwest with them. Guess a bit of that crawled up in me and stayed."

"That's where you get your friendly personality, that polite, easygoing style you have with everyone."

"I guess."

Jack placed his chin in his hands and stared at Millicent, a polite grin on his face. She smiled, then became uncomfortable. "Okay, Mr. Kirtz, staring at people is not all that polite."

"Lord, I'm Mr. Kirtz. I must be in real trouble. Excuse me, ma'am," he said with a drawl. "I didn't mean to make you uncomfortable. I just like looking at you. I'm sure you know you're a beautiful woman."

"Thank you."

Tenny brought the orange juice. Millicent took a drink and exclaimed, "This is delicious." She hoped the conversation could return to food or states or the weather, anything that wasn't on such a personal level as her looks. She was becoming more comfortable with Jack, but still reserved.

"I wish I had the outline of the Divine Daughters Celebration with me. I'll be sure and get a copy to you next week." Millicent gave him the rundown, and explained the topics for the three seminars. "That Saturday will be a full day," she concluded, "starting with breakfast, a four-hour seminar with lunch served between topics, then an afternoon of play and pampering before the commitment ceremony and dinner in the evening."

"This sounds like a lot of work," Jack said.

"It is, but the ladies are excited and believe we can pull it off. We're keeping the group small. There're only twenty girls, and almost that many adults helping, so it should be fairly painless. Organization is the key."

Jack knew he was staring at her again, but he couldn't help it. "You know, God really smiled on us when He brought us you."

"Oh, Jack . . ."

"No, seriously, the women speak highly of you. They say you've really contributed and have bright, innovative ideas. It's just what we've needed." From her smile he knew she was warming to him. She'd even called him Jack.

"I admit it feels good to be doing this kind of stuff again. I've missed it."

"Was it a big church where you were active back in Portland?"

Millicent had initially told the members she was from Portland, had left out the decade-long stop she'd made in Los Angeles. She hadn't corrected Leah, who thought her work with Ladies First in Los Angeles had been something she'd been called in specifically to organize. She felt that one day that omission might come back to haunt her. But until then, she divulged little, while speaking as truthfully as possible. "It was a small church actually. My mother's been there since I was young. But I've worked with larger ministries, helped out with seminars, things like that."

"Oh, I see." Jack had astutely picked up on the evasiveness Millicent was trying so hard to cover. He'd had the knack since he was a boy, could almost know what people were thinking sometimes. He felt there was a lot Millicent wasn't telling him, felt there was much she was keeping to herself. Everyone had baggage, a past. He hoped in time she would feel comfortable enough to share some of it with him, especially the part that kept her so guarded, so reserved, even when she donned an open, friendly facade.

Tenny walked over with two huge platters. She sat them down and returned with toast, extra butter, and a carousel of jellies. The aroma that drifted up from the plate was tantalizing. Millicent hadn't eaten a meal like this since she'd left her mother's house.

"Wow, I'm getting full just looking at this," she said as she picked up her fork and dove in to the crisp hash browns and onions. "Oh my goodness," she said, savoring the mouthful. "This is heaven."

"I thought you'd like it," Jack replied, dousing his pork chop with ketchup, before slicing off and devouring a huge piece. "It's the best food like this on the coast. And it's all organic."

They ate and talked and laughed and ate some more. Millicent was full after barely eating a third of the meal, but enjoyed it. She pushed back her plate, satisfied yet guilt-free for not eating more than was comfortable for her flat stomach.

Jack stopped, fork in midair. "You're not done."

"I'm stuffed. But it was delicious, thank you."

"May I?"

Millicent nodded. Jack reached over and placed the remaining piece of pork chop on his plate. An idea came to him in that instant. "Sounds like after all the hard work for this commitment ceremony, you might need a little vacation."

Millicent looked up quickly. *Does he know about my plans for Mexico? No, surely not. Play it cool, girl.* "You're absolutely right. In fact, I've planned one for right after everything's done."

Jack's heart dropped. He'd planned to ask Millicent to go away with him. He covered his disappointment with a smile. "Oh, really? Where are you going?"

"Hawaii," Millicent said, without hesitation.

"One of my favorite places. The big island?"

That was general enough. "Yes."

"I know a great resort there. It's—"

"Not to cut you off," Millicent said, effectively cutting him off, "but we've already planned everything."

Jack's heart dropped further. He'd assumed Millicent was unattached. "Sorry, didn't mean to interfere. I hope you and your, uh, friend enjoy yourselves."

"Thank you." Millicent didn't comment on Jack's assumption. The less he knew about her, the better.

"I was just going to invite you to take a trip with me. . . ."

Millicent raised her eyebrows.

"Separate rooms, of course. My travel agent is surprising me with some kind of exotic package she's putting together, said I was long overdue for a break. And she's right."

Jack went on to tell Millicent how he'd worked almost nonstop since his wife, Susan's, passing, and how the strain of continuing on as a single dad and maintaining the ministry had taken its toll. He wanted to go someplace and renew himself, physically, mentally, and spiritually.

It had been two years since Millicent had taken a trip with a man, and over a year since she'd had sex. A longing she didn't know existed sprung up from nowhere. Maybe after she saw Cy and Hope together, saw him face to face one final time, she could move on to someone else. But not Jack. Not her pastor. Still, his invite had been a nice gesture.

"Where are you going?" she asked.

"Probably the Caribbean," Jack responded. "Leah knows how much I like the islands."

"Leah's your travel agent?"

"Yes."

Millicent was impressed. If Leah was handling Jack's travel plans through Exquisite Journeys, his was going to be an expensive vacation. "Well, you're in good hands," Millicent said, reaching into her purse for her wallet. "I hope you have a nice, relaxing time."

"Please, allow me," Jack said, reaching into his pants pocket and pulling out a money clip bulging with cash.

"No, it's okay," Millicent said.

"Look, I think I can handle potatoes and eggs. This is my treat. Next time can be on you."

Millicent didn't miss the presumption that there would be a next time. Jack seemed nice enough, but even thinking about dating someone in church made her nervous.

Millicent stood. "Thanks again for the wonderful meal."

"You're welcome."

Jack paid the check and walked Millicent to her car. He gave a smile and wave, watching as she maneuvered out of the full parking lot and started down the winding road. Today was a big advance. He'd spent over an hour with this marvelous woman, alone. She'd been just slightly skittish and had conversed quite easily. But considering the cold shoulder he'd gotten that first day on the beach, she'd been a siren. He had a feeling that there was a lot of passion beneath that cool exterior. Yes, he'd be patient with Millicent Sims. A scripture floated across his mind, Romans 5:3: . . . *But we glory in tribulations also, knowing that tribulations worketh patience, and patience, experience, and experience, hope.* . . . Jack had high hopes for his future, and with whom he could spend it.

28

Strictly Business

Frieda escaped the unusually hot, July heat by stepping into the Peninsula, an upscale hotel in Beverly Hills. She was there to meet Gorgio, who was almost off work. When he'd first asked her out, she had been a bit intimidated, with his model good looks and extravagant demeanor. When he told her he worked in Beverly Hills, it only added to her hesitation—until she found out it was as a waiter at this five-star establishment. Her first visit to see him there had been memorable. Having good friends both in management and in the kitchen, he'd sat her at a discreet table and plied her with banana martinis and a sampling of almost everything on their luncheon menu. They'd been together almost four months, and in addition to the good food and great sex, Gorgio lived rather large on those wealthy businessman tips.

"Hey, Frieda," the host said as Frieda entered the Belvedere, the hotel's patio-styled restaurant. "Gorgio said you were on your way. He wants to grab a bite, and we've saved a table."

"Hey there, Frieda-lay," another of Gorgio's coworkers, a waiter, greeted her. They'd partied together once or twice; he was familiar with Frieda's zany side. "Come with me."

He led her to a table for two tucked in the corner. "I've got a banana martini with your name on it," he whispered with a wink. "You game?"

"Absolutely," Frieda replied.

"Coming right up," the waiter said, and disappeared to the bar area.

Frieda took out a compact and checked her makeup. She hadn't taken the time to freshen up after handling the dense traffic along Santa Monica Boulevard. She was just about to put the compact away when two men caught her eye in the mirror. She put down the mirror and turned around. It was *him*. It was both of them, the men from the Hollywood Hills party—one of whose name she now knew was Darius.

She turned back around, smiling slightly. Even though they'd never met, she felt a certain familiarity with him. After all, she'd seen his bare ass, not to mention his other asset in all its rigid glory. She discreetly turned around again. They were being seated, and appeared to share a comfortable camaraderie. She noticed Darius squeezed his friend's shoulder before sitting down in his own chair.

Frieda's mind was going a mile a minute. There hadn't been enough drama in her life since moving to California, and Frieda's life was normally swimming in it. *I should go over there.* Frieda imagined what she would say if she did walk up to them. *Hi, remember me? I was at the party in the Hollywood Hills . . . the private one that was going on upstairs.* She laughed out loud at their imagined reaction. Would they deny it? Would they be pissed?

"Ooh, I should do it," she said with a devilish giggle.

"Do what?" the waiter asked, setting down a frosty banana martini.

"Yeah," Gorgio asked, kissing Frieda before sitting opposite her. "Do what?"

"Remember those gay dudes I told you about, the ones who were fuckin' in the bedroom the night I met you?"

"Yeah."

"Well, keep it on the DL, but they're right over there."

Gorgio leaned to the left and right, trying to see around Frieda. "Who?"

"Those two Black guys sitting over there, behind us." She cocked her head toward them to emphasize the direction.

"Those all-about-business-looking brothers over there? One of them is in a suit, the other in, what is that, Sean Jean?"

Frieda sipped her martini, her eyes sparkling. "That's them!"

Gorgio perused them critically. "Hmm, very interesting. I never would have thought . . ."

"You can't tell these days. Athletes, corporate execs, politicians, everybody's getting it in the booty."

"Girl, you are crazy."

"But you like it."

"That I do."

"So," Gorgio said, still checking out Darius and Bo. "You hungry?"

Frieda wasn't listening, she was deep in thought. "I want to go over there and say something."

"Frieda, you are not going over there." And then, "What would you say?"

Frieda's voice dropped to a whisper. "I'd say, 'Haven't I seen you before?' Then I'd say, 'It was either at *church* or a booty-full party in the Hollywood Hills!' "

"No, Frieda," Gorgio said, afraid his girl might follow through on her insane plans. "Let that man handle his business. You worry about handling what's over here."

Frieda slipped off her shoe under the table and reached her leg across to Gorgio's lap. "It's about time for me to handle something over there," she said sexily, rubbing his crotch with her foot.

"Stop, woman!" Gorgio said, grabbing her foot. But instead of pushing it away, he rubbed it against the bulge in his pants.

Frieda smiled, her foot sliding up and down his leg.

"Let's get something and take it home," Gorgio said. "I'm tired, ready to get out of these clothes."

"Uh-huh," Frieda said, still smiling and rubbing.

"Come on then," Gorgio said as Frieda finished her martini. "Let's get you out of here before you start something."

They placed their order and soon had "to-go" boxes on the table. With thoughts of a naked Frieda on his mind, Gorgio hurried toward the exit.

When Frieda reached Bo and Darius's table, she slowed her pace. "Hey, fellas. Hello, Darius." She smiled secretively, as if withholding information. "Enjoy your meal. The gazpacho with huge *cucumber* chunks is delicious." Without waiting for a response she moved past the table toward the exit. Gorgio shrugged toward the men and followed her out.

She could barely contain her laughter until they'd gotten outside.

"Frieda, you're crazy as hell," Gorgio said, laughing. "How you gon' front somebody like that?"

"What do you mean?" Frieda asked innocently, between giggles. "I just suggested a meal I thought they'd enjoy."

"Sure you did."

"A meal for later maybe." He squeezed her affectionately as they walked to Frieda's car. Gorgio, who lived relatively close to the restaurant, had caught the bus that day.

"Yum, like the one I'm getting ready to have?"

"You know the deal."

"Well?" Bo asked, waiting for an answer to his inquiry as to who Frieda was.

"I don't know her," Darius said for the second time. "She's probably seen me at church."

"She didn't act like she'd seen you at church. And that line about cucumbers? That skank has nerve."

Darius loved Bo but at times became annoyed with his possessive, prissy attitude. "Look," he said firmly and slowly for emphasis, "I don't know her."

Bo squirmed in his chair, but sensing Darius's exasperation, wisely chose to let it go, in a way. "First there's Stacy, and now this hootchie. I just can't stand these twats twittering around my man. Waiter!" he said, catching the man passing. "Bring me a double scotch on the rocks, please."

Darius couldn't totally blame Bo for being agitated. He didn't know how he'd handle Bo telling him he had a date. But going out with Stacy seemed like a safe enough move, definitely like a necessary one. No one at the church had questioned his sexuality directly, but he knew there were rumors, had been since his divorce from Gwen. And while he thought Derrick might let him continue playing for the church, even if he were outed, it wasn't something he wanted to find out. Not only did the gig pay well, but it was perfect and constant exposure for his music. Maybe after the second album dropped, after he blew up, things would be different. But he'd worked too hard, waited too long, for the success he was now experiencing. He wasn't going to let his sexual orientation fuck things up.

Plus, he'd already cancelled on Stacy twice; it had been a month since they'd made plans to meet. After signing with Arista Records, his schedule had gotten insane. The execs were trying to push up the release date, wanting the title track, "A Timeless Love," to drop on Valentine's Day. Stacy hadn't been happy, but she was determined to go out with him no matter how long it took. He knew the girl would bug him until the return of Jesus.

Darius tried to soothe Bo. "Baby, you know it means nothing with Stacy. This coming Friday is strictly business. And it's the perfect cover. She and I will hang out—"

Bo heaved a dramatically heavy sigh.

Darius placed a hand on Bo's arm and finished quickly,

"Every now and then. Just enough to, you know, make it look cool." He leaned over, lowering his voice. "And you'll be by my side, and in my bed, every step of the way."

Darius's words and the quickly downed, hard liquor had the desired calming effect. Bo sat back, grabbed the menu. "I think I'll try that damn gazpacho, with the *cucumber* chunks."

Darius laughed. He loved Bo, his sense of humor was infectious, and the way he viewed life, refreshing. Plus, he was a good businessman. Bo didn't know it, but Darius was busy figuring out how he could legitimize Bo traveling with him, being with him all the time, as the album neared completion and tour dates were being tossed around. Darius had suggested Bo to the record company as his choice for personal assistant. Not that he could use that title with Bo. With him, Darius would need to come up with something flashy, something that sounded important. But he was working on it. He couldn't see going on tour and leaving his love behind—or his lover's *behind* either.

29

What's Done in Darkness . . .

Her hands full, Tai used her shopping bags to push open the unlocked front door. She'd dropped the twins off at the recreation center, and with Princess working at her new, part-time job, Tai relished thoughts of a quiet house after a day spent shopping. Mama Max's car was in the driveway, perfect since she'd seen and purchased one of her mother-in-law's favorite pieces of clothing, an oversized cotton top in bright colors. Tai was just about to announce her arrival when she heard what sounded like raised voices coming from King's office. *That's unusual.* It was rare that anyone ventured into King's self-proclaimed private domain.

Later, Tai would wonder why she'd snuck up on her husband and mother-in-law. Maybe it was instinct, maybe premonition, maybe both. But that's what she did—gently placed down her shopping bags and tiptoed toward King's office. As she neared the door, Mama Max's voiced dropped a bit. Tai stood to the side of the doorway, absolutely quiet and still.

"There's a reason that girl ain't talking," Mama Max said. "And I think it's because she knows that's your child!"

Tai took a step back and looked at the wall, as if she could see through it. Her mouth opened, even as she questioned if she could have really heard what she heard. *King's child? What girl? What is Mama Max talking about?* There was only one way to find out. She burst through the door.

"Who's got what child, King?" Tai didn't even try to stay calm. Still, she crossed her arms and willed herself to not yell.

Both Mama Max and King were stunned at Tai's entrance. They stood silently, the unfinished conversation hanging heavy in the air, like a fourth body. Mama Max looked away. King looked down.

Tai asked again, "What child? King, Mama, what is going on here?"

"Now, Tai, I don't even know if there's any truth to it, probably just the wonderings of an old woman." Mama Max tried to speak with lightheartedness. She gave a little laugh. "I didn't hear you come in. Where are the kids?"

"Mama Max, we've known each other too long for you to try and patronize me by changing the subject."

Silence.

Tai persisted, agitation rising. "Don't you two think I have a right to know what you were discussing when I came in? Now whose baby are we talking about?"

King knew there was no easy way to break this news. It had been hard enough carrying the possibility around alone, even with Derrick as a sounding board now and again. He thought the best approach would be a direct one. "Tootie's," he said simply.

The name was a bullet. Tai sat down, as if shot, in the chair opposite King's massive desk. It seemed moments before her heart beat again. She couldn't think, not even of how to react. So she just sat staring.

Mama Max walked over and sat in a chair next to her beloved daughter-in-law. "Now, Tai," she began.

Tai held up a hand, cut her off. "Mama, I need some time." She looked at King. "Tootie is saying she has your child?" Tai remembered what Vivian had said about Tootie having three children. Until this moment, she'd not given those words a second thought.

King jumped at the chance to ease Tai's fears. "No, but—"

Mama Max did, too, at the same time. "She ain't said—"

Both stopped, then started again. "King doesn't believe—"

"Mama thinks—"

Mama Max placed a hand on Tai's arm. "When Tootie first came here, I asked about her children. She seemed evasive about the third child, the oldest. Then when I asked for a picture, she said she didn't have one, even though she proudly showed off her two youngest kids."

Tai exploded. "You've been suspecting this for months? And didn't say anything?"

"I didn't want to start trouble." Mama Max turned more fully toward Tai and continued, "But as time went by, it kept bothering me, the fact that Tootie has a child around the—" Mama Max stopped, not wanting to say what she thought. But she'd already started, so she continued, "Around the same age as Princess. I asked Nancy if her daughter's child was my grandchild. And that's when it got real interesting, too interesting for me to leave it alone."

"What did she say?" Tai asked.

"She said she didn't know, that Tootie refused to name the daddy."

"So why do you think it's King's? If you'll remember, Tootie's been around."

"I hope it's not," Mama Max said quickly. "I just wish I could know for sure."

Tai looked at King a long moment. He was sitting behind the desk, hands steepled, looking off in the distance. "And what about you, King? What do you think?"

King answered truthfully, looking directly at Tai. "I don't know. As much as I'd like to state emphatically that there's no way the child could be mine, the truth is, that's when—" King chose his words like steps taken in a minefield—"that was the last time I was with her."

"You mean the affair, *after* we were married." Tai was surprised at how quickly and intensely the anger about King's past infidelities came rushing back. She thought she'd moved way past anger and hurt. She was wrong. And to think when she'd encountered Tootie, she'd been cordial!

Mama Max assumed the voice of reason. "It doesn't help nobody to get upset until we know for sure there's something to get upset about." She was unaware that it was her raised voice in the first place that alerted Tai to something out of the ordinary going on in her house. "I think we need to come up with a way to find out for sure if that's King's son."

The fact that "King's son" was not referencing her boys, Michael or Timothy, was too much for Tai. She stood. "I can't do this right now. This is too much; I need some time alone. If Tootie has your child, King . . ." Tai didn't finish the sentence. She didn't know the ending. She got up and left the room.

Mama Max and King watched Tai walk out of the office. "Well," Mama Max began in a low voice after the door had closed, "it was bound to happen. What's done in the dark always come to light. Best she knows, 'cause if that boy's yours, it will not just be you but Tai, and your kids, dealing with this."

Mama Max and King sat silently for a long moment. "Well, son, I'm going to go. I'll be praying for you." She walked around the desk and kissed King's forehead. As she did, an old Baptist standard, one of her favorite songs, popped into her head, "The Lord Will Make a Way Somehow." She took some assurance in the words of this hymn. Because God was the only one who could make a way out of this.

30

To Friendship . . .

The potato salad was mixed, the grill was hot, and a bottle of champagne chilled in a bucket on the bar counter. Stacy looked around her apartment, satisfied. She wasn't rich, but had a knack for making the most of what she had. Her decor was Afrocentric. A grouping of masks adorned one wall, wooden figurines occupied end tables. One intricately carved ebony piece was of a couple entwined. It was her favorite, and held a place of prominence on her coffee table. Colorful works of Black artists were showcased throughout the apartment, complementing tan leather furniture.

Stacy had pondered what to wear and finally decided to go casual with cut-off jean shorts and a tank top with spaghetti straps. She wasn't wearing a bra, but didn't need to. Her breasts were small, firm, and fit the top nicely. She'd kept her makeup light as well, only lip gloss and mascara, wanting to give the appearance that tonight was no big deal.

But it was a very big deal. Stacy had high hopes for the evening. If things went okay, she'd get a kiss. If they went good, a feel or two. Great, some deep French kisses and maybe other oral action. And if things went perfect, Darius would wake up at her house in the morning.

Stacy walked out on the patio to check the grill. The charcoal was grayish white, a red glow beneath them. She went into the kitchen to prepare the meat for the burgers and, using one of her brother's tricks, added finely chopped onions, peppers, and chili powder to the ground round. If the way to a man's heart was through his stomach, she hoped this meal would hasten the journey.

She'd just looked at her watch when the doorbell rang. Darius was right on time.

"Hey, you," she said, opening the door and giving him a big hug.

"Hey, back," Darius said, returning the hug. Even with her crush on him, Darius was comfortable with Stacy. She and Tanya had been best friends for years. He'd already planned how he would handle the friendship—as if she was a best buddy. He would be friendly and funny and caring and kind. He'd maybe throw in a kiss or two, just enough to keep things interesting and keep the questions down.

He walked into the living room. "Hey, where's the food? I don't smell anything cooking." He pointedly sniffed around. "Don't tell me you ordered pizza!" This was one of his sister's commonly and widely known meal solutions.

"Look, I can cook, okay?" Stacy teased. "I hope you brought your appetite. But you'll eat this food even if you're not hungry, it's that good."

"Oh, look at her, the woman is sure of herself," Darius said. He walked around the living room, checking out the statues and artwork. "I like your decor."

"Thanks."

"You've got good taste, an eye for color."

"I try. HGTV is one of my favorite channels." At times, Stacy entertained the thought of hosting a show on the Home and Garden network.

Darius walked over to the entertainment center and began browsing Stacy's CDs.

She'd forgotten music! How could she invite a musician

over and not have the sounds playing? "Put on anything you want," she said, walking out to the grill with a plate of burgers.

When she came back in, Jill Scott's melodious voice filled the room. "Don't you just love her?" Stacy asked, joining him in the living room with the bottle of champagne.

Darius turned around. "She's, oh, what are we celebrating?"

"Your butt finally coming over to my house," Stacy said jokingly. "Even though you kept a sistah waiting. I've only been asking you out for a year, and waiting a month!"

"You've never asked me out."

"Strongly hinted."

"Well, maybe that. But see what happened when you just came straight out with what you wanted? That's what women do, throw out these little hints and innuendos and expect us to figure out a whole story."

"Maybe, but you can't tell me you didn't know I liked you."

"No, I can't tell you that. Here, let me do it." Darius took the bottle and walked toward the kitchen. "In case it sprays," he said over his shoulder.

While Darius popped the cork and poured the bubbly, Stacy flipped the burgers. A subtle yet distinct smell of onions and peppers wafted in before she closed the patio door.

"Um, something smells good!" Darius said, handing her a glass.

Stacy just smiled. "So, I would like to toast us going to a new level. We've always known each other casually through Tanya, but here's to us knowing each other as really good friends." She hoped that sounded light enough. Although she wanted more, she knew nothing could scare a guy away from commitment faster than telling him that's what you wanted. Better to try and stay loose and easy and, as things progressed, let nature hopefully take its course.

"To friendship," Darius answered. *And friendship is the only thing I want.*

Later, Stacy's succulent hamburgers and potato salad gone,

and Darius pleasantly full, she pulled out the game she'd purchased for the weekend.

"I just got this," she said, opening the disk. "It's the latest
X-Man. I've got Halo Two and some other ones, too."

"Word?" Darius said. "I've been wanting to check that out."

Stacy gave Darius the box and went into the kitchen to
straighten up. Moments later, the noise began, both the game
and Darius. "Aw, man. Got you, sucka!"

Stacy smiled. This is what she wanted, the sound of Darius
in her house.

He glanced around and noticed her sitting on the couch.
"Come on, woman! It's time to take this beating I'm getting
ready to serve up."

"In your dreams," she said, but only halfheartedly. She wasn't
very adept with the game.

"Oh no, you've got to get in on the action. Here, I'll show
you how to play."

Stacy walked over and sat down on the floor next to Darius's chair. He joined her on the floor, leaned into her, showing
her how to work the controls. She was a fast study. While there
was no way she was going to beat Darius that or probably any
other night, she held her own enough to not be too embarrassed.

An hour and another bottle of champagne later, Darius
and Stacy were still absorbed in the game, trash-talking the
whole time they frantically pushed the controls. Darius's level
of play had slipped a notch with the third and then fourth glass
of bubbly, and Stacy seemed to have found her niche in how to
play rather effectively. As the game continued, there looked to
be a real chance that Stacy might win.

"Watch out, Darius, watch out! Looks like somebody
might get beat up!" She punched the button and took out another man, his ace.

"Oh, no you don't." Darius put his whole body into it,

maneuvering this way and that as he navigated the game. He playfully pushed Stacy over, trying to leverage an advantage.

Stacy pushed him back. "Don't think you're going to distract me, trying to start a fight," she said. "I'll beat you on the TV, then beat your butt in the living room!"

They tousled back and forth, pushing buttons, laughing. Having grown up in a house full of boys, Stacy was a hearty competitor at anything she tried, so getting into a game that she had little personal interest in wasn't difficult. The more she got into it, the more Darius enjoyed her. She really was like one of the boys.

And then something happened. Stacy, seeing she was going to lose to Darius for the umpteenth time, began tickling him. It was done innocently, only to try and stop his game. What she didn't know was that Darius was extremely ticklish.

"Stop, stop that," he laughed, trying to grab her arms and pin them behind her.

"Oh, you're ticklish, huh? Where? There? There?" Stacy was enjoying herself, avoiding Darius's hands while aiming for his sides. Darius rolled over on Stacy, stopping her with his body weight. Stacy struggled underneath him, trying to free herself from his grip. Darius stayed on top and finally managed to grab her arms. He held them straight out from her body. They both panted.

"Now, what do you have to say now, huh?" Darius held Stacy's arms immobile out to her side. He looked down. Stacy's nipples had hardened with her excitement, and protruded through the tank top fabric. Darius's dick jumped. He paused, surprised. Stacy kept tussling and his dick kept jumping, getting harder. For the first time in a long while, he was getting a hard-on because of a female. This rarely happened, was one of the reasons his ex-wife had finally sought pleasure elsewhere.

Stacy noticed Darius's grip had loosened on her arms. She'd noticed something else, too. He lay on his side, appeared to be thinking. *Probably about that bulge between his legs and what he wants to do with it.*

Stacy chose to help him decide. She rolled them both over; now she was on top, he on the bottom. "You know what just happened," she said triumphantly. "I won."

With that, she leaned down and brushed her lips against Darius's. She'd waited for this moment a long time and went slow, savoring the taste, the feel, the moment. She outlined his lips with her tongue, then kissed him on the mouth. She was excited, but tried to keep the mood light. "What are you gonna do now? Huh? Huh?"

Darius tried not to think, tried to just be in the moment. He'd planned this, had planned to kiss Stacy. *Just get it over, man.* He grabbed the back of Stacy's head and pulled hers down to his. Then he mimicked her movements; outlined her mouth with his tongue and kissed her mouth. She parted her lips. He slipped his tongue inside.

Stacy was hot. This man drove her wild, he was fire! She plunged her tongue into his mouth, grinding her pelvis against his throbbing manhood. Her tongue made the same circular motions as her body as she tried to mold herself to Darius's hard frame, leaving no space between them. She wanted him, all of him. *Go slow.* She didn't want to scare him, wanted to keep it light. But her body had other plans. It was aching for release. Stacy tried to speed things up. She slid to the side of Darius and grabbed his dick through his shorts. She began rubbing the length of it; slowly, caressingly. Their kiss deepened even more as Darius fumbled underneath Stacy's top. It had been so long since Gwen, playing with her breasts felt almost new to him. But they felt good, firm, not very big. And the nipples, they were small, beady, like Bo's.

Bo. Darius stopped the kiss, grabbed Stacy's hand. "I can't do this."

These words were water on Stacy's flame. She hadn't had

sex in months. She'd wanted Darius for so long, and he felt so good. "Why? What's wrong?"

Darius's throbbing penis was affecting his ability to think. *What is wrong? Why am I attracted to Stacy like this when I've never been attracted to women?* The champagne, he rationalized. It had to be the combination of that and the game and her one-of-the-boys personality. He'd felt totally comfortable in her company.

"We need to slow it down, that's all," Darius said finally. He lay on the floor with his eyes closed, trying to gather himself.

Stacy lay next to him, smoldering, like her grill's charcoal. She couldn't give up. When would she get the opportunity again? She didn't want to scare him away, but she didn't want him to leave without her feeling she'd done all she could to attract him either. She slowly reached out her hand toward Darius's shorts. She undid the button and grabbed the zipper.

"No," Darius began.

Stacy shushed him. "It's okay, just let me do this. We don't have to do it or anything, but just let me make you feel better."

Darius said nothing. Stacy reached for the zipper again and pulled it down slowly. She reached inside. *Nice.* Stacy straddled Darius's legs and took his manhood out of his shorts. She thought it was beautiful, curved and dark, a thick vein running from the base to the tip.

That's where she started. She traced the vein with her tongue, slowly, leisurely.

Darius inhaled sharply. He had expected her to want to have intercourse, not this. "Head" was his weakness.

Stacy continued to lavish her attention on Darius's penis. Darius moved and moaned under this targeted and undivided attention. Stacy's eyes closed, she thought of nothing but pleasing Darius, of giving him the best blow job he'd ever had. And she did.

31

No Mountain We Can't Climb

A week had passed since Tai heard the news that Tootie might have King's child. In that time, she'd looked at the situation from every possible angle. The only one that worked for her was King not being the father. But the more she'd thought about it, thought about how close King and Tootie had been, of how the time of the affair and the age of the child matched, and how quickly Tootie left town afterward . . . The chances that King was the father were much greater than that he was not.

Vivian, as always, had been understanding, sympathetic, and a voice of reason. "It was a long time ago," she'd said. "It doesn't change what you two have now." She was right, technically. Tai couldn't fault King almost twenty years later for a child he knew nothing about.

The affair *had* been totally his fault. She still remembered how devastated she felt, finding out King was having an affair at the same time she was carrying their second child. It had taken her years to release the anger, years to feel healed. And she could tell she had healed. Before, this news would have sent Tai on a rampage. She would have been a bellowing fool, maybe even a violent one. But this time, she had remained basically calm and basically rational. What was done had been done and losing her mind over it wouldn't change anything.

Their marriage felt like a fortress, and this was definitely new. King and Tai had talked the evening she heard the news; talked, not argued. They'd discussed how best to handle the situation, how to confront Tootie. That definitely had to happen. If Tai was sure of nothing else, she was sure of that. God said the truth was the light, and nothing short of knowing beyond a shadow of a doubt that the boy was not King's child, would allow the family to live in peace, to get back to a sense of normalcy.

And that's what they'd decided to do tonight, find out the truth. King and Tai would meet Tootie at Miss Smith's house. They'd ask the question. They'd hear the answer: simple, over, done. And then she could breathe again.

"Man, all you can do is what you're doing. This wouldn't be easy for anybody, let alone what you guys have already faced the past year. So keep your head up. It's gonna be all right." Derrick truly believed his last words were true.

"Yeah, we're gonna know one way or another in just a few hours," King replied. "It's what's best but not necessarily what's easiest. If that child is mine . . ."

"Don't forget your faith, King," Derrick said. "I don't have to tell you that with God, all things are possible or that faith moves mountains."

"Yeah, but can it remove a child?"

"Faith will make finding out you have a child, *if* that's even true, easier to handle, because you know that if God brought you to it, He'll bring you through it."

King paused. "Have you ever thought about becoming a preacher?"

Derrick smiled. "A time or two."

King looked at his watch. He knew he should be leaving now to pick Tai up. They were expected at Miss Smith's at seven o'clock. "Well, it's about that time, brother. But listen, can you say a prayer for us?"

Of course, Derrick didn't hesitate. "Let's do it right now. Father God, we come to you this evening knowing that with your grace and mercy, there is no problem we can't solve, no mountain we can't climb, no river we can't cross. . . ."

"But, I don't want to talk to them!" Janeé was furious. How dare her mother set up a meeting and then trick her into coming over. It would serve all of them right for her to leave right now.

"Rita Janeé," Miss Smith said, wringing her hands. "It's the right thing to do. I know you're mad at me, but would you have come over if I'd told you why beforehand?"

Janeé responded with a scathing glare at her mother.

"You know you wouldn't have. And this thing needs to be resolved. Now, all these years I've honored your request and not said a word about Kelvin. I haven't bugged you about who his daddy is, although I've wondered many times. I've done all that you've asked. But now it's time for you to do what I'm asking. It's time to bring this situation into order. That boy deserves to know who his real father is, and the father deserves to know his son. Who knows? What you're fearing so strongly may turn out to be a blessing.

"God don't make mistakes. And don't a soul come into this world that God don't bless. So, for whatever reasons, Kelvin had to be born, and he had to come here the way he did. I know you've gone far away from your church training, but you've got to believe that God is *still* on the throne; ain't nothing too hard for Him. Ha! I know that." Miss Smith thought about the open-heart surgery she'd come through and got happy. "Hallelujah! There is nothing too hard for my God!"

Janeé looked at her mother. It really wasn't her mother she was mad at. It was herself. This could have been handled years ago, when Kelvin was younger. But the more time that passed, the more Janeé believed it best to leave well enough alone. Then she'd met Hans and he'd adopted Kelvin and she'd hoped that would be the end of it.

That had been wishful thinking. She'd known all along that this day would come, and now it was here. No matter how much she wanted to avoid it, she couldn't. And leaving would only delay the inevitable opening of this sixteen-year-old can of worms.

"You're right, Mom," she said, reaching for her phone. "But can you do me a favor? I need Hans here with me, but not the children. Can we ask your neighbor's son to take you guys for an ice cream when they come over?"

Miss Smith didn't want to leave. She wanted to be there for her daughter. But she knew it only right that her husband be by her side instead. "Of course I will," Miss Smith said, walking toward her bedroom. "Just let me get presentable."

Janeé punched in her husband's cell phone number. Her heart beat faster with each ring. Having made the decision to confront her past didn't make the moment easy. "Baby," she said when Hans answered. "Can you guys come over? I need you."

Forty-five minutes later, King and Tai knocked on Miss Smith's door. Janeé started to answer it, but Hans placed a hand on her arm and rose to do it instead.

"Hello, come on in," he said, opening the door. He held out his hand. "I'm Hans. You must be King."

King stepped in and gave Hans a firm handshake. "Pleased to meet you."

"And you must be Tai; Hans here." Again, Hans held out his hand. Tai shook it and followed King into the living room.

Janeé sat on the couch, rigid and unsmiling. She didn't bother to get up. With much effort, however, she managed to curve the corners of her mouth somewhat. "Hey, y'all."

"Tootie," Tai said simply. Ice had replaced the warmth of their meeting at the mall.

"Hey, Janeé," King said, hoping the use of her current name would put some distance on their past.

"Hi, King."

Hans motioned King and Tai to a loveseat. "Have a seat, guys. Can I get you anything to drink?"

"No, we're fine," Tai said, answering for the both of them.

Hans hadn't realized until this moment that he would conduct the "meeting." But being a corporate executive used to navigating shark–filled waters, it seemed the natural thing to do.

"Well, we all know why we're here," he began. "And I think the best thing to do is get right to it."

Various nods and replies of agreement followed, and then silence.

Tai looked at Janeé. Janeé looked at Hans. King looked at Tai. Hans looked around the room, waiting for someone to speak. Finally, he turned to Janeé. "Why don't you just tell them, dear?"

Why didn't she just tell them? Janeé couldn't understand why she was making this so difficult. The more she hesitated, the more the situation could get even trickier. If she could just lighten up, give them the answer they wanted, maybe everyone could go on with their lives. But then there was Kelvin. He wasn't going to stop questioning her about his father. But that could be dealt with another day. Today, Janeé just wanted this over.

She grabbed Hans's hand and tried to look directly at King and Tai. Instead, she looked just over them. "King, you're not the father of my son."

King visibly relaxed, sat back against the loveseat. He'd been taut with nerves, now he rubbed Tai's shoulders as if kneading hers could make his relax. He wanted to jump up and do a holy dance. He wanted to shout hallelujah from the rooftops. He wanted to run over to Hans and slap him a high five. He wanted to kiss Tootie—well, maybe give her a big, bear hug. He wanted to take Tai and go home. It was over, he was off the hook. The boy was not his son!

"Of course, we're relieved," he said, once he got his excitement and relief under control. "Nothing against your son, I'm sure he is a great kid, but for so many reasons, whew, thank you, God!"

Tai should have been overjoyed, too, but for some reason the ending felt too something . . . too anticlimactic. If the child wasn't King's, why all the secrecy? Why wouldn't she have told her mother, who she knew was close to Mama Max. This could have been over before it became a saga. And now here Tootie sat calmly saying King was not the father. She'd had them all tripping when the thing could have been nipped in the bud immediately, like when Mama Max questioned Miss Smith. And Tootie was not even able to make eye contact? What was up with that? Tai wanted to celebrate as much as King, but she couldn't find the joy.

"May I see a picture of your son? What's his name?" Tai asked.

"Kelvin," Janeé said after a moment. "Kelvin Petersen." She emphasized the last name as she reached over and squeezed Hans's hand. "Hans adopted him when he was five and has been an excellent father figure in his life."

"A boy sure needs that," King said before turning to Hans. "That's an honorable thing to do, man, take on someone else's responsibility. You're a good man."

"He's a wonderful man, a fabulous man," Janeé said.

"Do you have a picture?" Tai asked again.

Janeé looked at Tai a moment. This is what she'd never liked about her. This holier-than-thou, I'm better than you attitude. Janeé had tried to be civil with Tai, but she just didn't like the woman, never had, never would. Hadn't she done enough? Marched her ass into her mother's home like she owned it, demanding to know what wasn't her business, and adding insult to injury by basically implying she didn't believe what had been said. Well, fuck her. This party was over.

"I don't mean to be rude," Janeé said, "but I gave you the information you came for. And I don't appreciate my word being questioned by your asking to see proof." She stood, walked over to the piano, her back to the group. "I've said King is not Kelvin's father. Let's let that be the end of it."

Tai looked at King, her temperature rising. Was it too much to ask to see a picture? But she knew this wasn't about the picture. It was about the rivalry Tootie had felt with Tai ever since she came on the scene, ever since Tai became King's official girlfriend. Tootie had never been official. She'd always been the other woman, the booty call, the good friend. The fact was, Tai had gotten King. And after more than fifteen years, Tootie still couldn't stand it.

"Let's go, King," Tai said, standing up abruptly. "Tootie's right. We're done here." She walked toward the door.

King stood up, unsure of why the atmosphere was suddenly crackling around him. As much as he loved them, he'd never be able to figure women out. Shouldn't everybody be happy, in a celebratory mood? He was ready to pop a cork on some Dom Pérignon, and he didn't even drink!

Not knowing what to say to either Tai or Janeé, he walked over to Hans, who was now also standing. "It was nice to meet you. Thank you for, for everything." They shook hands warmly.

Janeé continued to stand with her back to them. "Take care, Janeé," he said simply. And then they were gone.

32

Looking for Love

Millicent stretched, yawned, and rolled over. After two weeks straight of ten-hour days and Saturdays at the office, she was more than ready for a day to sleep in. It was well-deserved rest. Millicent's marketing campaign and company branding strategy had been accepted by the partners of the firm. All of the subcontractors for its implementation had been selected. On top of that, organizing the Open Arms commitment ceremony was going smoothly. Leah and the other women had been tireless in their help.

You'll need a vacation after all this work. Jack's words floated up into her memory. She'd convinced herself that the trip to Mexico was just that, a well-deserved vacation. That it was the same resort Hope and Cy planned to visit, and at the same time, was purely coincidental.

But what are you going to do in Mexico? What is it going to prove? Millicent had pondered these questions ever since she'd booked the trip. She still didn't know. Maybe she'd purchase a thong bikini and give Cy an eyeful of what he'd turned down. Maybe she could somehow get Cy alone, drug Hope's drink, drug Cy, too . . . and have her way with him. *Is there a way I can get Hope out of his life?* Millicent didn't think so. She might be crazy, but she wasn't stupid. She wasn't doing jail time for anyone. And she wasn't going to make a fool of herself again. But maybe she could bring a little storm into the Taylor's marital paradise, cause Hope to hurt the way she had. Whatever she did, she'd have to do it quick. Millicent had only booked a weekend at Rosewood. Whatever was going to happen, it would have to happen like Jesus's resurrection, within three days.

Millicent's stomach growled, reminding her she'd been too tired to eat last night. She rolled out of bed and after morning ablutions, walked into the kitchen. Not much there. Cooking was not Millicent's forte, and she'd been so busy, even grocery shopping had been ignored. Scrounging around cabinets and the refrigerator, she came up with some granola bars, a couple spotty apples, and popcorn. It would have to do. And she'd order in dinner. Millicent planned to spend the day at home.

Ten minutes later, she carried a plate into her office area and turned on the computer. She hadn't checked personal e-mails all week, and wanted to shop on-line for the girls' commitment rings. Amid the scores of spam mail was a message from Alison. She replied that no, she hadn't dropped off the face of the earth and would call her later. Millicent had never had many female friends and appreciated Alison, and now Leah, in her life.

She was deleting the spam mail when a heading caught her eye: Christian Connections, Your On-line Dating Experience. *Hmm.* Alison had once suggested Millicent try an on-line dating service. Millicent had balked, believing it looked desperate to advertise oneself on-line. But crashing a church service in a wedding dress had been desperate, too. Millicent clicked on the link. She scrolled down their marketing information about finding the perfect mate with the same values, morals, and faith. These would be total strangers, with no connection to her past. *It may be the perfect solution.* She continued browsing the site, looking at the sample page of potential matches and reading their summaries. *These men are probably total losers.* But there was a free, trial membership. What could it hurt?

One would think a marketing expert would have no problem highlighting her own attributes, but Millicent struggled. Who was she? What was she looking for? The questionnaire stirred up questions she had never asked herself. For the past year, all she'd wanted was Cy. And what was it about him, besides everything, that had made him so attractive to her? After a long moment, she typed a succinct paragraph in the "What I'm Looking For" box:

> Looking for intelligent conversation, inspiration, and passion. One who is successful yet modest, strong yet sensitive, religious but not dogmatic. Good looks, toned body, great teeth: big pluses. Sexy, romantic: even bigger pluses. Will exchange pics with right person.

Millicent read it once, again and pushed "finish." She'd have to take her chances with who would reply, because she refused to post her picture for the world to see. Nor would she use her first name, posting under her middle name, Rose, instead. One never knew who visited these sites, and she didn't want anyone knowing she was looking for love on-line. If it was meant to be, the person would be willing to respond to her post without a picture. After all, who wouldn't want to meet someone who was intelligent, adventurous, sensual, beautiful, and financially secure, as she'd accurately described herself in the ad?

Two hours later, Millicent turned off the computer, satisfied with the commitment rings and gold-gilded frames she'd found for the girls' ceremony. Rarely one with time on her hands, she contemplated what to do with the rest of her day. After a moment, she headed for the shower. She'd wash and condition her hair, give herself a facial, and maybe find a good movie on television. Or perhaps she'd get back on the computer. And find that someone had answered her post, someone who, like her, was looking for love.

33

Game On

King, Tai, Derrick, and Vivian sat inside the Azul Restaurant at the beautiful Mandarin Oriental hotel in Miami. It was a beautiful August evening. The Total Truth Association's annual executive meeting had just ended. It had been intense, but successful. The more involved the four were with Total Truth, a group of churches that had broken away from the National Baptist Convention, the more excited they were to be a part of it. They liked the unorthodox approaches to biblical teaching, as well as its commitment to business and urban rebuilding. The focus for the upcoming year was going to be on recapturing the attention of today's youth, a task which all thought daunting, but not impossible.

"It's a different world they're coming up in," Tai said. "It's getting harder and harder to keep a rein on Princess, as much as we're trying."

"They're just so defiant," Vivian said. "All the anger and feelings of self-righteousness, as if the world owes them something. Where does that come from?"

"It comes from no home training," King interjected smoothly, between bites of prime rib eye. "No whippin's, no responsibilities."

"No fathers in the home," Derrick added. "Most of these

parents today need to have their behinds whipped. They're too busy trying to be their kid's friend instead of their kid's mother or father."

"I just hope," Tai began. "Never mind . . ."

"What is it, baby?" King asked.

"I'm just hoping we can get Princess through high school and college without having to deal with any *issues.*"

"You mean without her getting pregnant," Vivian stated frankly.

Tai nodded. King squirmed. Talk about babies, so close to his near-miss with Tootie, made him uncomfortable. Not to mention thinking of his daughter getting pregnant, and more specifically the activity she'd engage in to make that happen. Talk of babies, in general, was not a good idea.

"Speaking of children," Derrick said as if reading his mind, "I know you two are happy that whole Tootie mess is behind you."

"God knows I am," King said. "Tai and I were prepared to deal with it, but thank God we don't have to." He quickly changed the subject. "You think Shaq's going to stay with the Heat?"

While the men talked, Tai thought. Whether they'd been prepared or not was a matter of opinion. Tai had never fully come to grips with the thought of another member joining her family, no matter the circumstances. She knew a child would bind Tootie and King forever, in one way or another. And she hadn't been prepared for that at all. Their last meeting was proof that no matter how much growing each of them had done, Tootie and Tai would never be friends. There had been too much bad blood for too long. And Tai was still not comfortable with how things ended, cut and dried, with no explanation for all the secrecy. The way Tootie had acted when she'd asked to see a picture . . . She still couldn't get that out of her mind, still couldn't totally close the door on the issue.

King had closed the door, slammed it shut, and locked it.

When they'd gone home that night, and she'd brought up Tootie's behavior, King had been blunt. "Let it go, Tai. You know how Tootie can be. We have no right to see a child that doesn't belong to us, and we don't need to see Tootie, ever again. I say good riddance. Let it go."

He'd refused to talk about the subject again, and after a couple days, she tried to take his advice and release it. But a nagging doubt persisted.

Dessert over, the four walked toward their suites. Passing through the lobby, Tai spotted the lounge. "Hey, Viv, you up for a cup of coffee?"

"If I drink a cup of coffee this time of night, I will be up!" She'd had a feeling since dinner that Tai needed some "sistah-girl time." "I'd love a cup of tea, though."

"Great." Tai turned to King and Derrick, who were walking slightly behind them. "You guys go on up. Viv and I are going to hang out a minute, maybe hit the clubs."

Vivian turned to Derrick. "Yeah, I might be able to pick up a boy toy."

Derrick responded confidently. "Baby, you know you've got all the 'toy' you can handle." He turned to King. "You ready to call it a night? Or do you want to walk off some of that soufflé?"

"Let's step," King replied, turning to the ladies. "We may be able to find a little something ourselves." Waving, they turned and walked toward the exit.

"Oh, hell," Tai said, turning to Vivian. "Just look at the idea you've planted. And with King, he really might mean it."

"Please. King isn't going to do anything that would jeopardize his future with you, especially not with Derrick in tow."

Vivian and Tai walked into the lounge area. Immediately, a waiter came over and took their orders for decaf coffee and tea.

Vivian started right in. "So, what's on your mind, Tai?"

Tai was equally straightforward. "I want to go to California next month."

"Just you? Really?" Vivian was excited. She and Tai had had a ball during the S.O.S. Summit, when Tai had stayed in Los Angeles the entire month of September. "You know you're always welcome at my house, girl. Just tell me when."

"I just have to get a few things together, collect all of my information. Maybe in two weeks?"

The waiter brought their drinks over, giving Vivian a moment to think. As soon as he left, she asked, "What kind of information?"

Tai took a sip of coffee, set it down, and looked Vivian straight in the eye. "I want to see Kelvin. I want to see Tootie's son for myself."

Vivian got ready to respond, but Tai stopped her. "That's the only way I'll be able to truly put this behind me."

Vivian took a sip of her tea but said nothing.

"I know it sounds crazy, and maybe it is. But Tootie has been a thorn in my side for over twenty years, half of my life. I want to make sure she's out for good. I want to know in my heart of hearts that her oldest son is not King's child."

"But what's to say you'll know that by looking at him? He could look like Tootie."

"As a woman who has four of his children, believe me, if King is anywhere in there, I'll see him."

Vivian couldn't argue with that, nor could she argue with Tai. "If this will make you feel better, make you able to go on with your life in peace, then come on up. I'll help you any way I can. Now, how do you propose to find a virtual stranger in some private school in tony Santa Barbara?"

Tai's voice dropped to a conspiratorial whisper. "Remember my computer instructor, Bryan?" Tai's taking a computer class to learn the Internet had grown into a full-fledged pursuit toward an associate degree.

Vivian remembered. "Is he still flirting with you?"

"Yes," Tai said, smiling. "But it's harmless. He knows I'm married. We've become friends."

"Uh-huh."

"Anyway, he's a whiz when it comes to anything to do with computers, the Internet, and digging up information. I just gave him the name, the city, and said he was in a private school. And that's how he found Kelvin."

"What? You've already tracked him down?" Vivian looked at her friend with new eyes. "Somebody's been busy."

"By the time I get back, Bryan should have everything that can possibly be found out about this child on-line. Now, what we do when we find him, well, we'll just have to flow."

Vivian shook her head. Tai was full of surprises. Clasping her teacup, Vivian sat back against the cushy lounge chair and eyed her best friend of over twenty years. "Game on," is all she could say.

34

No Place Like Home

Cy punched in the code and unlocked the door to his penthouse. Stepping aside so Hope could enter, he helped the limo driver bring the suitcases and bags inside. The driver thanked Cy for the generous tip and was gone.

"There's no place like home," Hope said as she walked into the living room and fell on the couch. "I thought we'd never get here."

"It was a long flight," Cy answered. He walked into the kitchen. "How about a glass of wine."

"Sounds perfect."

Cy and Hope loved travel, and planned to do lots of it. Their first stop as a married couple: visiting family. Because the engagement and marriage had been such a quick, whirlwind experience, there hadn't been a real chance to interact with their families. The idea to do just that began with an invitation from Hope's mother for "the city folk to come spend a week in the country." They traveled to Oklahoma, where Cy spent time getting to know Hope's parents. He and Hope stayed in a hotel near Mrs. Jones, and spent equal time with both her and Earl, Hope's father, who lived on the other side of town. Always the hostess, Hope's mother helped her put back on the five pounds she'd just lost with her southern-inspired peach cobblers and pound cakes. "Nothing wrong with some meat on the bones," her mother would say, giving everyone a second helping.

From Oklahoma they traveled to Washington, D.C., and Cy's family, going from down-home country to the capital's elite. Cy's father had spent almost thirty years in the military, retiring at sixty-five as a commissioned officer for the United States Army. He'd handled classified assignments for the government and was good friends with General Colin Powell. They'd served together in the military and Mr. Taylor often entertained the general and his wife, Alma, in the exclusive Chevy Chase neighborhood where the Taylor's lived.

Although they'd met briefly before the wedding, Hope was initially intimidated by Mrs. Taylor's refined style. That dissipated her first night in the home, as over coffee and pecan pie, Mrs. Taylor and Hope became better acquainted. Turns out, Mrs. Taylor was born and raised in Beaumont, Texas, and beneath the reserved demeanor was a warm, compassionate personality. They had more in common than Hope had initially thought, and with Hope's fears eased, she settled into a wonderful time in the nation's capital.

As tired as Hope was, she was already thinking about where they could go next. She thought about Frieda's wanting to visit Cy's island in the Caymans, and thought that might be a possibly exciting way to bring in the New Year.

"Here you go, darling. Thought I'd keep it light with Sauvignon Blanc."

Hope accepted the wine. "Thank you, baby."

Cy joined her on the couch. "It's good to be home, huh?"

"Yes," Hope replied. "Though I was just sitting here thinking of where we could go next."

Cy knew exactly where they'd be going and smiled at the thought of the luxurious Mexican vacation he'd planned as Hope's Christmas present, complete with a private plane for their transportation.

"I thought maybe we could return to the Caymans," Hope continued, "bring in the new year. Frieda's been bugging me ever since I told her how gorgeous it was down there. Maybe we could invite a small group and throw a party."

"No," Cy said simply. "I have other plans for the holidays."

"Oh? What are those?"

"Those are for me to know," Cy said, taking Hope's hand and pulling her off the couch, "and for you to find out."

Hope tried to pull away, but was no match for Cy's strength. "What plans, Cy?" she asked, laughing. She allowed Cy to lead her into their massive master suite.

"All I can tell you is this: make no plans for the holidays. They're taken care of." Cy reached for Hope's dress and began pulling it over her head. "And now," he said, as he continued to undress her, "I'm getting ready to take care of something else."

35

Good Night, Theodore

"Lastly," Millicent announced, handing out glossy pieces of paper, "these are the best ten rings I found on-line, for the commitment ceremony, in terms of quality, style, and price. I have a couple favorites, but I'd like us to decide as a group which one is best for our girls."

Since working on the Divine Daughters Celebration with the women's fellowship, Open Arms had gone from being "the" church, to "my" church in Millicent's mind, and the young women participating, "her girls." She embraced the undertaking with passion, reminded once again of how fulfilling working on "God projects" could be. They were still almost four months away from the early December celebration, but Millicent had already finalized most of the details, including location, limousine company, caterer, and band for the evening program. An upcoming project for the girls would be writing, in their own words, what commitment meant to them, and the commitment they planned to verbalize to God. Then Millicent would have each one printed with gold-embossed ink on linen paper and framed, a memento to each participant of what the night meant. She and Leah planned to visit day spas to find the perfect one for the girls' massages, scented

steam baths, facials, manicures, and pedicures. This was going
to be a formal, black tie event. Millicent wanted each girl to
feel like Cinderella invited to the ball.

"They're all so beautiful," Leah exclaimed. "How can we
make a choice?"

"What about choosing a different one for each girl?"
Debbi asked.

"I thought of that," Millicent said. "But in the end, I think
it best that they're all alike. That way there's no friction with
one girl thinking another girl's ring is prettier or one wishing
they had another, and so on."

"You're right," Leah agreed. "With teenaged girls, we definitely need to keep the uniformity." She pointed to a ring at
the top of the page. "This one is truly beautiful. I like the simple design and the flowers inscribed around the band."

Millicent smiled. That ring had been one of her favorites as
well.

"I like this one," someone else said, pointing to a shiny gold
band outlined with a rope design and inlaid with small diamonds.

"I must say you ladies have great taste," Millicent said,
laughing. "Those are my two personal favorites."

"How should we choose?" one of the ladies asked.

"As you can see, the rings are numbered," Millicent answered. "I suggest we write the number of our favorite ring
down, and the one with the most votes wins."

"That's easy enough," Leah said. "Everybody agree?" Nods
and affirmative responses followed. Leah went into the dining
room and came back with blank pieces of paper and a box.
"Okay, ladies, write down your choice and place them in this
box. Millicent, you can tally 'em up."

An hour later, the ladies had made their choice—the ring
with diamond inlay—approved Millicent's program outline,
and finished off Leah's blueberry coffee cake. Millicent, as
usual, was the last to leave.

"Thank you for asking me to do this project, Leah," Millicent said. "It has given me back something that was sorely missing, working in the church and especially with you wonderful ladies. I really appreciate it."

"You're welcome. But we're the ones blessed. We appreciate you more than we can say. I've always enjoyed church work, too, and imagine you were pretty active back in Portland."

"No, the church I attended in Portland was very small." Millicent hesitated about clarifying her LA connection. "I was very active in a church in Los Angeles."

"You *lived* in LA before? I thought you'd just gone there to organize the summit meeting."

As close as Millicent and Leah had become, she didn't want to say too much. One never knew who knew whom, and if possible, Millicent wanted to keep her debacle a secret forever. "Oh, it was a while ago."

"Well, you're here now, and that's all that matters." Then, changing the subject, "How is it a beautiful, intelligent woman such as yourself is still single? Answer me that one!"

I'd rather not. "I guess everything happens in God's perfect timing," she answered diplomatically.

"No boyfriends, no prospects, no broken hearts scattered along the West Coast?"

Millicent laughed, but didn't answer. Actually something interesting was happening. It was why she was anxious to return home and check her e-mail. A few men had answered her post on the dating Web site and one in particular, Theodore, had caught her interest. They'd e-mailed back and forth a few times and had finally decided to exchange pics and telephone numbers. She'd sent hers that morning before leaving. He'd promised to send his later. It should be there when she got home.

"Oh, goodness, I've got to run," Millicent said.

Leah raised her eyebrows. It was unusual for Millicent to

take off so quickly. Normally they'd walk, chat, or catch a Life-time movie if an interesting one was on.

"I promised a friend on the East Coast I'd call before it got too late." That wasn't a lie. Millicent had told Alison about her foray into the Internet world and had promised to keep her posted. That would be her first call after she saw Theodore's picture, finding out what her best friend thought.

Millicent thought about Theodore on the drive home. She liked him. He'd found it refreshing that she didn't demand a picture immediately; they'd agreed to get to know each other a bit first. Looks, they both agreed, were often misleading. And physical attraction did not a long-term relationship make. As that was what they both were looking for, they'd decided to find out more about each other's personalities, dreams, and plans for the future before exchanging pictures and telephone numbers.

That was two weeks ago. In that time, they'd e-mailed back and forth almost every night. That had been another different, interesting thing. Theodore had wanted to e-mail for a short while before exchanging phone numbers. He felt there was something about the written word, actually seeing what you're thinking before pushing "send." Millicent preferred the tele-phone, but had gone along with Theodore's preference since he'd gone along with hers regarding the picture exchange. She'd actually gotten into it, looking forward to reading and responding to his witty letters. She'd never exchanged love let-ters or notes, so not only was it different, but also added to the uniqueness of the budding relationship.

So far, she knew that Theodore was intelligent, witty, thoughtful, and unassuming. He was forty-eight, had two chil-dren from a previous marriage, lived in San Diego, and was a motivational speaker. He'd not been in a relationship for a while, and was looking for a long-term commitment that would lead to marriage. He liked all things connected to the ocean including water skiing, snorkeling, and cruising along the coast in his sailboat.

Instead of dimming her desire, meeting Theodore had only made Millicent that much more excited to see Cy. Now she felt she could truly see him again without having her heart break. *Then why do you have to see him at all?* Millicent sometimes despised the good angel on her shoulder. "I don't know why," she said aloud. She only knew that she did, that for whatever insane reason, she had to see Cy again.

Ten minutes later, Millicent pulled into her garage. She unlocked her door, scanned her mail, then went to the fridge for a diet cola. Humming, she turned on her computer. The first item in her outlook was a response from Theodore. "Here I Am!" was in the subject line. She clicked on his mail.

> *Well now, God is truly amazing. You are beautiful, just like the woman for whom I've prayed. Thanks for your number. I'll call you tonight. I'm sure we'll have a very interesting conversation. Theodore.*

Millicent's heart fluttered as she read Theodore's e-mail. Feeling a bit like a schoolgirl, she clicked on the attachment with his picture. They'd not described themselves at all, and Millicent was curious how he would look. Would his hair be blond, brown, black? What about his eyes? How was he built? For some reason, she'd pictured him with dark brown hair, brown eyes, and tall. In seconds, she'd see how close her imagination was to the real thing.

The picture downloaded, and for some reason was off-center. Millicent saw only trees, and had to scroll down to see the person standing in a grassy, mountainous area that looked to be northern California. When the picture of her secret correspondent of the past two weeks hit the screen, Millicent gasped. She could *not* believe it. Staring back at her were sparkling blue eyes in a familiar face, the face that belonged to her pastor, Jack Kirtz.

"No! This can't be happening, I cannot *believe* this!" Millicent was excited and angry and embarrassed all at once. She thought back to every word of every e-mail they'd exchanged: the subtle flirtations, the double entendres, the joking comments about preferred positions and whether nighty or naked sleep was preferred. She'd told him she slept nude. She'd told Pastor Jack Kirtz she slept nude!

"Oh my God," Millicent said, reaching for her phone. She sure hoped Alison answered, because she wanted someone to tell her she was dreaming, and to wake her up. As she reached for the phone, it rang. Private call.

"Hello?"

"Millicent, did you get my picture?"

Oh-my-God.

"Millicent, I know you're there. Please, don't hang up."

Millicent was flabbergasted. Hanging up is *exactly* what she had in mind. "You said your name was Theodore!"

"Yes, probably for the same reason you said yours was Rose. My legal name is Theodore Jackson Kirtz, but I've been called Jack since childhood. Is Rose your middle name?"

Millicent couldn't believe Pastor Jack was talking in a normal, conversational tone as if nothing was out of the ordinary.

"Well, is it?"

"Is what?" she said, exasperated.

"Rose, is it your middle name?"

"Yes, it is but, but, oh God, I'm so embarrassed. I cannot believe this."

"Millicent, please, don't be embarrassed. I think this is great, amazing even. It's like Providence, Divine Order. There can be no other way to look at it."

"But I never would have said—"

"Which is probably the exact reason why things unfolded

the way they did. You would never have come from behind that wall you construct where I'm concerned, the wall that allows for nothing other than strict, professional, church business."

"That's not true." It was true. "We've gone to lunch, we talk at the gym."

"You never would have gone to lunch with me had you not wanted to talk about the celebration." Jack paused. "Millicent, I don't know what's happened in your past, or what you're afraid will happen here, but I'm a really simple guy. I'm human, with the same needs and desires as any other man on the planet. I want love, companionship, a confidante, best friend, nothing out of the ordinary. We're both adults here. You liked me when you didn't know who I was. Why can't you continue liking me now that you do?"

"Because I can't. I have a rule to not become involved with anyone at church or on the job."

Jack was silent. He'd had that rule, too, until he saw Millicent. There had to be a reason she was being so adamant. However, he felt it best to tread lightly.

"But, why not? I think those are perfect places to meet people. We usually spend so much time there. There's already common goals, common beliefs.

"Tell me something. If I weren't the pastor of Open Arms, or you weren't a member, would you go out with me?"

Millicent knew the answer was yes. She enjoyed Theodore, now Jack, and the lively e-mails they'd exchanged. She'd looked forward to the phone call until the moment her pastor's face appeared on the screen. But it was too much, it was too complicated. Although it was completely different and irrational to think it similar, it felt too much like she and Cy. She knew it didn't make sense, but that's how she felt.

"Well, would you?"

"Look, Pastor Jack—"

"Oh boy, there's the wall. I'm 'Pastor' again."

"Look, Jack, there's a lot about me you don't know. A lot

of . . . things have happened to make me think as I do. I just think it best to not pursue this. I've just become happy again for the first time in a long time, with the church, with the women's fellowship. I don't want to do anything to jeopardize that."

"And you think going out with the leader of those sources of your happiness will do that?"

"What will people say?"

"For starters, who cares? But if it matters, we can be discreet, at least until we find out if this is something serious or not. But I think we owe it to ourselves to just see what could possibly happen here. That won't cost you or me anything. Dinner, a movie, walks, just simple things, to talk and find out if the connection we made via the e-mails is something that can be sustained and built upon in real life.

"I'll be honest, Millicent. I've been attracted to you from the moment I saw you on the beach. And look at all the things that happened, seemingly coincidental, that led up to this moment. First, the beach. Is it a place you go often?"

"No, that was the first time." Come to think of it, Millicent had never gone back to that spot again.

"And then the gym, and us both being members there. And your deciding to accept my invitation and visit Open Arms."

"Actually, uh, that wasn't planned either."

"What do you mean?"

Millicent told Jack what had happened, how she'd been shopping for furniture when she heard the harpist play.

"All the more reason," Jack implored. "It would be ludicrous not to give this a shot. I'm sure you've heard the story about the man who was drowning and prayed for God to save him. A huge log floated by but the man didn't grab it, wanted to show his faith by waiting on God. Then a rowboat went by and the occupant tried to help the man, but the man shouted he was waiting on God. Finally, a large ship threw out a life buoy for the man to grab, so they could pull him aboard. Again, the man declined, so he could receive a miracle. He didn't, he died.

"When he got to heaven he searched God out, perplexed at how God could not answer the prayer of someone so faithful in tithing, in praying, in serving his fellow man. I'm sure you know the story. God tried to answer his prayer, and was turned down, three times.

"Maybe, like me, it's been your prayer to meet someone kind, sincere, with the same values, the same beliefs, as you. Someone who loves God, but isn't so holy they can't let their hair down and have a good time. Who could be romantic and sensual . . ." Jack thought of how he'd imagined Millicent, sleeping in the nude. "I think that might be you and me."

Millicent remained silent. There wasn't one thing Jack had said that wasn't true.

"Can we at least discuss it over coffee? If you feel the same afterward, I'll act like this never happened. I'll respect your wishes for a professional, platonic relationship, and move on."

Millicent's thoughts were divided. A part of her wanted to reach out to Jack, to take him up on his offer. He was the first man who'd interested her since Cy, and she was more than ready to get that part of her life going again. On the other hand, she was afraid to get involved with Jack because he was her pastor. What would that mean? Would they remain celibate? Millicent had no intentions of doing that. And what about Susan? It hadn't been that long since his wife died. Two years, but people grieved differently. If he wanted to wait until marriage to have sex, that might be years from now.

"Hey, Millicent Rose, do you want to think about it?"

No one, except her mother, ever called her Millicent Rose. And no one had ever done so, so sweetly. "Yes, let me think about it."

"Good. That's a start. Is it okay to call you in say, a week or so?"

"Okay."

Jack let out a breath. It wasn't what he'd hoped for, but it was enough, for now. He spoke to her softly. "Good night, Rose."

In spite of her fears, Millicent smiled. "Good night, Theodore."

36

One Big Mess

"Maybe we'll see Oprah while we're there." Tai ignored her scattered thoughts by imagining the chance to meet her favorite celebrity. "How far did you say it was again?"

Two months had passed before Tai could get away to California. The October breeze felt good; somehow, California air always seemed to feel better than Kansas.

"Oh, we should be there in about an hour," Vivian replied. "Montecito is about ninety minutes from LA. But remember, we're going to Oxnard first. Maybe afterward, we'll comb the neighborhoods and see if we can spot Oprah and Stedman out for a stroll."

"Girl, that would be so much fun, even better if it were Oprah and Gayle. They've been best friends longer than we have. I'd invite myself over to see that beautiful garden she has in her backyard that is the size of Connecticut, ask her if she wouldn't mind me having a spot of tea."

"Please, Tai, you'd barely be able to ask for an autograph."

"You're probably right." Tai laughed, but it was empty. Her real thoughts smoldered just beneath their light banter. An hour to Oxnard, where Tootie's son worked. An hour to know for sure that Kelvin was not King's child, so she could get on with her life. It wasn't lost on her that their names both began with K. Was that coincidence? Or a mother's veiled attempt to form some sort of connection?

In the time since Tootie's denial that Kelvin was King's son, Tai, with her teacher Bryan's help, had become an ace detective. She didn't know how he did it, but Bryan quickly located Kelvin through the Internet. It was amazing what one could find with just a name and general location. The only thing he hadn't been able to find was a photograph.

Finding out that the boy worked, and where, had been Tai's stroke of genius. She'd gotten the idea one day to call the school he attended, Laguna Blanca, pretend to be Tootie, and see what kind of information she could get. It had taken three calls. On the first two, she'd gotten a stern, no-nonsense woman who'd asked Tai as many questions as Tai had wanted to ask her! Tai had acted like the connection messed up. "Hello? Are you still there? I can't hear you. Let me call back." She didn't.

The second time the same woman answered and Tai hung up. The third time was the charm. The young woman who answered, probably a student working part-time, had been friendly, bubbly and very informative about her friend Kelvin. Tai had felt a bit guilty about how excited the girl had been over meeting "Kelvin's mom." So much so, that she had to think quick to make sure her cover wasn't blown. "Don't tell Kelvin I've called. He hates to think I'm checking up on him but, well, you know how mothers worry." The girl had agreed, in a conspiratorial whisper, to not divulge a thing. *Good girl*.

But that's when she'd found out Kelvin worked part-time at a Best Buy about forty-five minutes from the school. "You know how your son likes his electronic gadgets," the girl had said. Tai had no idea, but thought of how King was always the first to buy any new electronic gizmo that came out. Hmm.

"A penny for your thoughts." Vivian noticed Tai had been quiet for some time.

"I can't believe I'm actually going to do this. It was one thing being at home and planning it. But now that I'm here . . ."

"You know, I'm uncomfortable, too. I think this is the first time I haven't been totally honest with Derrick about what I'm doing."

"I appreciate it, Viv. But you know how close Derrick and King are. I just don't want to take the chance of King finding out I'm doing this. He'd be pissed, and that's putting it lightly. He can't understand why I can't just let it go, count my blessings. Sometimes, I don't understand either."

"It's not always clear what motivates us. But listen, here's another way to look at it. All we're doing is going shopping. You're going to buy some CDs, and I'm going to get a new organizer. Yes, you could have gone to the Best Buy in Kansas City and I could have gone to the one in LA, but we both needed a breath of fresh air. All we're doing is going shopping."

Tai rolled her eyes. "Leave it to your eternally optimistic ass to find a spin like that to put on it. Only you!"

"What, it's true isn't it? I told Derrick we were going shopping. Did I lie?"

"Not as long as we buy something."

Tai had told King she was visiting Vivian so they could better plan the second S.O.S. Summit. That was partly true. They did plan on talking about the summit during the trip. In actuality, they probably wouldn't get past the general outline stage. But having something to take their minds off whatever they found in the electronics department was probably a good idea.

King had been happy to hear about the trip, had encouraged her to go. Mama Max agreed to help watch the kids along with the twin's babysitter. Both hoped this meant Tai had moved on from the whole "Tootie and child" scenario. Tai had been uptight since the meeting with Tootie and Hans. Hearing her talk about the S.O.S. Summit was a sign to both of them that maybe Tai was over the ordeal.

"You know, Tai," Vivian began, "it still isn't too late if you're having second thoughts about this. There's nothing saying we have to go through with finding Kelvin. You can never guess how something like this might affect you. What if we get there and you believe he is King's son? Are you really ready for those consequences?"

This wasn't the first time Vivian had asked the question. Tai's answer was the same as when Viv had asked the night before. "As ready as I'll ever be."

They passed a sign indicating Oxnard was ten miles away. "What's the address again?" Vivian asked.

Tai gave it to her and Vivian spoke it into her Navigator system. The Best Buy exit was coming up very soon.

"You want to know something interesting?" Tai asked.

"What?"

"If it hadn't been for King's affair with April last year, I don't think I'd be strong enough to do this."

"Hmm."

"It's true. The strength I found getting through that situation is amazing. I found *me* again, found my power. And King and I found the strength of our marriage again. Found the love that brought us together in the first place. That's why I know I can handle this. If Kelvin is King's son, we'll just have to deal with it. We'll take it one day at a time, one situation at a time, and do whatever's best for all involved."

"How do you think King will react if it's true?"

"First, he'll go off because I didn't tell him I was doing this. But I know King. He would have tried to talk me out of it, raised hell about my coming out here. Besides, the boy may look nothing like King. That's my prayer; and if God hears and answers me, no harm done. I will have eased my mind, kept King's blood pressure down, and everybody will be happy."

The women were quiet as Vivian followed the Navigator instructions and exited the freeway. Vivian thought about Tai and all her friend had gone through with King. She continually counted her blessings. How had it ended up she got someone like Derrick, someone who'd been faithful to her from day one of their marriage? She was aware of how fortunate she was and thanked God every day. Over fifteen years, and though they'd had their share of women trying to cause disruptions, women like Robin, the Montgomery marriage and the love in their relationship had remained strong. Their children were healthy, the church was thriving, all was well. *God, you are so good to me . . . thank you.*

Vivian turned into the Best Buy parking lot. Although it was in the middle of the day, in the middle of the week, it was full. She pulled into a space and turned off the engine. No one moved.

"Well," Vivian said, turning to Tai. "This is it, girl."

Tai took a deep breath. "Let's do this." She grabbed her purse and opened the door.

Vivian opened her door as well. *God, help us.* She caught up with Tai, slowly walking toward the store's entrance.

"We've been through some things, you and I," Tai said.

Vivian grabbed Tai's hand. "God's got your back, and so do I. You know that, right?"

Tai stopped and looked at her friend. "If I know nothing else, I know that."

"Well, then," Vivian said, starting toward the store. "Let's do this."

"Good afternoon, welcome to Best Buy." The greeter smiled and handed Vivian and Tai each a sales paper as they walked inside. Vivian was nervous. What in the world were they doing? And how would she help her friend if the boy was King's spitting image? She prayed silently for the strength to help her friend. . . . *Yea, though I walk through the valley of the shadow of death, I will fear no evil, for God is with me. . . .*

"Where should we start?" Vivian asked Tai.

"Why don't we start at the end, over there by appliances, and work our way down each aisle."

"That sounds good. But wait? Didn't his friend say he was into electronics? Let's start on this side, by the computers and televisions, work our way from there."

"Okay."

The women walked over to the far right wall and started browsing the televisions there, trying to look like casual customers. Within minutes, a cheery voice sounded behind them.

"Hello ladies, looking for a new television set today? We've got some great ones on sale, and some new plasma screens in the back."

"No thank you, we're just looking. We'll let you know if we need help." Tai was polite, but firm.

"No problem, ladies. My name is Jeff. Just let me know if you need me."

Vivian looked beyond Jeff to a group of workers congregated in the back of the store, near the plasma screens he'd pointed out. One was a tall, gangly, Black boy, his back to them.

"Hey, Tai," Vivian said after the store employee had walked away. "See that group of workers? Let's walk that way."

Tai nodded, and they started walking a few feet behind Jeff, who had headed in the same direction. They tried to stay casual, but both of their hearts were beating, hard. The young Black man, obviously telling a story, was the center of attention. He was gesturing with his arms, faking a jump shot, as the boys around him laughed. Tai grabbed Vivian's arm, signaling her to walk along the far aisle. They'd go to the end of the store and walk back down the aisle where the group was standing. That way, they'd be able to see his face without looking obvious.

"Ooh, girl, my heart is beating fast," Vivian finally admitted.

"Mine, too." Tai laughed nervously. "We're crazy as hell, acting like we're CSI California or something."

"Shhh . . . Okay, he's around this corner. You go first."

"No, you go." Tai had stopped and pulled Vivian in front of her.

They were whispering, acting like kids. Vivian looked at

Tai, a smirk on her face. "You old scaredy-cat," she said, boldly stepping into the aisle. "He probably isn't even going to . . ."

The rest of the words died on her lips as the boy looked up. Tai, just steps behind her, stopped, too. Kelvin had obviously finished his story and had broken away from the group. He was standing in the aisle repositioning product, not fifteen feet in front of them. He looked up as they turned the corner: shiny brown eyes, a smile revealing straight white teeth, a whisper of a mustache.

"Good afternoon. Can I help you find something today?"

Tai couldn't move. Vivian couldn't breathe. He'd already helped them, more than he knew. They'd found something all right, found just what they were looking for. The boy's face told the story. It couldn't have been any clearer, the smooth brown skin, sharp brow, prominent cheekbones. He looked just like his father.

Kelvin, Tootie's son, was the spitting image of his preacher dad, Derrick Anthony Montgomery.

"Vivian, you okay? Here, drink some water."

Tai grabbed her friend's water bottle, uncapped it, and handed it to her. Vivian was sitting perfectly still. She hadn't moved, had barely blinked since getting back in the car. Tai had immediately taken over inside the store. She'd grabbed Vivian's hand, mumbled something to Kelvin about forgetting her wallet in the car, and practically dragged a still-staring, shell-shocked Vivian out of the building.

In a thousand years, neither woman had expected this turn of events. How could the child look so much like Derrick? It was impossible that he'd fathered Tootie's child. Wasn't it? Vivian was aware that Derrick knew Tootie, that they'd all known each other since their high school days in Kansas. But she'd never, ever dreamed there'd been something sexual between them.

Vivian tried processing what couldn't be denied. Their features were so much alike: the eyes, nose, mouth. His forehead was a bit different, and where Derrick didn't have a dimple, Kelvin did. The head shape was slightly different but . . . that boy looked like her husband, resembled her son. *Kelvin, Derrick's son?* It was too much. It was unreal. Where before she'd been concerned for Tai, it was now *her* life that was shattered, *her* family that looked about to enter mass turmoil, *her* future that suddenly looked unpredictable. The prayers she'd prayed for Tai, fearing no evil because God was there . . . Ha! She'd had no idea how much she'd need God. Not for Tai, for herself.

"What am I going to do?" she asked Tai, hurt and confusion surrounding every word. The shock started wearing off, replaced by anger. "I can't believe it. I can't believe Derrick would do something like this to me, to our family! All this time, he's said he was faithful, and I believed him!"

"Slow down, Viv. I know you're upset, but let's think this out, okay? Remember, Mama Max said Kelvin was sixteen. That would mean he was conceived before you and Derrick were married, maybe even before you met."

"But in all these years and all the talk about Tootie, Derrick never mentioned he'd slept with her . . . not once!"

"And why would he? What good would that have done? Has he told you about the other women he slept with before you were married, or have you shared with him your former lovers?"

They'd talked generally about their premarriage relationships, but nothing specific. It hadn't seemed necessary; they'd always been so in love.

"This is different," Vivian said, tears starting to stream silently down her face. "This is somebody who's in our life *now.*"

Until five minutes ago, she was only in my life, Tai thought, but didn't verbalize. Sometimes silence was golden; this was one of those times. "What do you want to do?" she asked, after a moment's pause.

Vivian wiped her eyes, reached for a tissue, and blew her nose. "I don't know," she said softly, staring off into the distance, trying to see the perfect life she'd left in the parking lot. "I really don't know." New tears flowed.

"I'm so sorry, Viv. This is all my fault. I just had to know about Kelvin, just had to know the truth." She rubbed Vivian's shoulders as Vivian sat with her head bowed. "I'm so sorry."

"This isn't your fault," Vivian said. She wiped her eyes once more, straightened her shoulders, took a deep breath, and started the engine. "It's Derrick's fault. And Tootie's. And now we've got one, big mess."

Tai was silent, thinking back to the meeting with Tootie. Now the strange behavior made sense. Why she'd been so close-mouthed, why she hadn't wanted to show a picture. She knew how close King and Derrick were, knew that they would have known immediately. So she'd told the basic truth. King was not Kelvin's father. It's what she hadn't said that was today's revelation.

"Has King ever mentioned anything that would suggest Derrick and Tootie had been together?" Vivian asked.

Tai gave Vivian a look. "Girl, King and I don't talk too much about Tootie, trust."

"I want so much to hold out for the small chance that Kelvin is not Derrick's son. But he looks just like him . . . like Derrick spit him out. It's not fair!" Vivian screamed, hitting the steering wheel with her hand. "We've tried to live a good life, follow the word, do what's right. First, Robin brings her crazy ass into town, and now this. What is the devil going to try and throw at us next?" She looked at Tai for answers that Tai didn't have.

The normally calm, cool, and collected Vivian Elise continued to rant. Tai completely understood. Now, it was her turn to soothe a troubled friend. "God won't put on you more than you can bear, Vivian. I can understand how hard this is for you right now. But fear not. Trust God."

Vivian's heart clutched as she heard the door open. She sat in the den, alone, curtains drawn. D-2 and Elisia had gone shopping with Aunt Tai, in Vivian's car. Tai had taken her packed things and made reservations to spend the night in a nearby hotel. She would wait there, with the kids, until Vivian let her know the coast was clear to bring them home.

"Hey, baby," Derrick asked, kissing Vivian on the forehead. "I called you earlier, but you didn't answer. Did you leave your phone on silent again?" When Vivian didn't respond, Derrick sat down beside her. "Is something wrong, Vivian? What are you doing sitting here in the dark?"

Vivian turned to face her husband. "I need to ask you something, and I need a straight answer. I'll explain why in a minute, but I need you to answer a question for me, honestly. Deal?"

Derrick hadn't seen Vivian this serious in a long time. But there was nothing he wouldn't share with his wife. His answer was immediate. "Sure baby, deal."

Vivian took a deep breath. "Did you ever sleep with Tootie?"

"Whoa," Derrick said, clearly taken aback. "Baby, where is this coming from?"

"I'll explain in a moment. Just answer me. Did you ever have sex with Tootie Janeé Smith? Yes or no?"

Vivian barely breathed as she awaited the answer. Far away from Oxnard and the brown-eyed boy in the Best Buy store, she'd been able to be more rational. There were thousands, millions of boys that could resemble Derrick, she'd reasoned. How many brown-skinned boys had brown eyes? And what was so unusual about full lips and prominent cheekbones on a

Black man? Those were common traits. She'd convinced herself that her initial reaction had been rash; that she'd jumped to conclusions, let her imagination work overtime. She could barely remember what the boy looked like now, and convinced herself that she'd gone overboard in her assumptions. She couldn't believe she was being so silly. Why was she tripping, and involving Derrick as well? She needed to start the conversation over, and not assume she knew something she didn't.

"Yes."

Wait. Did I just hear Derrick say yes? "Excuse me?" Derrick had answered softly. Maybe Vivian had misunderstood.

"Yes, Vivian," Derrick said clearly. "I slept with Tootie. Half the basketball team slept with Tootie. But, baby, why are you asking me this? It was a long time ago, before I met you."

"Oh, baby," Vivian murmured. She felt like a weight was crushing down on her chest, making it difficult to breathe.

She grabbed Derrick's hand. "Derrick, I have some news. I hope I'm wrong, but everything in me is saying I'm not. And this news is going to affect everyone, and everything, in our lives."

Derrick's mind was spinning. What news could Vivian possibly have about Tootie that had anything to do with them? He thought the saga with Tootie was over. Now that King and Tai knew Tootie's boy was not theirs, he thought the book was closed. What did Vivian know? Only one way to find out. "Talk to me, baby," he said.

Vivian did just that. She talked to him, told him everything: the real reason for Tai's visit, how Tai had researched and found information on Tootie's son. How they'd gone to Oxnard to find him, and did, in the Best Buy store. And how the boy was Derrick's spitting image.

"What? Oh, hell no." Derrick jumped up from the couch. "Baby, baby, look. I know you're upset and I'm sure the boy must have bore a strong resemblance to me for you to react like this, but please, are you kidding me? You cannot be serious. There's no way the child can be mine."

"So you're telling me you used a condom every time you guys screwed?"

"No, but—"

"Then how can you be absolutely positive the child isn't yours? You know I'm pretty levelheaded, Derrick. I'm not prone to go off on ridiculous tangents. And I don't want this to be true any more than you do, believe me. But I can't deny what my eyes saw, and I'm telling you, the boy looks like an older version of D-2, and a younger version of you."

Derrick looked at her with skeptical eyes.

"You don't believe me?"

"I'm sure you saw what you saw, but no, baby, I don't believe the boy is mine."

"Great, perfect. Let's go back to the store. I want you to see for yourself."

"You want us to get out right now, in rush-hour traffic, to Oxnard?"

"I want you to see what I saw; I want you to tell me I'm tripping. Believe me, I want to be wrong."

"Vivian, you know tonight is Bible study."

"Yeah, well, tonight we need to study something else. This is important to me, Derrick. Call Cy or one of the other associate ministers. I need you to do this for me."

Derrick stared at Vivian for a moment. Vivian stared back. "Okay," he nodded. "Let me change my clothes. You're right, it's probably best to nip this madness in the bud right now."

He walked slowly out of the room, turning once to look at Vivian. She got up, put on her shoes, grabbed her purse, and walked to the doorway. She called Tai, told her the plans, and asked if she could keep the kids for the night.

"Of course, Vivian. Don't worry about them, we'll be fine.

You will, too. I know it doesn't look like it right now, but you'll be fine, too."

It was time to go back to Oxnard. Maybe Derrick was right. Maybe it was totally preposterous to think that Kelvin was his son. But Derrick had confirmed that he had slept with Tootie. So, preposterous? Maybe. Possible? Yes.

37

Wait on God

Stacy was happy and frustrated at the same time. Happy that she and Darius were dating. Frustrated that since that explosive first night, the dating had been strictly platonic.

His reasons had been noble enough, that he wanted to go slow, take his time. He reminded her he'd been married before and was cautious when it came to relationships. Yet he really liked her, respected her. He admitted that he'd had his eye on her, too, and that he was glad they were taking things to a new level. Then he'd mentioned the "C" word. He'd told her he was celibate.

Stacy felt as if she was walking a tightwire. On one hand, she wanted to take things one day at a time, too, not appear overanxious. It had taken her a long time to get to first base. She didn't want to scare him off the field before she'd had a chance to hit a home run. Or get another real good look at his bat anyway.

On the other hand, they were both grown, and grown people had needs. Neither of them was a virgin, and she was on the pill. She didn't see any problem with getting a little bit every now and then, especially since she'd seen what she'd be getting. They'd barely been dating a month, but Stacy had been patient for more than two years. She'd go along with his plan for a little while, but eventually, he'd have to go along with hers. She wanted to be with Darius in every way, and every moment they spent together intensified this desire. Whether it was a movie, or dinner, or sitting at home playing that murderous video game, Darius exuded the sexual energy Stacy craved. *Give it a rest, Stacy!* She stood up abruptly, deciding to find something else to occupy her mind. She was getting wet just thinking about Darius's thickly built manhood.

Stacy gathered up the notes on the youth program she'd been working on with Tanya and headed over to the church. She didn't even try and fool herself into thinking she wasn't going over there with the hopes of running into Darius. He'd had to travel with Pastor Derrick unexpectedly the week before and wasn't at church on Sunday. It had only been a few days since she'd seen him, but it felt much longer.

As usual, there were dozens of cars in the office parking lot. The staff at Kingdom Citizens numbered almost fifty, with a host of volunteers in and out everyday as well. Upon entering the lot, Stacy looked around for Darius's car, but didn't see it. She pulled into the closest available space, by a yellow MG.

Hope, who'd met Cy at the church for lunch, was just coming out. "Hey, Stacy!"

"Hey, Hope. Long time no see."

Stacy and Hope had met at one of the Montgomery summer dinners. They'd exchanged numbers and agreed to keep in touch, but Hope and Cy left town shortly afterward. This was the first Hope had seen Stacy since then.

"I know, and I'm sorry for not calling. Cy and I went out of town and stayed longer than expected."

"Oh? Where'd you go?"

"Visiting family; Oklahoma, D.C."

"You are one blessed sistah. You've got a few of the women

seeing green in this place. Do you know how many had their sights set on Mr. Taylor?"

"I can imagine, and have felt more than a couple daggers at my back. It's all God though. I'd have been the last one to believe Cy would be my husband."

"How did you do it? How did you get him to commit?" Stacy frowned, looked toward the church. "Men are so skittish when it comes to a real relationship."

"Hmm, sounds like this is coming from personal experience. Anybody I know?"

"Actually, yes." While Stacy had talked to Tanya about Darius, there was only so much one could discuss with a man's sister. Hope was married, so she was no threat to Stacy. She was new to the church and with all the jealousy, a bit isolated; little chance of Stacy's business getting out. Not that she didn't want *everybody* to know that she and Darius had a thing going—she did. It would be good to get another woman's perspective. Hope seemed like good people. She liked her.

"It's Darius," she said after a thoughtful pause.

Hope hid her shock. *Darius? Does she know he's gay?* "Darius Crenshaw?"

"Yes, our music director. Why are you looking so surprised?"

Hope tried to change her expression. Obviously she hadn't hid her feelings well enough. "I just didn't know he was dating anyone, that's all."

"We just started going out actually, about a month ago. But I've liked him for a long time and believe he's the man for me. He really likes me, too, but wants to go slow, too slow. It's driving me crazy."

Hope didn't know what to think. There were a zillion questions running through her mind. Did Stacy know about Darius's past, or his present, for that matter? Were they having sex? Were they using protection? Was he still having sex with the man Frieda caught him with that night? Did that man know about Stacy?

"Believe me, I know *exactly* what you're talking about. I was celibate for two years before marrying Cy, and there were times I thought I'd lose my mind if God didn't send me my husband. But if I can give you some advice, some you probably don't want to hear . . . Wait on God. Pray about this situation, ask God about Darius. And don't rush things, Stacy. Everything will happen the way it's supposed to, in God's perfect timing."

"You're right; I don't want to hear that. And between you and me, I'm not trying to be celibate for two more months, let alone two years. Girl, let me get in this church. You've got me talking crazy. I barely know you and I'm telling you all my business. See how not getting any is clouding up my mind?"

"Just don't let it cloud your judgment," Hope said in what she hoped was a lighthearted tone. She pulled out a card and gave Stacy her number again. "Call me this week, okay? I could use more friends up here and I really want us to do lunch or something soon. And don't worry about your business; your story's safe with me." She opened her car door. "Remember what I said, now. Don't do anything crazy."

"Don't worry. Darius seems to be making sure of that."

"Good for Darius. That shows he's a true man of God. You'll appreciate that if things get serious. Call me."

Stacy watched Hope drive away before turning toward the church offices. It just may be that in Hope, she'd found a perfect confidante.

"Ooh, give me that big dick, baby. Give it to me, hard, yes, just like that. Ahhhh."

Bo growled. Darius moaned. Both men lay exhausted after intense orgasms. Darius gave Bo a quick kiss, rolled on his back, and looked at the ceiling.

Bo turned to face him. "That bitch ain't *ever* gonna be able to give you what I just did."

"I told you about calling her that. Her name is Stacy."

"Well, Stacy needs to stay the hell on away from you." He reached over and massaged Darius's limp penis. "This will always be mine. Does she know that?"

"What she knows is that I'm celibate. I told you how I was gonna handle it. Why do you keep bringing her up?" Darius jumped out of bed and headed for the shower. "Stop being so insecure."

Bo jumped up behind him, knew he'd crossed the line. "I'm sorry, baby," he said, following Darius into the bathroom and turning on the water for him. "I just know you're going to see her tonight, and you're going to ask her out to keep up this damn charade, and I'm jealous. I just can't help it.

"That's my dick. I don't want anybody else touching it. Especially some funky old stank pussy. It would probably shrivel up like beef jerky as soon as it touched her stank hole."

"Bo!" Darius said, laughing. Bo was jealous, possessive, obnoxious, overbearing, and funny as hell. He loved him.

"Just remember, I'm going to be checking my merchandise for use as soon as you get home. With a magnifying glass and everything, baby. Just call me Agent Double-oh-eight."

"Don't you mean Double-oh-seven?"

Bo looked down at his long penis. "No . . . eight."

Darius laughed again. "You nut."

Bo stepped in the shower. "Get on in here so I can bathe you. It's almost time for your choir rehearsal. Are we still going to the party afterward?"

One of their wealthy gay friends was having an underground party, one of the many clandestine, strictly gay, male-only parties hosted all over Los Angeles on any given weekend. "Of course," Darius said, leaning back as Bo expertly cleaned every nook and cranny of his body. "You know I wouldn't miss the opportunity to show off my one and only baby."

"Turn around, let me get your back." Bo soaped him all over and hugged him from behind. He was grinning from ear to ear. Stacy might be able to be with him on the outside. But Bo was his on the inside, in his heart, where it counted.

38

The Truth Is the Light

It had been days, it had been a lifetime. Vivian was in a place she'd never expected, but in the typical "stiff upper lip" style she learned from her father, and with her broadcast journalism background, she tackled the life-changing event of learning Derrick had a son like a treacherous work assignment.

Derrick had taken one look at Kelvin and felt Vivian was right in believing the boy could be his son. They'd reached Best Buy around eight that evening, Derrick hidden behind dark glasses and a baseball cap. They'd gone to the TV/stereo section but didn't see him. So they'd browsed around the CDs and DVDs, until Vivian heard his voice coming from the back of the store. She'd nudged Derrick, and he'd looked around to see a younger version of himself. His heart flip-flopped. He didn't want to admit it, but a part of him instantly knew there was a connection. He'd stared thirty seconds, sixty, and left the store quickly, not wanting the boy to see him.

Once back in the car, Vivian had been emotionless, matter-of-fact. "What do we do?"

"We call Tootie. Ask her point-blank. No need beating around the bush about it. If he's my son, I need to know. We all need to know."

Derrick started the car then, and the long drive home.

There seemed to be an eternal silence. Then Vivian spoke. "Tell me about it, the history with you two. And how is it that I never knew?"

Derrick told her everything: how Tootie was known for being an easy target in high school, and how several boys had been intimate with her on a regular basis. More importantly, he told her about the night after King had broken things off with Tootie for the last time. How she'd come over to his house, cried on his shoulder. Out of all of them, Tootie had genuinely loved King. She was heartbroken to know it was really over, that he was committed to Tai, and would not sleep with her again.

One thing had led to another and Derrick's comforting Tootie took on intimate proportions. They'd slept together that night, and again the next morning. Not long after that, Tootie had moved to Los Angeles, and then to Germany. Derrick hadn't spoken with her since. He'd thought of her infrequently, and of that night, not at all.

Vivian tried to keep from getting upset by constantly reminding herself that this all happened before she came on the scene, before she'd met Derrick. She almost succeeded, but not quite. She wasn't too happy with Derrick or Tootie at the moment.

For now, however, the situation had to be dealt with. She was sure at some point the full reality would hit her and she'd go off: scream, cry, throw things, curse. But for now she relied on the detachment honed as a former broadcast journalist. Do what needs to be done to get the story and solve the problem.

The next day, she'd told Tai everything, including what she was going to do. Tai called Mama Max and got Miss Smith's number. Vivian called Miss Smith immediately, introduced herself, told her why she was calling, and asked for Tootie's number. Just like that.

Miss Smith, knowing this moment was long overdue, had given her the number without question. It was time to put an end to this mystery, this mess. It was time for the truth to come out. She called her daughter and told her what she'd done. Told her someone named Vivian would be calling, and suggested that Tootie "tell that woman everything she needs to know. Enough's enough."

And it was. When Vivian called, Tootie was ready. Interestingly enough, the truth had been surprisingly easy. It had gone like this:

"Hello?"

"Tootie, Janeé, this is Vivian Montgomery, Derrick Montgomery's wife."

"Yes."

"Do you know why I'm calling?"

"Yes."

"Is Kelvin his son?"

"Yes."

"Kelvin is Derrick's child."

"Yes."

"Would you be willing to have his DNA tested?"

Sigh. "Yes."

"When can you fly out here? Or we can come to Kansas to meet you. Either way, we need to talk."

That phone call had occurred the very next day following Vivian and Tai's trip to Best Buy. All the calls had been made from Tai's hotel room. Words could not express how invaluable Tai's presence was. Vivian had never experienced anything like this in her life, but Tai had lived through marital upheavals many times. During these times, Vivian had been her anchor. Now, the favor was being returned.

That was two weeks ago. Today, Vivian and Derrick sat in the lobby of the Hotel Sheraton, waiting for Tootie and Hans to come down. They'd agreed to meet in Los Angeles, since the Petersens had already planned to visit Kelvin before returning to Germany. Vivian still felt detached from the whole situation. It had happened so fast and had been so unexpected; she had still not been able to wrap her brain around the fact that Derrick had a child that was not hers.

As for Derrick, he'd been all about business. They'd talked long into the night after Tootie revealed that Derrick was Kelvin's father. Vivian had found out things she'd never known about the man she'd loved for so long. He told her all about his high school days, about how Tootie and King and Derrick used to hang out, she acting like one of the boys. How the camaraderie of their middle school years had turned into sexual liaisons in their high school ones. Vivian asked how two good friends could sleep with the same girl, at the same time. Weren't there feelings of betrayal, trespassing, something? Derrick had looked at her with compassion then. "No, baby," he'd said. "You know men don't feel the same emotional bond the way women do. By the time I slept with Tootie, she and King were just casual friends. Yeah, he was still hitting it, but he wasn't exclusive. And honestly, I didn't for a second think any big deal about sleeping with Tootie the night King broke up with her. I even told myself I was doing her a favor, making her feel a little better, easing her pain. It just goes to show what the consequences of casual, unprotected sex can be."

Vivian had asked Derrick how he felt about knowing he was the father of another boy. His answer had been simple. "I've always handled my responsibilities, and I won't stop now."

They'd decided to wait until they'd talked with Tootie to determine how to proceed as far as the children were concerned. They didn't even know if Kelvin knew who his father was. Would he want to meet Derrick? Would he want any involvement in their lives? Was he resentful, curious, indifferent? There were a lot of questions that needed to be answered before the next moves were made.

Derrick and Vivian looked up at the same time to see a well-dressed couple walking toward them. Hans looked distinguished, his salt and pepper hair newly cut, sporting a casual jacket and khaki pants. Tootie was dressed casually as well; navy slacks with a paisley printed blouse and sandals. Her hair was pulled back in a ponytail. She wore little makeup.

Derrick and Vivian stood as they approached. Both couples were nervous, unsure of each other. Both Hans and Derrick held out their hands at the same time.

"Hi. Derrick Montgomery."

"Good to meet you. Hans Petersen."

Derrick nodded at Tootie. "Tootie."

Tootie's mouth turned up in a slight smile. "I haven't been Tootie in over fifteen years. I really prefer Janeé."

"Alright, Janeé, good to see you're looking well after all these years."

"Father Time and I are fighting, but I'm holding my own."

Vivian held out her hand. "Janeé, I'm Vivian."

There was a look of sincerity in Janeé's eyes as she responded, "It is nice to meet you."

The civil formality helped to relax both couples. They stood awkwardly for a moment, as if both were unsure what to do next. This was the first time Vivian had seen Janeé, but since she'd lived through so much of her past through Tai, it was as if she knew her. Something was moved inside Vivian's heart as she observed Janeé fidgeting unconsciously with the strap of her purse, trying to look calm in what had to be an extremely uncomfortable situation, for her most of all. Vivian had expected to feel anger, coolness, chagrin, judgment. Instead she felt compassion, and that surprised her.

Janeé tried to look at Derrick without staring. Like King, he'd aged nicely. He still looked good. But unlike what had happened when she saw King, her heart didn't flutter at the sight of him. Yes, he was attractive. But there were no feelings of longing or vivid memories of shared intimacies.

"Well." Hans broke the awkward silence. "Should we get some coffee? Or do we want to find a spot in the lounge?"

"There's a nice patio where we can have a bit of privacy," Vivian answered. "Maybe we'll order tea from out there?"

"Sounds perfect," Hans answered as Vivian and Derrick led the way.

Once seated, their drinks ordered, Janeé followed Hans's advice. He'd suggested to his wife that the best place to start with this saga was at the beginning. Somehow, since Vivian was basically a stranger, it didn't feel hard to do.

Janeé began without preamble. "When I found out I was pregnant, I didn't know what to do. I was as confused as a woman could be about anything in her life. I'd been screwing half the town, seeing a married man, doing drugs, drinking. I didn't know who the baby's daddy was, and quite honestly at that time, I didn't care.

"I knew Mom would be devastated, her 'good Christian daughter' having a baby out of wedlock. Even though I was grown, I still felt a responsibility to Mom's reputation. You know how active she's been in the church all these years, and you know how folk talk. Hell, they'd been talking about me for years anyway. I could lie about all the screwing, deny it all. And that's what I did. But it's not as easy to deny a baby."

"So I ran away. This dude and I went to Los Angeles. I was going to have an abortion but then he said he'd help me raise it. And as much as I detested all the dogma I endured, being forced to go to church as a child, something inside felt better about having the baby than not. So I agreed to keep it.

"The man left me when I was eight months pregnant. Just didn't come home one night. It wasn't until the next morning I noticed his stuff was gone. No note, no phone call, no letter, nothing. Just left. And there I was in LA, broke, pregnant, and alone.

"So I hooked up with another guy, this older man, who let me stay with him until I had the baby. But he started trippin', getting violent, shortly after Kelvin was born. After a couple knocks upside the head, I knew I had to go. That's when I auditioned for and got a part in the European tour of Dreamgirls. Without thinking of how I'd take care of myself, much less my baby, I caught a plane to Germany.

"For the first couple months, I didn't know who Kelvin's daddy was. He looked more like me at first. I really wanted it to be King's." Janeé, who'd either been looking down at her hands or away from the table during her historical recount, glanced briefly at Vivian. "I'm not proud of what I did, but I was in love with King. And when you're in love, sometimes you do stupid things. But after a few months I realized it wasn't King's baby, it was Derrick's."

Janeé looked at Derrick. "I called Mom for your number then, Derrick. I was going to tell you that you had a child. But when I called home, Mom told me you'd just gotten married. And I was right back where I was with King, getting ready to chase a married man. And I just couldn't do that anymore. I had grown up, and I realized just how uncool it had been to be with King after he got married. That's when I made the decision to raise Kelvin alone and never tell him or you the truth. After I met Hans, and he adopted Kelvin, I thought I was home free.

"At the time, I did what I had to, to survive. But now I know it wasn't the best decision, trying to bury the truth." Janeé looked at Derrick, her eyes filled with tears. Hans grabbed her hand.

"Kelvin's been asking about you," Janeé said. "He wants to know his real father."

She stopped then, unable to go on. A weight of sixteen years had been lifted off her conscience. The relief moved her to tears.

The rest of the table sat quietly, letting Janeé's story sink in. They all could see the picture she'd painted: a young woman, scared, confused, unsure of what to do, thinking that if the situation was hidden it would go away. Vivian remembered the joy she'd felt at the birth of Derrick Jr., married to the love of her life, her parents and Derrick by her side. How different it had been for Janeé. Suddenly, the woman she'd despised for the pain she'd caused Tai became human, and in the end, more like her and Tai than not. A woman who'd done the best she could at the time.

"There's not an act outside of God's forgiveness," Derrick said, speaking Vivian's thoughts. "He's forgiven you, now you have to forgive yourself."

Janeé looked up but said nothing, as tears flowed anew.

Vivian took her hand. "We've all done things we're not proud of, Janeé. But when we know better, we do better. My mother always said that anything dark looks better with a little light shined on it. Well, now you've told the truth, and the truth is the light. I think things are looking a little better for you already."

Janeé smiled and blew her nose. Vivian was right. She did feel better, lighter, freer than she'd felt in over fifteen years. But she knew she wasn't finished. Things wouldn't be totally right until she'd apologized and received forgiveness from another woman, a woman she'd wronged for years. But things hadn't gone so well when they met. Feelings hardened through years of deceit, denial, and unforgiveness had erupted amid Janeé's lack of total honesty when Tai had asked about Kelvin. It felt good to make things right with Derrick about his son; she wanted to make things right with Tai as well.

"Do you think Tai would talk to me?" she asked Vivian. "I've really treated her unfairly. It was wrong of me. And I want, need, her forgiveness, too."

Vivian pulled out her cell phone. "Only one way to find out." She dialed Tai's number. "Hey, girl."

"Hey, Viv, how are you? Have you talked to Tootie yet?"

"We're talking right now. In fact, Janeé asked me if you

would speak to her, says she has some things to say that she should have said before. Can you talk to her? Do you have a minute?"

Tai didn't know whether she was more incredulous or pissed. Had Vivian lost her damn mind? "What does she need to say to me?" she asked defensively.

Vivian understood her friend's reaction. But she also understood that God was at work here. It was time for healing.

"She wants to ask your forgiveness, Tai. She knows that she has treated you badly, and it wasn't right. She wants to apologize and ask you to forgive her for these sins against you."

"Well, hell, now that you put it like that . . . I guess I would come off like the wicked witch not to talk to her ass. Put her on."

Vivian hid a smile. Just like God to use what looked like a negative situation to work his perfect will. All things really did work together for good for those who loved the Lord. *Work it, Jesus.* She handed the phone to Janeé, who got up and walked to the edge of the patio that looked out over the ocean.

"Thank you, Tai, for taking my call. It would be understandable if you didn't." Janeé took a deep breath. "Tai, I'm sorry, for everything. I'm sorry for all the pain I've caused you, for the affair with King, for being uncooperative during our meeting, and not telling the whole truth when you asked about Kelvin. I've been jealous of you for so long, hated you for so long, for getting what I thought was mine, for marrying the man who wouldn't marry me, even though I begged him to.

"I am truly sorry. And I hope that someday you can find it in your heart to forgive me."

Both women were silent, both wiping away tears. Until now, Tai hadn't realized how heavy hate was. But now, her animosity for Janeé was lifting, through the power of forgiveness, and she recognized her feelings toward Janeé for what they were—a burden.

"It's amazing what we women do to each other," Tai said, after a long silence. "And I never thought the day would come when I'd say these words but . . . I forgive you, Tootie, I mean Janeé." The presence of God, like a gentle, summer breeze, caused chill bumps on the arms of both women. "I really mean it, too. It's crazy, but I really mean it. I forgive you."

"Thanks, Tai," Janeé whispered. She wiped her eyes and tried to recompose herself. "I really need to get back to the table now. We've still got a lot to work out."

"I'll be praying for you."

Janeé smiled as she hung up the phone. Her mother told her she'd been praying for a positive outcome to this situation for fifteen years. Without a doubt, Janeé knew that God answered prayer.

When she walked back to the table, Hans was regaling Derrick and Vivian with stories of growing up in post–World War II Germany. Even though the war had been over for years by the time he was born, its affects were felt for decades afterward. It shaped the staunch, hardworking, no-nonsense persona for which Germans were known. It was partly true, but not all. As they were seeing, Germans could be kind, lovable, generous, and funny. Janeé loved Hans more with each passing day.

She sat down and noticed pictures of her two younger children on the table. "Oh, so proud Papa has shown you Daniella and Sophie?"

"And rightly so," Vivian answered. "They're beautiful children."

"So," Derrick said, steering back to the reason they were there. "What's next? How do we handle this situation?"

"Well," Janeé said. "Hans and I are on our way to visit Kelvin tomorrow. What we tell him depends largely on what you guys want to do. Yes, he has a right to know who his father is, but you guys also have the right to not have your lives disrupted because of my mistake."

"God doesn't make mistakes,"Vivian interjected. "The circumstances may have been unsatisfactory and in poor judgment, but Kelvin was born because he was supposed to be here."

"Thank you," Janeé said simply. Vivian's comments were a sign that maybe Derrick would accept his son.

Vivian looked at Derrick. She knew there was a part of him that wanted to know Kelvin. She was sure Janeé wanted them to know each other. She knew that the best way to deal with the situation was open, up front, and above board. Sooner or later, everyone would know about Kelvin. Heads would turn and tongues would wag, but the fact of it was, Derrick had another son. And his name was Kelvin. The chips would have to fall where they landed.

"What do you think?" Vivian asked, looking at Derrick.

"I say let the boy decide. If he wants to meet me, I'm open to doing that. We'll welcome him into our home, and into our life. If he wants to keep a distance, that's fine, too. He's probably been through enough turmoil within himself about this. We'll do whatever works best for the boy."

Once again, Janeé's eyes filled with tears. She reached for a napkin. "I'm sorry, I just can't stop crying. I was afraid to even dream the ending could look like this. And here you guys are, so understanding, so kind. . . ."

"It's not us, darlin'," Vivian said truthfully. "It's the Lord. In my own flesh, I might have another reaction. In fact, I most definitely would be thinking about a beat down. But when I love you with the love of Christ, unconditionally, the way God loves me? It feels like this. This is what God's love feels like."

Janeé sniffled, looked into the distance. "Maybe it's time for me to get to know God again." She laughed sarcastically. "He probably doesn't even remember who I am."

Vivian grabbed Janeé's hand, looked her straight in the eye.

"You're His precious daughter. How could He forget you? He loves you, and has had you in His arms this whole time."

Unbidden, a childhood song Janeé's mother used to sing rose up in her mind. ". . . little ones to Him belong. They are weak, but He is strong. Yes, Jesus loves me. Yes, Jesus loves me. Yes, Jesus loves me. The Bible tells me so. . . ."

39

A Father's Pride

"It doesn't matter that you're on the pill," Hope said in an aggravated tone. "You still need to be using protection. How long have you known the guy, not even six months? Do you know he's being monogamous? Do you know anything about his past sexual partners, his sexual history?"

"Ah, girl, who wants plastic in the pussy? Ain't nobody gonna get AIDS. Lighten yo' ass up!"

"Everyone who has AIDS probably thought that very thing. I'm serious, Frieda—"

"And I am, too. Look, we both got tested. Satisfied?"

"You both took an AIDS test?"

"That's right, went down to the clinic together. He doesn't like wearing a condom any more than I like feeling one. So we went and got tested and that's that."

"Well, and I don't mean to put thoughts in your head, but what's to say he won't get busy with someone else?"

"What's to say Cy won't?"

"We're married; there's a difference."

"Is it? Because there's about a million cheatin' husbands out there who'll prove yo' ass wrong."

Hope resisted the urge to get even more aggravated than she already was. Frieda had never listened to her. *I don't know what led me to believe she'd listen now.* Besides, Frieda was right. Married men did cheat.

"Whatever, cuz, just be careful."

"I always am. Gorgio's dick's too good for me to mess it up."

"I didn't mean like *that*," Hope said, rolling her eyes.

"I know, but I did," Frieda said, laughing. "What about you and Cy? You're giving him head, right?" Frieda asked this as nonchalantly as commenting on the weather.

"Frieda Lemay Jackson, no you didn't!" Hope exclaimed.

"I'll take that as a yes," Frieda replied calmly.

Hope's big smile could not be hidden. And it didn't go unnoticed by her curious cousin, who added, "Oh, and he's giving it pretty good, too. That's good, that's good. That'll keep a man around."

"I'm not even going to talk with you about this, Frieda," Hope said with feigned indignation. "Some things should remain in the bedroom."

"Not really. It's much better when it's done in the kitchen, on the dining room table, and if you can sneak and get it on the balcony under a full moon. . . ."

"Frieda, shut up!"

"You're getting wet, huh?"

"You are a trip."

"But that's why you love me. I keep it real."

Hope shook her head, while silently contemplating balconies, full moons, and Cy's holiday surprise.

Derrick and Cy headed back to the church in Cy's Azure. They'd just left the restaurant where Derrick had shared the news with Cy, the first person in his ministry to hear about Kelvin. Derrick wanted to see Cy's reaction and get his opinion. His reaction was subdued and opinion straightforward, both as Derrick had expected.

"It was something that happened a long time ago, that you knew nothing about," Cy said. "You have nothing to be ashamed of. I'd take the wind out of any would-be gossiper's sails by putting the information out there myself. Invite him to church, make a grand introduction, and use it as a teaching tool, both as to the value of safe sex and how God can turn what looks like mistakes into blessings."

Derrick liked what Cy had to say, but admitted saying it and doing it were two different things. He and Vivian hadn't met Kelvin yet, or told the children about him. Hans and Janeé had phoned from Germany, shortly after their visit with Kelvin. They'd told Kelvin what happened, that his father knew about him and was prepared to meet him whenever Kelvin was ready. Kelvin had told his mother he had to think about it. He was frightened that the reality would not equal the dream—his dream of a wonderful biological dad. In truth, Derrick would surpass his dream.

"When the time comes, we'll handle it as gracefully as possible. I don't plan to try and hide him, that's for sure. And I don't plan on flaunting him, either. I've prayed about it and released it to God. When the time comes, I trust I'll know what to do."

"And so you will, my brother."

"What about you?" Derrick said. "When are we going to be seeing a Cy Jr.?"

"Funny you should ask." Cy smiled. "We're working on that now."

"Oh, I suspect you've been working on something or other since the wedding night. Am I right?"

They both laughed.

"I never thought of a baby much, man. They always seemed to be a big responsibility, and a big hassle to my freewheeling lifestyle, if you know what I mean. But Hope's changed that, got me thinking of diapers and things. So maybe in a year or so. . . ."

"Like I said . . . whupped."

Cy didn't disagree. "It sounds pretty bad, huh?"

"Man, you need prayer."

"I need prayer, huh? Please, you think I don't see those sly looks that pass between you and Viv when you think no one's watching? The little winks from the pulpit, licking your lips like you want to take a bite right there in church?"

"Ah, dang brother, you see that?"

"I see that."

"I guess we'd better work on our signals a little bit. We're getting sloppy."

"I just hope I'm still trying to signal Hope like that in fif-teen, twenty years."

"Just keep it fresh, man, and keep it between the two of you. And it won't get older, it'll get better."

"Even after the baby comes?"

"Even after the *babies* come." Derrick continued. "Now, it'll interrupt it for a minute. You'll be ready to climb the walls and strangle your own child. But even that's worth it. Ain't nothing like looking at one of your own." Derrick paused. "When I saw Kelvin, even with everything else that came with him, there was a sense of pride in the fact that he's mine."

"It must be how God feels when He looks at us, huh?" Cy speculated. "No matter what else comes with us, all our mess, crazy acting, disobedience, and what not? He still feels a sense of pride that we're His."

Derrick nodded and put out his fist. Cy gave him "dap."

Enough said.

40

Satisfied

He'd promised himself it wouldn't happen again. But here he was, naked, in Stacy's bed. And she was doing what he'd repeatedly envisioned since the last time it happened. She was satisfying him orally, and royally, for the second time that night.

"I want to feel you inside me," Stacy whispered between licks. She teased him, a touch here, a nip there, just enough to take him to, but not over the edge. They'd been together intimately half a dozen times and this time, she was determined the night would end with her being as satisfied as he was.

"C'mon, baby," Darius moaned. "It feels good."

Stacy straddled Darius and tried to put him inside her. He grabbed her hand. "No, Stacy, we can't do that."

"Yes, we can," she countered, bending down to please him once more. "Is this good?"

"Oh, yes."

"Well, just close your eyes and enjoy the ride, baby."

Stacy went to work then, all mouth and fingers. Darius tossed and turned, in delirious pleasure. And just when he was about to climax, Stacy mounted him.

It happened so fast, Darius was pumping before he realized it. And once he started, he couldn't stop. *Ooh, this feels good.* Better than it had ever felt with Gwen. It was different, softer, wetter. Stacy had him in an iron grip. The friction generated by her muscle control had him freaking, for her.

He flipped Stacy over, positioned her on her knees, and entered her in a more familiar way, from behind.

"Oh, yes. Do it baby, do it." Stacy was wild with passion. This is what she'd wanted for so long, and it was as good as she'd dreamed it would be. Darius! She was with Darius, completely. She pressed herself against him as he pounded hard, relentless.

Stacy grabbed the headboard as Darius grabbed her hips and continued his frenzied lovemaking. They were both sweating, the bed creaking loudly.

"Oh, Darius," Stacy panted.

"Bo," Darius whispered.

Did he just say Bo? No, I'm trippin'. He must have said boo. Whatever he said, he was doing it to her so good. "Yes, baby, I'm your boo, I'm your boo. Ooh . . ."

Oh, damn! I think I said Bo! If Darius hadn't been so far gone, he would have lost his erection. As it was, thinking of his lover only heightened his pleasure. As he climaxed it was Bo, not Stacy, who was on his mind.

Stacy rolled over, into Darius's arms. She softly kissed his face. "That was incredible."

Darius's thoughts were totally different. *What have I done? Bo is going to kill me!* "We shouldn't have done it, Stacy."

Oh, hell. Here this nucka is getting ready to ruin a good night. "Look, let's not get into guilt tripping. I have no regrets about sleeping with you. I'm *glad* we did it."

Darius rolled out of bed and grabbed his pants. He looked down at her as he stumbled to put them on. "We can't tell any-body, Stacy. I don't want people thinking I sleep around."

"What? Is that what you call this? Sleeping around? I don't want to think you sleep around either. I want to think you make *love* to the woman you're *dating*. Why are you being so uptight?"

Because Bo's gonna have my ass when he smells your pussy on my clothes. Darius started removing his pants. "Can I take a shower?" he asked, already walking to the bathroom.

Stacy watched his muscular ass ripple out of her room. "Well," she said to the four walls. "That's not exactly the ending I expected." She fell back on the bed, grabbed the pillow, and smiled. "But it's a start."

"You fucked her, didn't you, didn't you?" Bo was furious, walking from one end of the living room to the other.

"Look, just because I come home late—"

"Smelling like new soap. We don't use no damn Dove, or Ivory, or whatever the hell that is on you."

"You're trippin'."

Darius was getting the reaction he'd expected after coming home at two-thirty in the morning. He'd already decided to lie though, or there would be even more of an explosion.

"I knew that bitch was gonna give me problems. I just knew it." Bo flopped down dramatically on the couch, biting his fingernails.

"I'm gonna tell her," he said, jumping up again. "If you don't stop seeing her, I'm going to tell her about us, tell her why you'll never, *ever* invite her to *your* house."

Darius walked over to Bo quietly and calmly. He stood staring at him, his nose inches away from Bo's. "If you ever threaten to out me again," he said with a voice just above a whisper, "I'll walk out that door and not look back. Do you understand?"

Bo bit his lip but said nothing.

"Do you understand me, Bo? I will not be threatened, not by you, not by anybody."

Bo tried to grab Darius's arm, but he pulled away.

"I'm sorry," Bo said. "But you promised. You promised you wouldn't fuck her."

"And I didn't."

"Swear on a stack of Bibles?"

Darius heaved a heavy sigh. "Look, you either believe me or you don't."

Bo didn't miss the fact that Darius didn't swear. But he decided to let it go. There were things he could do for Darius that Stacy could only dream of.

He grabbed his man and hugged him tightly. Darius hugged him back.

"Hey," Darius said, pulling Bo toward the couch and taking his hands in his as they sat down. "I wasn't going to tell you this until we were at dinner tomorrow, but I guess this is an even better time."

Bo perked up. "What?"

"I got you a job."

"What?"

"You are now my manager—a full-time, paid position."

Bo screamed.

"Of course this means you're indispensable. You'll have to travel with me everywhere, especially when we go on tour."

"Oh, Darius, I knew you loved me!" Bo's eyes glistened with tears. And to think he'd almost ruined the moment, fretting over a shriveled up pussy. How did he ever think that could replace his eight-inch hammer?

Bo gave Darius a big hug and kissed him passionately. *Go ahead and give Stacy what she wants,* he thought as he maneuvered Darius toward their bedroom. *I'm getting ready to give him what he needs.*

Darius smiled at Bo as they both undressed. Life was good, and getting better. He'd made two people very happy tonight. And he felt great, too. Both Stacy and Bo seemed determined to have him. They probably wouldn't be sharing Thanksgiving turkey together, but maybe there was a way to keep everyone satisfied.

41

Divine Daughters

"We are very, very proud of our young ladies," Millicent said, as the young ladies stood in front of the audience, radiant in white. "These Divine Daughters have taken a stand for God."

The audience cheered, parents beaming. After months of planning and preparation, the day had been a rousing success. She could hardly believe how fast the time had flown. Last December saw her at her mother's home, sad and disheartened, the holidays subdued. This year, she was happy, an emotion she had often wondered if she would ever feel again. And it was all because of the Divine Daughters Celebration, Open Arms, and Jack.

Millicent and Jack had been seeing each other, quietly and covertly. She refused to call it dating. She told him emphatically that all they'd ever be was platonic friends. Jack had been disappointed, but had agreed. This understanding allowed Millicent to feel comfortable with him, to loosen up. They hadn't gotten together often—coffee after a workout, the occasional lunch, but never dinner. That would feel like a date. Mostly, they talked on the phone and exchanged e-mails, sometimes funny, sometimes steamy, but always respectful. Once or twice, she'd almost shared everything about her past. Jack was a good talker, but an even better listener. She'd even considered cancelling her trip to Mexico and joining him in the Caribbean. But in the end, she did neither.

But no doubt, Jack had added to her happiness, and being in her element, planning and organizing elegant events, made her heart sing. She was so thankful, so aware of how miraculous it was to be standing in this beautiful hotel, with a warm, loving church family, and a handsome, caring friend and pastor cheering her on. Millicent's smile widened.

"Now it's time for the commitment ceremony. This is a very special time. Each young lady has written her own promise, or commitment, to the Lord, a commitment to sanctity, to purity, to treating her mind and body as the vessel for the Spirit of God that it is. These ladies do not enter this moment lightly. The past two Friday evenings and in this afternoon's seminar, we've discussed what this vow to God means, and why they should make it. We asked them to consider it carefully, as a commitment to God should not be made lightly. Each of these ladies approaches this moment with sincerity, and has written, in her own words, what she will declare tonight, to us and to God. And now, I present to you, the Divine Daughters, beautiful brides, dancing for their bridegroom."

As the audience clapped, the lights dimmed and a spotlight shone on a single microphone in the front of the room. Off-stage, a violin began to play, joined by a flute, then a harp, then a keyboard. Eleven of the ladies began to dance slowly, gracefully, swaying as they moved seamlessly, forming a circle and then opening wide, revealing Jack's daughter, seventeen-year-old Sarah, at the microphone. From memory, she recited her vow to God:

"I offer myself to you, oh God, a vessel pure and good.
I vow to be of virtue, as the Bible says I should.
Until the day you send to me, an apple of Your eye,
And then we'll dance, a divine romance, and You'll be
    glorified."

Tears formed in Jack's eyes as he watched his daughter, looking so much like her mother, stand and proudly declare to remain chaste until marriage. He was so proud of her, and so wished Susan could share this moment.

He looked over at Millicent and smiled. How he wished he could openly profess his love for her. How he wished he could show how deeply he cared. Soon, he hoped.

As each young lady approached the microphone and declared her personalized vow, the other ladies danced, unobtrusively, in the background. Some of the young ladies cried as they promised God with all their hearts, joined by parents and other adults, who knew how hard it could be to keep such a vow. But something could be said for what they desired, the power of their intention. That alone would help them remain virgins far longer than their peers.

Leah squeezed Millicent's hand. "This is so beautiful, Millicent," she said, her eyes shining as she watched her daughter, Jazz, recite her commitment vow. "It's even more beautiful than I'd imagined." As the last girl spoke, and the music swelled, she continued, "I actually feel it might work. That we might save some of these girls from the heartache we've experienced."

"I hope you're right," Millicent answered. If just one girl could avoid the kind of pain she'd endured in the past twelve months, all the work put into the day would have been worth it.

And what a day it had been: breakfast, the spa, manicures and pedicures, an afternoon tea, and now this. The final girl recited her vows, and the crowd applauded their agreement as the girls took their seats.

As the applause died down, Jack and Millicent walked to the podium. Pastor Jack picked up a commitment ring from the velvet box and motioned the first girl forward. Millicent opened her Bible and began to read from the book of Isaiah. As she did, the girls approached one by one for Pastor Jack to place a ring on her finger. The celestial sound of the harp accompanied Millicent's words: "Thou shalt also be a crown of glory in the hand of the Lord, and a royal diadem in the hand of thy God . . . for as the bridegroom rejoiceth over the bride, so shall thy God rejoice over thee. . . ."

42

God's Work

Derrick, Vivian, King, and Tai sat expressing their gratitude. God had seen them through another year. And what a year it had been, with the reappearances of Robin and Janeé, and the surprise appearance of an addition to the Montgomery clan, Kelvin. Through all the turmoil and changes, which also included Tai getting a breast augmentation, and Derrick's weathering Cy's near resignation, both marriages remained strong. Mount Zion Progressive and Kingdom Citizens' Christian Center were growing steadily. Everyone was healthy, children were fine. The Montgomerys and Brooks were mutually thankful for their blessings.

"See how God works?" Vivian asked, as she reached for another roll. "He broke Evan and Princess up just in time, so you didn't have to worry about them on this, your second honeymoon."

"I am relieved they're not together, but I hate to see my baby with her heart broken. That boy always seemed too slick for me, and I tried to tell her, but you know kids don't listen. And his sleeping with her former best friend, Gayla—that didn't surprise me either. Life's lessons, huh?"

"Yes, live and learn."

"So, she told me she's sworn off boys until she's twenty-one. But she doesn't know that I know she's already talking to Rafael, another one of our Kingdom Kickboxers. I feel better about him, though. He comes from a good home, close-knit family. They've been members for years. King baptized him."

"Hard to believe you have a daughter that's dating age," Derrick said.

"And a son in college; don't forget about Timothy and his throng of admirers," Tai interjected.

"Man, I'm still not ready. I don't think as a father you ever are," King said.

"I know I'm not," Derrick agreed. "If I could send Elisia to a convent until she was, oh, about thirty-five, I'd sign her up."

Vivian laughed because she knew her husband was serious. "Seems like just yesterday they were crawling, and today they're courting. It's crazy how time flies."

"Tell me about it. The twins are next. Tabitha is still a bit of a bookworm, but Timothy has his eyes on one of the girls at school. Again, he doesn't know I know. Kids always think their parents were born yesterday."

Everyone nodded, thinking of how fast time passed.

"Doesn't it seem like just a few months ago we were vacationing in the Caribbean?" Tai asked.

"And now you two are on your way to Fiji."

"Yes," Tai crooned. "For our second honeymoon."

Derrick raised his glass. "Well, I'd say it's long overdue. So here's a toast, for you two to have a fabulous time in the South Pacific."

"I'm glad you guys stopped in Cali first," Vivian said. "And remember, you're welcome to lay over on your way back, too."

"I thought you guys would be gone by then," King said.

Derrick looked at Vivian and winked. "No, we've pushed our leaving back to Valentine's week in February."

"Ooh," Tai teased. "Sounds like somebody else is planning a second honeymoon."

"Just a little getaway. We've been talking about going skiing for about ten years and finally decided to do it this year. We're going to Aspen."

Tai rolled her eyes. "See, you gotta live in California before you'll fly to some snow. As for me, give me seventy-five, eighty degree weather every day of the week."

"From what we hear, it's not so bad," Vivian responded. "Plus, they've got that delicious hot chocolate and those roaring fireplaces to keep us warm."

"Hmm," Derrick said, reaching over to hug Vivian. "I'm all the chocolate and fire you need, baby."

Vivian kissed his cheek. "Touché."

The couple took a moment to enjoy their dishes: buttery lobster, jumbo, deep-fried shrimp, king crab legs, and prime rib filets. The wind off the ocean swirled around the couple, keeping them comfortably cool.

King sat back, having demolished a lobster tail. "Say, Derrick, did y'all ever hear from that crazy woman again, what was her name, Wanda?"

"Crazy woman?" Derrick asked.

"Robin," Vivian answered for him. "Thankfully no, and I hope it stays that way."

Tai turned to Vivian. "Have you heard much from Janeé?"

"We've talked a couple times. Didn't I tell you we received a Christmas card from her?"

"I think you did tell me that."

"Yes, she wrote that she and Hans were coming back to California around the time of Kelvin's spring break, and that maybe we can all meet then."

King looked at Derrick. He and his friend had talked little about Kelvin. Such irony—if anyone had a child with Janeé, one would have thought it'd be King. But Derrick had faced it stoically, just another challenge along life's road. "How do you feel about that?" King asked him.

"I'm okay with it, especially since Vivian and I have had a chance to digest this whole thing. It worked out best that he wasn't ready to meet me right away, because I wasn't ready to meet him either. Now though, I don't have any qualms about it. I don't have any expectations either. What will be, will be. Vivian and I have decided to deal with it when the time comes, and not before."

"Good, good," King said. "That's the right attitude."

"Well, Vivian," Tai said, "you're a better sistah than me, the way you've handled this. I don't know if I could have been so strong."

"Sure you could have," Vivian responded, thinking of all the battles Tai had fought and won. "But it helped that I don't have the same history with her as you do. Helps me to not resent Kelvin, because he had no choice in the matter."

"I never thought I'd forgive her but"—Tai looked at King—"I've felt better ever since. It's strange, something can be affecting you subconsciously, and you have no idea. Then, when it surfaces and you deal with it? You realize how much it affected you by how different you feel afterward. Y'all know what I mean?"

They did.

"I'd held hatred, animosity, all this negative energy in my soul against her. And now, it's not there anymore. I know God gets all the glory for that, because Lord knows it would have been a cold day in hell for me to do that on my own."

"We've all come a long way," King concluded. "And it's a blessing that the four of us have been able to travel down life's road together."

"May our journey together continue," Vivian said.

"Here, here," they said, and raised their glasses again.

Robin peeked out from the menu she'd used to hide her face. She'd been following Derrick and Vivian whenever she could, trying to learn their schedules, their habits, their friends. She'd gotten a job in a hot, noisy, toy manufacturing plant in downtown Los Angeles, and was renting an equally hot, shabby motel room for $125 a week. But she was determined to not leave the city of angels until she got what she wanted—revenge.

Yeah, y'all think you can treat folk any kind of way. Well, I got news for you muthafuckas. . . . Details at eleven. . . .

43

Hallelujah

Millicent shifted nervously in her seat, eyeing the beautiful Mexican waters below. During the plane ride, she'd repeatedly asked herself what the heck she was doing. And why she was doing it. She didn't know; it was almost like someone else was doing it and Millicent was just along for the ride. *I might not even see them,* she thought to herself. This thought made her feel better. While the resort was small, it was exclusive. Each couple's suite afforded total privacy. For the first time since the ridiculous idea entered Millicent's mind, she actually thought it might be better *not* to see Hope and Cy. Too bad she hadn't thought of this stateside.

"Ladies and gentlemen, we are making our final descent into Cancún, Mexico. Please move your seats forward and make sure your tray tables are up and in their locked position. Please stay seated for the remainder of the flight. We'll be on the ground shortly."

Millicent's nerves returned. Her thoughts raced a mile a minute. If she'd made different choices, she could have been in the Caribbean with Jack right now. *What was I thinking? What am I doing?!*

A private helicopter took Millicent from Cancún to her

final destination, Riviera Maya, Mexico, and the Rosewood Mayakobá Resort. Nestled amid a tropical jungle and surrounded by translucent blue waters and white sand beaches, the resort offered an unspoiled view of both the ocean and the second largest coral reef in the world. *This is beautiful,* Millicent thought. That she was here alone, however, was not so attractive.

Millicent checked in quickly and was escorted to a beautiful suite. The bellboy smiled, tipping his hat as he pocketed her gratuity. "*Muchos gracias, señorita,*" he said with a wink.

"*De nada,*" Millicent said absently. "This really is nothing," Millicent said to herself once the man had gone. "Just a time to relax, a simple vacation."

But she knew there was nothing relaxing, or simple, about it.

Hope moaned softly as Cy made delicious love to her. What they'd done since arriving was only eat, sleep, and make love. How had she been chosen to be blessed like this?

Cy kissed his way up from his personal paradise to Hope's mouth. They shared a passionate kiss, exploring each other with their fingers, drinking in the joy of true love.

"I love you," Cy said, between kisses.

"I know," Hope replied. "I love you, too."

Cy spent the next hour showering Hope with his love, making love slowly, tenderly, with unabashed sexuality. He had prayed that God would send him a woman who was uninhibited, and God had more than answered his prayers. Cy felt he would never grow tired of Hope, never get enough of her. His rhythm increased as he thought of her, his priceless treasure. *This is my pussy,* he thought, pumping faster. *Mine!* His orgasm was loud and sustained, spilling his seed deep into Hope's waiting womb.

It took them several minutes to catch their breath and float back down to earth. They stayed locked in each other's arms, hearing each other's heartbeats.

Separately, they were thinking the same thoughts—how happy they were, how blessed. Just as Cy perched up on his elbow to look into Hope's eyes, both their stomach's growled; their lovemaking had worked up ferocious appetites. They'd ordered room service for three days straight. Maybe it was time to eat out, for a change.

Cy smiled as he kissed Hope's nose. "Hungry?"

"Yes," Hope answered, as she rolled out of bed and headed for the shower. "Starved."

Millicent sat at the bar, slowly sipping a perfectly minty Mohito. She rarely drank, but had decided to try the drink when she saw the bartender make it for the man next to her. She had to admit, it was much tastier than the regular iced tea she'd been drinking.

Millicent felt relaxed, refreshed. This vacation, especially from Jack and Open Arms, had given her time to think. She'd been able to rethink as well, rethink her position about Jack being just a friend. She finally could admit to herself that she was attracted to him physically, attracted to him beyond friendship. Maybe she would relax her rule, make an exception. He'd been trying so hard to please her, to assure her that his intentions were honorable. He'd been patient and kind, sensitive, loving—just the kind of man she had always wanted.

The day after arriving at the resort, Millicent had also made the firm decision to not see Cy, and had made every attempt to not run into the Taylors. Within a span of a few days, having decided to come here at all looked totally ludicrous. *What was I thinking?* Truth was, she hadn't been thinking, but somehow she'd gained clarity. Maybe it was God. Maybe God had stepped in, stopped her from doing something that, once again, she'd regret.

It hadn't been hard to dodge the Taylors. From her discreet inquiries to the well-tipped bellman, she learned that Cy and Hope rarely left their room. Neither had she; for the most part she'd been content to enjoy late night walks along the beach and soak up the sun from her balcony. But tonight was her last night; she wanted to soak up a bit of the resort's nightlife. After the drink, she thought to perhaps venture into the resort's club. She'd heard a live band's music emanating from there the other night. *Maybe it's time for me to let loose on the dance floor.* Millicent smiled at the thought. She hadn't been to a club in years.

The more Millicent thought about it, the more she was in the mood for fun. She slid off the barstool feeling tipsy; the rum, hidden behind mint, lemon/lime, and Angostura bitters, packed a punch. She giggled to herself as she headed to the ladies room. "Time to freshen up, before I bust a move," she said aloud, to no one in particular. She wasn't aware that someone had heard her, and his eyes followed her every step as she headed toward the door.

Hope and Cy enjoyed a companionable silence as they shared a decadent slice of triple-chocolate layer cake. The dessert was a perfect ending to his lobster, her traditional Mexican fare of spicy tamales, beans, and rice, and their afternoon of lovemaking. Hope was glad they'd decided to leave the room. As usual, in public Cy commanded attention, and she had to admit she was proud to be on his arm, an arm that often stayed draped around her possessively. She was aware of the eyes that kept straying in his direction, and of a couple *mamacitas* wearing low-cut blouses and thigh-high skirts, who'd blatantly sashayed by the table.

Cy seemed to have eyes for only her. He'd seen the women checking him out, but he'd seen the men checking out Hope's assets as well, displayed fabulously in a form-fitting halter dress that hugged her booty as if she'd been born into it. Her four-inch-heeled, strapped sandals showed off her curvy calves to perfection, and her smile lit up the room. The scent she unconsciously gave off was more than the ylang ylang and vanilla in Clive Christian No. 1. It was the fragrance of someone who had been thoroughly sexed, and who'd enjoyed every minute of it.

"Hey, baby," Hope said as she put down her spoon. "Let's go dancing."

Cy's eyes lit up. It had been a while since he'd hit the dance floor, although in college he had definitely been "the man" to watch. "That sounds great, baby," he answered. "I could use the movement to work off all this food I just ate. I'm stuffed."

"Me, too," Hope agreed. "But it was good, though. Let me use the restroom, and then I'll be ready to go."

"I have to go, too," Cy said, standing up alongside Hope. "Let's both go and then meet in the front."

When they got near the front, Hope turned toward the left and went inside the women's lounge. Cy headed to the men's lounge, on the other side. As he walked toward the door, he looked out the restaurant's window and saw a tall, attractive woman standing near the entrance of La Caliente. *That looks like . . . No, that's impossible. . . .* Cy shook off the absurd feeling and went inside the bathroom.

Millicent was having the time of her life, receiving more attention than she could handle from a variety of Spanish cuties. Millicent had often dated other cultures, but never a Hispanic. She thought now might be the time to try something new. She'd started off on the dance floor alone, but quickly had her pick of partners. Free drinks lined the bar near her seat;

sweat ran down the valley between her breasts as well as her legs. She gathered her long, loose hair to the top of her head as her hips gyrated in time to the music. The action caused her breasts to lift, her cleavage to deepen. Several pairs of eyes went to the spot, and lips were licked in appreciation. Millicent looked beautiful in her abandon, the sheen of perspiration causing an ethereal glow, her sexy moves raising libidos around the room. She'd been followed from the restaurant, but was oblivious to the fact that she was being stalked.

The sound of Latin hip-hop was pulsating through the room, lights blinking on and off in time with the beat. The dance floor was packed. Cy and Hope moved against each other, in time to the music. She turned around and ground her booty against Cy's manhood. He grabbed her hips and pretended to ride.

Millicent's body turned and churned, a group of dance partners around her. She danced with one, and then another, totally absorbed in the music, dancing freely around the room. It seemed her joy was contagious; everyone was letting loose. Millicent left her circle and continued to dance, free and fanciful, laughing and loving life. She got to one particularly crowded part of the room and stopped, closed her eyes, and simply bobbed to the rhythm. She blindly reached out, touching women and men alike, innocent movements, a chest here, an arm there. Millicent was having a blast.

Now it was Cy's turn to get the booty treatment. Eyes closed, he turned his butt toward Hope. She came up behind him, her arms around his waist. Cy raised his hands in the air and bobbed his head, keeping perfect time to the music and Hope's hip-shaking moves.

Suddenly, Cy felt a pair of hands on his chest. They felt good, massaging his pecs; and one lightly tweaked his nipple. *Hope, you are insatiable.* He took his hands and placed them over the ones on his chest, encouraging this dance floor seduction. It took him a while to realize that Hope's hands were still around his waist. *Wait, what's going on?* Cy and Hope had shared a bottle of wine with dinner; his head was deliciously foggy. The hands on his chest started to massage it. This wasn't his imagination, and this wasn't Hope. Cy's eyes flew open. He couldn't believe who it was . . . Millicent.

Cy froze for a split second before he reached up and took Millicent's hands from his chest. The rough move brought Millicent out of her dance daze and she opened her eyes. *No, it can't be,* her mind screamed. But all she could do was stand there, mouth open, eyes wide. They both stood motionless for a moment, staring at each other. Soon, Hope noticed Cy was no longer dancing, felt the rigidity of his back. She moved around to see what had caused him to stop.

"Millicent?" she said incredulously, coming from behind Cy in disbelief. "What the hell are you doing here?"

Millicent was speechless. She could look in both their eyes and tell what they were thinking. That she'd followed them, that she was after Cy. True, she had followed them. But it had taken this trip to finally convince her that while Cy may have been the man she wanted, Jack was the one she needed.

"I—I—" Millicent stammered. As intelligent as she was, at the moment she was incapable of putting a coherent sentence together.

Hope looked at Cy, confused. They hadn't talked about Millicent in months, had almost forgotten about her. Almost, but not quite. The scene from that fateful Sunday began playing in her mind's eye.

It was playing in Cy's as well, causing his heart's pace to quicken. He didn't want to think Millicent had planned this, but what were the chances that she'd "just happened" to pick the same vacation spot as he and Hope, and at the same time. He hadn't seen or spoken to Millicent since that Sunday. But obviously, it was time he made some things very clear.

Cy took Millicent's arm, gently but firmly, pulling her off the dance floor. Millicent didn't object. Hope followed.

As soon as they reached the outside air, Cy turned to Millicent. "We asked you a question, Millicent. What are you doing here?"

Still, Millicent didn't have an answer. She stood, rubbing her arm, vacillating between truth and fiction. She cleared her throat, ready to come clean.

"She's with me," Jack said, walking up next to Millicent and putting his arm around her. "And who are you?"

Three pairs of brown eyes looked at Jack, tall and handsome, blue eyes blazing.

"Jack!" Millicent said, shocked, yet never so happy to see anyone in her entire life. She realized how surprised she sounded, and added, "Here you are! Uh, I've been looking for you."

Jack looked into Millicent's eyes with unadorned desire. "And I've been looking for you, beautiful." He looked pointedly at Cy, then asked Millicent, "Is everything all right?"

The sight of Jack cleared Millicent's cloudy mind. Finally, she was coherent. "Jack, this is Cy and Hope, his wife." That Millicent had not choked on *wife* was a welcomed surprise. "We belonged to the same church in Los Angeles."

Jack knew there was way more to this story, but decided to act civil. "Jack Kirtz," he said easily, his hand outstretched.

"Uh, yeah, nice to meet you," a somewhat befuddled Cy said, shaking Jack's hand.

"Let's go, honey," Jack said to Millicent. He could sense more than see that she was upset. With his arm protectively around her, they turned toward the path that led to the resort. Two pairs of eyes stared after them silently. Jack and Millicent didn't know it. They never looked back.

Jack took Millicent to his suite. Once there, Millicent collapsed on the couch, visibly shaken but silent.

"Wanna tell me what happened back there?" he asked, after he'd brought Millicent a glass of sparkling water and ordered a pot of coffee from room service.

Millicent looked up, staring at Jack. She thought at any

moment he'd disappear, that she'd wake up and be alone confronted by Hope and Cy. "How did you know I was here?"

I didn't, but God did. "I didn't," Jack responded. "This is the package Leah planned."

"But I thought you were going to the Caribbean."

And I thought you were going to Hawaii. Intuition told Jack that now was not the time to bring up the discrepancy. "This is the Caribbean," he said instead. "Seventy-five miles of beach stretching from south of Cancún to north of Playa del Carmen," he added, as the resort's brochure had described Mexico's Yucatán Peninsula.

"But I was thinking Barbados, Bermuda, Bahamas. . . ." Millicent's voice trailed off. "How long have you been here?"

"Just arrived this afternoon," he answered. "I checked in, unpacked, took a nap, and headed down to the restaurant to grab a bite. That's when I saw you."

Millicent wondered why he hadn't approached her, but didn't ask. He was there. It was enough. "Oh, Jack." Millicent put her head in her hands. The realization of what just happened hit her, as did the tears.

"Shhh, it's all right, honey, I'm here," Jack cooed. He sat down and took Millicent into his arms. That supportive act made Millicent cry harder. Jack didn't say a word. He just sat and rocked her, holding her until the tears subsided.

Millicent decided to tell Jack the truth. It took a while, but eventually she told it all, about her obsession with Cy, about their brief dating, and about how it all ended one bright, Sunday morning. She told him about her stay in Portland, and how she ended up in La Jolla, and at Open Arms.

Jack listened intently, without interrupting. He listened with compassion, without judgment. God had prepared him for this moment. Jack knew that as sure as he knew Millicent would be his wife. He felt they were one already, that any ceremony would be a mere formality.

"Come here," he said, after she'd finished. He lifted her

gently, effortlessly, from the couch and walked into the bedroom. He tenderly placed her on the bed and began removing her shoes.

"What are you doing?" Millicent began.

"I'm just going to help you relax," Jack said.

"Really, Jack, I should probably go back to my room," Millicent said, although leaving Jack is the last thing she wanted to do.

"Only if I come with you; I don't want you to be alone tonight." Jack didn't want to be alone either, but that was beside the point.

Jack encouraged Millicent to lay back and began massaging her feet. Millicent was tense at first but with Jack's expert ministrations, relaxed quickly. She felt his hands on her calves, her thighs. . . . *This feels good,* she thought. And then she fell asleep.

When she awoke, it was to a pair of loving, crystal blue eyes looking down at her. Jack was slowly, lazily, brushing up and down her arm with one finger. It took her a moment to realize she was naked, and another one to realize it felt perfectly right. She'd bared her soul to Jack the night before. In comparison, baring her body was easy.

"What happened to my clothes?" she asked timidly.

"I took them off," Jack replied.

"Obviously," Millicent said, suddenly self-conscious. "But why?"

"Didn't want them to get wrinkled," he said matter-of-factly. "Plus, I remembered that you sleep in the nude. And so, since you were sleeping . . ." He smiled an impish, boyish smile.

Millicent tingled. "I don't know whether to thank you or slap you for being insolent," she said, trying to sound stern. Just then, a thought came to her. She reached under the sheets. As she'd suspected, Jack was naked. "You're nude, too!" she exclaimed, this time with real righteous indignation.

"You never asked," he said calmly. "But I, too, sleep in the raw."

Jack continued to caress Millicent's arm, shoulder, face. A part of Millicent felt she should stop him. This was her pastor, after all. They were friends, *friends*. They hadn't even gone on a date! But another part of her, particularly the lower part of her body, wanted him to continue. It had been so long since she'd been loved. Her practical, sound mind was fighting a losing battle with her pulsating pussy and humming heart. She tried to summon some will, some anger, but with Jack drawing lazy circles around her taut nipple, it was very hard to do.

Jack kissed her. His lips were soft, tongue strong. He plundered her mouth with raw passion, his hands aching to explore every inch of her. But he refrained.

Millicent kissed him back. Jack's passion became her own, their tongues swirling, arms entwined. Jack's workouts were evident as Millicent rubbed his large, hard chest. She placed a leg over his, silently consenting to the moment. It was almost Jack's undoing.

"Let me love you, Millicent," he said, even as a scripture popped into his head. *Behold, old things are passed away. All things become new.* It was as if God were talking to him. "Yes," he said, and then to Millicent, "let me make you new."

Millicent simply nodded and reached for him. It was all the encouragement Jack needed. He kissed a trail from her mouth to her breasts, feasting upon each one, even as his finger found her soft, waxed nether lips, and began its exploration. Millicent moaned, her hands beginning a journey of their own. She paused when she reached his manhood, balls big and heavy, shaft long and thick. *Oh, goodness,* she thought, a smile on her lips.

Goodness, gracious, Jack thought, as he cupped Millicent's slender, tight bottom, pressing her up against his hard rod. He was ready to plunge into Millicent's wetness with abandon, but not yet. First, he wanted to savor every square inch of her honeyed sweetness. With that thought in mind, he started at her toes, blowing and sucking first the big toe, then the rest, and worked his way up.

The sunlight kissed Millicent's skin, waking her. She stretched, her hand hitting Jack's rock solid form. For a split second she was confused, and then she remembered. Her sore yet sated body was further testament. She hadn't been dreaming; she'd spent the night, all night, making love to Theodore Jackson Kirtz.

She turned to face him and softly touched his forehead, pushing his tousled grayish blond curls away from his brow. Jack's eyes fluttered, then opened.

"Good morning," Millicent said, her voice shy, tentative.

Jack kissed her lightly. "Good morning," he replied. He pulled her close.

"Thanks for last night," Millicent began. "For everything: saving me from a scene with Hope and Cy, bringing me here, loving me. . . ."

Jack touched Millicent's mouth softly with his finger. "There's no thanks necessary," he said tenderly. "It is what a bridegroom does for his bride."

Millicent turned to look at him, the question in her eyes.

"Yes, darling," Jack said, answering the unasked. "I fully intend to make an honest woman out of you. And, no, this is not the proposal. I know you well enough to know that I'll have to . . . how do the kids say . . . come correct?"

Millicent laughed at his slang. How had she even for a moment thought to pass on this blessing? Her thoughts drifted to the night before, how Jack had made love to her. He'd been tender yet thorough, with a passion she'd never before witnessed. But it hadn't simply been physical; she'd felt their minds and their souls connect, as well as their bodies. She had felt the oneness of sacred sex.

"Last night was amazing," Millicent said softly. "The way

you made me feel. It was incredible, so wonderful, so right, like, like . . ." Millicent searched for the word.

"Like love, like hallelujah," Jack whispered, completing the sentence and hugging her tighter.

"Yes," Millicent agreed, hugging him back. Hallelujah was the perfect word. Millicent stared upward, toward heaven, and thanked God for Love.

LOVE LIKE HALLELUJAH

LUTISHIA LOVELY

ABOUT THIS GUIDE

The following questions are intended to
enhance your group's reading of
this book.

DISCUSSION QUESTIONS

1. Is Millicent finally over Cy? Does she truly love Jack?

2. How do you feel about the fact that Millicent and Jack had sex before marriage? Do you think most Christian couples in committed relationships are abstaining from sex before getting married?

3. What do you think about single pastors dating? Is it okay for them to date women in the congregation? Why or why not?

4. Did Janeé have plans to "shake up" King and Tai's marriage? Does she still have a thing for King?

5. Does King still have a thing for Janeé, or was he just fondly remembering their shared past?

6. How do you think everyone handled Kelvin's existence: King, Tai, Derrick, Vivian?

7. After learning the whole story, do you think Janeé's actions regarding keeping Kelvin's paternity a secret, and the initial way she treated Tai, were justified?

8. Hope and Cy seem to live a fairy-tale life. Is such a relationship possible? Do you think a man like Cy exists? Why, or why not?

9. Is Robin really crazy, or is she just playing crazy to get what, or who, she wants?

10. Today, women are often the aggressors in relationships. Was Stacy too aggressive in going after Darius, or did she do the right thing by going after what she desired?

11. The Bible states that homosexuality is a sin. Do you agree? Do you believe that homosexuals choose their sexuality or are they born with this same-sex preference?

12. Is it possible for someone to be homosexual, yet also be attracted to the opposite sex?

13. How prevalent is the "down low" in churches today? Since most churches do not openly welcome gay parishioners, do they come anyway, but stay "in the closet?"

14. What are your thoughts on Internet dating? Any personal horror stories? Successes?

15. What are your thoughts on commitment ceremonies, where teenagers promise to remain chaste until marriage? Is this a realistic expectation for today's young adults? Does such a ceremony add pressure, or alleviate it?

Don't go anywhere!
Things are just heating up,
literally,
in the next book of this series. . . .

A Preacher's Passion

I

Like Fire

People said Passion was fast from the womb. That when she heard men talking, she'd make a motion in her mother's belly that felt like a tickle. When she heard women, her mother would get gas. Before she was born, she established that men were to be loved, women tolerated, and only when necessary.

She'd had one real girlfriend growing up, Robin Cook. They'd gotten along like peas in a pod since meeting in first grade at Martin Luther King Elementary School in Atlanta, Georgia. For one, they were big tomboys, and bigger than most kids their age. For another, they both hated most of the other girls at school, and were always baking up evil schemes to right some imagined wrong done to them. Whether it was putting cayenne pepper in a classmate's food, or glue on a seat, or trying to beat somebody up at recess, they were always getting into trouble, and usually together. But Passion and her family moved from Georgia to California when Passion was fifteen years old. She hadn't seen Robin since.

Passion sat in her living room, painting her toenails and watching the MLM network, a new, progressive, Black-owned network that was finally giving BET some competition. A pastor, Derrick Montgomery, was speaking at a convention hosted by a group called Total Truth. He looked as fine on TV as he did in person.

I want me some of that, Passion thought, as she turned up the volume. *That man is fine fo' real, like fire.* Passion wasn't a member of Kingdom Citizens but her church, Logos Word Nondenominational Church, pastored by Stanley and Carla Lee, fellowshipped with KCCC often. Passion loved Pastor Montgomery's fiery style, not to mention how fine he looked in a designer suit. She could always expect a word and some men worth watching when she visited Kingdom Citizens, and was one of the many who'd visualized Pastor Montgomery without his clothes, or his wife. Even now she was wondering if there was any way she could get some ministerial counseling—after hours.

An hour later, Passion pulled into her favorite strip mall. It housed an inexpensive clothing shop, a video store, a nail salon, a greasy Chinese food restaurant, and the reason for her trip, Gold's Pawnshop. Passion loved this shop. It had kept her lights or gas or phone on many times right after her divorce, when she'd been struggling to raise her daughter. She'd pawn her gold, diamonds, china, silverware, anything she could just to make it to payday. She prided herself on the fact that she'd always bought back her stuff, and in the process, would sometimes find a couple bargains, enough to keep her coming back every few weeks or so, though she hadn't had to pawn anything in years.

She stepped into the shop. As she'd expected for the middle of the day, it was quiet. Lin, the Korean owner, was behind the counter, helping his one, lone customer.

"Hey, Lin," Passion said cheerfully.

"Hey, Passion," Lin said. "What you buy today? I got tennis bracelet you like, just came yesterday."

"How much you want for it?" Passion asked. "I might be interested if you give me a good deal."

"I give you very good deal," Lin said. He unlocked the

showcase and pulled out a bracelet, effectively shown off in a black faux-velvet case.

"Ooh, that is nice," Passion said. She put it on her arm, turned it this way and that.

The other shopper, a woman, looked at the bracelet as well.

"This is pretty, huh?" Princess said to her, being friendly. "You think it's worth three hundred dollars?" That's the deal Lin said he'd give to Princess, because "she good customer."

The woman didn't answer, just stared. Princess looked up and stared back. The face was familiar. Then it dawned on her.

"Robin? Robin Cook? Girl, is that you!"

Robin was shocked, her response subdued. "Passion Perkins?"

Both women were incredulous. It had been twenty years.

"What on earth are you doing in LA?" Passion exclaimed, stepping forward to grab her former best friend in a bear hug. As she did so, she felt something cold, hard, in her stomach. She pulled back, looked down.

"And why are you buying a gun?"